THE KISS OFF

ALSO BY THE AUTHOR

The Come On

THE KISS OFF

A
Novel
of
Suspense

JIM CIRNI

F

Published in the United States of America by
Soho Press, Inc.
853 Broadway, New York, NY 10003.

Library of Congress Cataloging-in-Publication Data

Cirni, Jim, 1937–
The kiss off.

I. Title.
PS3553.I76K5 1987   813'.54   87-9184
ISBN 1-56947-036-7

Manufactured in the United States

10   9   8   7   6   5   4   3   2   1

For my wife Linda,
and for my daughters,
Karen, Susan, and Lauren

THE KISS OFF

CHAPTER 1

A fortune teller told me that Thursday the twelfth was my lucky day. Actually it was somewhat after midnight, on the thirteenth, when disaster struck—like about two A.M. But let's not split hairs. The gypsy lied. My life as it was came to an end that Thursday night in January.

The wind outside was howling. Which was a far cry from what was taking place inside. Inside, the lounge was deader than Chernobyl after the leak. I was tending bar with Tommy Milano, though neither of us had poured a drink in the last half hour. The only guy on a stool was a beleaguered salesman from West Virginia. He had his nose buried in a Stephen King thriller, rolling an olive pit in his mouth while his martini slowly evaporated. I kept replacing the napkins under his glass just to have something to do.

"Freshen it up for you, sir? Sir," I said louder. "*Sir,*" I shouted.

He jumped back a little. "Say what? Oh, no. I'm fine." He turned a page and went right back to Mr. King.

I glanced over at Tommy. He was reading, too. Not a

novel. The last book Tommy read was a goodie called *Whips and Lace*.

Now he was hunched over the bar reading the night edition of the *Daily News*. Like most gamblers I knew, Tommy liked to read the paper from back to front. It saved time in getting to the heart of the matter, the tout sheet. He'd already killed an hour circling his picks for tomorrow and was now busy licking his thumb. He flipped the page and chuckled. Which meant he'd hit on Bill Gallo's cartoon. That's the little box that brings humility to million-dollar jocks and the tycoons who pay the freight. Cartoons of Donald Trump, for example, sketched as King Midas waving ta-ta to the likes of Doug Flutie and Herschel Walker. Or Lou Piniella catching a kiss from Basement Bertha. For Tommy, Gallo was to the *News* what Mickey was to Disneyland.

Tommy slammed his hand on the bar. "That's it. I'm going fifty times on the Browns." Fifty times meant $275 with the vig: about a week's pay if things ever picked up.

"Is it still three points?"

I wasn't much of a bettor. A ten-timer was about all my nerves could take. But in the bar business it was more important to know point spreads than the ingredients of a Harvey Wallbanger.

"Yeah," Tommy said. "I gotta go with Cleveland." He showed me Gallo's handiwork, a playoff special featuring John Elway. "Look at this fag."

"Elway?" I said. "The man's got a girl. I've seen them on TV together."

"Why would a broad marry a fag like that? Look at him. Fucking fairy."

There wasn't much you could say to Tommy when he was on a losing streak. I'd seen him yank the cable box out of his TV because the Jets went for it on a fourth down, instead of taking the sure three, and didn't make it. Tommy went down by two, losing a hundred bucks, plus service costs on the set.

"It's a lock," he said as if his own certainty would

cement the win. He started licking his thumb again and I made a mental note to bet Denver ten times.

The salesman was finally coming to. He'd placed the book on the bar and was stretching, yawning loudly without covering his mouth. He picked up his drink and swallowed it in two mammoth gulps. "Aah, that's good." He turned toward Tommy. "Denver should run those Brownies right off the field."

Tommy looked at the salesman, then me. His eyes opened wide and his forehead shriveled up to his hairline. "Who's this guy?"

"Name's Harold Willis," said the salesman. He made a sucking noise with the olive pit, then pulled a business card out of his billfold and slid it down the bar to Tommy. "Pulp and paper out of Wheeling."

Tommy picked up the card, studied it while bobbing his head. "Wheeling? Where the fuck is Wheeling?"

I had an idea what was coming and backed away.

"West Virginia," the salesman said.

"And where the fuck is West Virginia?" Tommy said. "I never heard of West Virginia. You got a football team in West Virginia?"

"Steelers," piped the salesman. He hesitated now, still not sure if Tommy was serious. "We root for the Big Steel Curtain back home in Wheeling."

Tommy walked slowly over to the man, held the business card in front of his face. "Here's what I think of Wheeling." He tore the card down the middle, placed the two halves together. "And here's what I think of the Steelers," he said, tearing it again. He crumbled the pieces in his fist, then opened his hand and blew everything in the salesman's face. "Go on, take a hike. Pay your tab and get the fuck back to Wheeling while you still got legs to get there."

The salesman searched me out of the shadows. I stepped forward. "He can't talk to me like that," he said.

I shrugged.

He started to protest. Tommy cut him off. "Go on, settle up and get out of here. What's his tab?"

"Two-fifty."

The salesman fumbled with his billfold. "That's okay," I said. "It's on me."

He left without a word, sneaking a look at Tommy before dashing off. He was out the door before I noticed his book on the bar. I grabbed it and tossed it to Tommy.

"What's this?"

"Whips and Lace Revisited," I cracked.

He didn't even glance at the cover, just threw the book in the pail under the sink. "You believe that Jonah? And you give him a free ride. How many times I gotta tell you. Don't never do nothin' for nobody that can't do nothin' for you." A mouthful of negatives but I got the gist. "I should have whacked him," he said. "Douche bag."

The Skyview Lounge is on high ground overlooking Grand Central Parkway and LaGuardia Airport. From behind the bar I had a good view of the planes taking off. Tonight I could see the runway lights like rows of fireflies. Pretty. A jumbo jet screamed its distant ascent and I felt a sudden sense of envy for the lucky bastards inside her.

It depressed me. Got me thinking about my marriage and my career, both of which were something less than a tale of Horatio Alger.

Tommy sighed. "This joint sucks."

What he meant was we were dying. A yard was all we'd rung up for the night. And we hadn't done much better last night, or the night before.

It was hard to figure. Last year we were packing them in, doing close to twenty thousand a week. None of us knew why. Not me, not Tommy, not even the boss, Dusty Sands. I figured that was the reason we were dying now. I mean if you don't understand the components of success, you can't possibly know the reasons for failure. That was my theory, though no one ever paid much attention to it.

I had another notion, one I kept to myself—clientele. We had some heavy hitters in the place. During our heyday, rare was the night that unsuspecting customers wouldn't rub elbows with the underworld. Bookies, shylocks, pimps,

4

pushers, and punks of all color and size. We had more godfathers in the Skyview than married guys doing their "my-wife-hates-me" routine. I never cared though. The hoods were good tippers, and besides, they dressed up the place, gave it dramatic flare.

The problem was, too frequently they'd scare the drawers off the women. And if they couldn't scare them off, they'd yank them off. We had three rapes in the parking lot in one month. And whether a girl said yes or no, she was still referred to as a rag, skank, hump, bimbo, or cunt. It was a rough bunch we had coming in.

Before long the ladies began migrating to more digni-fied discos, leaving us with a cast of flat-nosed wise guys. As a former bar hopper, I know it was damn disheartening to deck yourself out, drive an hour for a place to park, and then bop into a joint full of gorillas owned by a gorilla like my boss.

I met Dusty Sands through Tommy four years ago, at a point in my life when I was single and sleep-walking through the corporate chain of command at Lester Morris, Inc. Three years on a job that had all the thrills of a coma. And all because of a parental legacy: "Be an accountant, son. Better to tell someone he's lost his shirt than to have someone tell you." This from an aging mother whose husband had died leaving her a chain of two hardware stores in Akron.

So I shunned the world of sole proprietorships and came to New York City bearing a BBA and an army discharge. No medals though. As a finance clerk in Ahnkhe I had spent a year dispatching script instead of shells. Seemed the 1st CAV was disinclined to issue Purple Hearts for paper cuts.

With Akron on fast-fade I took to the Big Apple like a worm. An apartment in Queens, singles bars every night, the whole tacky scene. I loved it. The only snag was that my nine-to-five job was becoming more and more like a daily dose of radiation.

Enter Tommy M. It was a few months before the

Skyview opened. Tommy was mixing in an eastside disco. The place had been running hot, and for a time there I was scoring more than Larry Bird. Then suddenly the place went sour, and so did I. I started drinking, feeling down on everything, especially women. I turned to Tommy who seemed to know more broads than any guy I'd ever known. He also knew the town, went through it like it belonged to him. I can't explain why, but being around Tommy gave me a lift, made me feel like I was finally a part of what I'd been reading about as a kid in Akron.

We started making the after-hours scene. I'd wait for him to get off and we'd bounce until brunch. I found Tommy to be a certified lunatic: cruel, selfish, and ignorant. But most of all, he was totally irresponsible. It was a quality I began to envy.

Meanwhile, at Lester Morris, my attendance record showed more X's than an algebra quiz. I wanted to get fired, played for it, yet when it happened, I got pissed.

"Don't fucking worry," Tommy said. "From now on you'll work with me."

He introduced me to Dusty with the phony story that I used to have my own place in Akron until the cops busted me for selling grass instead of booze. That appealed to Dusty, and he hired me. A week of on-the-job training and I had myself a new career.

I suppose I've always been taken by the notion that on the crooked side of the fence lies grass not only greener but softer. When you've been straight all your life, you can't help wondering what it's like. At the Skyview, I quickly learned that a wise guy's life wasn't green or soft. It was black, and hard.

Take Dusty Sands. Most people hated him. He was a pimp and a dope dealer, slicker than a politician and with twice as many pockets. Yet there was something about the man I liked. He was a rebel, arrogant enough to bullshit his way around and through the Mob. Never made, he never let it stop him from doing what he wanted. His key to success was to "fuck 'em all."

Me, I'm not immoral. I wouldn't sell dope or mug old ladies. But guys like Dusty and Tommy, who do it without conscience—I know it sounds wacky but I just can't help it—the bastards fascinate me.

Dusty also had a hobby, an expensive one. He gambled. Loved to lay it in big. Like most high rollers, it wasn't long before he found himself drowning in loanshark lagoon. It's easy to get chewed to pieces by sharks, particularly if you swim with a bloody steak dangling from your teeth. And Dusty Sands had dangled one juicy T-bone when he offered part of the Skyview against a $75,000 loan from a kingpin named Charles "Candy" Gizzo. To a man like Gizzo, buying into a legitimate front was like a small nuclear weapon falling in the hands of an aborigine.

Personally, I didn't care why Dusty borrowed the money or who gave it to him. Why should I? I was just trying to make a living. The seventy-five large had saved Dusty as well as myself and the fourteen others who toiled nightly at the Skyview. We were working when many like us were lined up at their local unemployment office. We were getting paid and that's all that mattered.

Tommy, though, didn't see it that way. He had a hard-on for Gizzo that went back twenty-five years when Tommy was ten. His mother's sister had married Charles Gizzo, and from that time on Tommy had envisioned himself the big man's protégé. It was not a fantasy shared by Uncle Charlie. Candy Gizzo barely acknowledged his nephew's existence. And when he did, it never quite lived up to Tommy's expectations.

Take last week. Late Saturday night Gizzo had dropped in with one of his boys. He had a mouth as big as his biceps and a face like Lucca Brazzi. We knew him simply as Nunze. As soon as he'd bellied up to the bar with Gizzo, he started on Tommy.

"Hey, retard!" he shouted. "Give us two Johnny Blacks."

The ladies snickered and the gents guffawed. Tommy

pulled at his collar as though a yellow jacket had crawled down his neck. But I'll say this for him, he knew how to eat shit when he had to. So he readied himself for a three-course meal, offered his hand to Gizzo, and said, "Good to see you, Uncle Charlie."

To which Gizzo responded by poking his nephew in the chest with a swizzle stick.

Rumor was that Gizzo's voice had been fucked up by cancer. I'd never heard him talk so I didn't know. When he had something to say, he'd motion to his sidekick, who would lean in, listen, and then bark out the order, "Two more Blacks!" Nunze bellowed.

How sick Gizzo was I didn't know, but to me he hardly looked like a man who would give in to anything or anybody. He may have been small and thin, yet from the waist up with that Bahamas tan and those think-lines chiseled into his bony face, he could have passed for a bronze bust of Marcus Aurelius.

He kept whispering to Nunze, pointing at his nephew as though Tommy was the regional distributor of gonorrhea. I sympathized with Tommy but I kept out of it. Better him than me, I figured. If there was one place I didn't want to be, it was on Gizzo's shitlist. Mercifully, Uncle Charlie and his pet hadn't been by since.

Tommy was still buried in the late Thursday edition of his *News*.

"What do you say we pack it in?" I called to him.

He looked up at the Seagram's clock above the register. It read 2:20. "What's the rush? We gotta wait for Carol, anyway."

Carol Antonucci was a busty cocktail waitress with a moon face and carrot hair. She'd been with us a few years, waiting tables while her husband Leo finished up a ten-year stretch in Dannemora. On slow nights like this she'd taken to serving up a little extra for the boss. We knew better than to interrupt and we couldn't close the damn place until Carol squirmed back into her mesh tights. It was something I never had to put up with at Lester Morris, Inc. But like any job, you learn to cope with the idiosyncrasies of management.

"They've been in there for almost an hour," I said, waving my hand toward Dusty's office.

Tommy smirked. "Maybe they're talking new wears for the hired help. Fashions by Frederick of Hollywood."

"Well I don't care. I'm breaking it up. This is bull-shit."

"Be my guest," Tommy said, and went back to his point spreads.

At the end of the U-shaped bar was a panel that lifted like a drawbridge. I raised it and stepped out from behind the bar. Spinning slowly over my head, the mirrored ball rolled checkered patterns across the dance floor. The only sound was that of my heels clicking on the hardwood surface.

The office was in the rear where the outer walls were covered with red velvet drapes to cut the sound. A slit allowed access to Dusty's office. Near it was a fire door secured by a heavy metal bar. An exit sign above it cast a dim red glow on a man I'd never seen before.

I jumped like I just stepped in dog shit.

Some time ago I'd seen a horror film in which Dracula was of African stock. "Blacula" it was called and that was exactly what this guy looked like. He wore a wide-brimmed hat and a knee-length fur coat with a large collar that fanned up and out along his broad shoulders. His teeth looked pink in the pale light and his eyes were two white holes in a vermilion mask.

"Watcha want here?" he said. His voice was a bit too high, but still menacing enough to unnerve me.

"That's my line," I said as a feeble counter. "How did you get in here?"

"Beat it!" he said.

Now I'm a rational man. I believe in self-preservation. Had this been broad daylight, in an open field where I could have seen his face, read clearly the fear or confidence in his look, well then maybe I would have gotten cute. But in the dark, talking to a shadow with eyes, I had no choice. I backed off.

It's a heist, I thought. His partner must be in Dusty's office tearing it apart. It had happened a few times before word got out that Candy Gizzo had acquired a financial interest in the place. With Gizzo, we were insured against this type of hazard. The Gizzo organization, like Allstate, had spread their good hands over the Skyview Lounge.

I checked his hands for weapons. He was holding a pair of leather gloves. Nothing lethal.

"You got business at the bar," he said.

"Listen, ace," I said, not quite so anxious now that we were engaged in conversation. "If this is a ripoff you'd better think twice." My adrenalin was flowing. Fear or anger, I wasn't sure which. But I was delighted with the biological effect. A real high.

He started toward me. I squared off.

Then Carol came busting out of Dusty's office and saved my ass.

"Jeez, Frankie," she said, wide-eyed. "You scared the living shit out of me." Under the pale red light, with her brown eyes bulging and her mouth agape, she resembled a jack-o-lantern.

"Tell Dusty there's a guy out here giving me a hard time," I said, keeping a close watch on the gloves.

"What's going on?" Dusty said from his office. The door was open and a bright glare flooded over us. I thought the guy would hiss at the light. Instead, he just stepped back into the darkness. Dusty came out.

"You know this guy?" I asked. He was angry, I could tell. If he was flushed with rage, I couldn't say because Dusty was blacker than the other dude. But his lips were drawn tightly across his big teeth and a vein pulsed at his temple.

"For Chrissake, Frankie," he said. "He's all right."

"Well, what's he doing here? How'd he get in without me seeing him?"

Tommy hollered from the bar. "Hey, what's happening?"

"Carol," Dusty said, "settle up and close it down. And you," he said, glaring at me. "Come over here." He pulled me aside. "What's wrong with you, man?"

"Nothing." I'd positioned myself to face his associate and the office. Dusty was shorter than me, about five-feet-ten-inches, and over the frizz of his hair I saw in his office the back of a man holding an attaché case. On the desk rested a second case. The man in the office was stocky and the reflection from his bald head left no doubt that he was white.

"Since when do you start nosing around?" Dusty said. He was still hot—too pissed for the offense he thought I'd committed.

"Ah," I said.

It hit me that I'd interrupted a score. I knew Dusty was transacting but I never thought he'd use his office for a drop. I should have known as soon as I'd spotted the doorman. Even with Dusty's African heritage, we rarely saw blacks in the Skyview any more. Which meant he must have come down from the Bronx where Dusty had owned a club called Levine's, locally known as the drug store.

"Oh, wow," I said. "Like, ah . . ." I get inarticulate when embarrassed.

"Okay then," Dusty said. "You didn't see nobody, right?"

I nodded.

"Good." He came closer to me. "Do me a favor, Frankie?" He was whispering and the scent of scotch wafted up at me. "Take Carol for some breakfast. She's a little edgy. Can't explain it now but I might have to split for a couple days. I'll want you and Tommy to run the show while I'm gone."

He was putting me on a spot and I didn't like it. Gizzo was the underboss here and I didn't think he'd appreciate Dusty's turning the place over to Tommy and me. Particularly since Gizzo had placed his own man here as sort of second in command. That was Peppy DeSimone, who, beside being Gizzo's spy, was also employed as our bouncer. Which meant he was big and mean, not the kind of guy I wanted to mess with.

"What about Peppy?" I said. "Shouldn't he take over until you get back?"

"Fuck no, man. This is my place. I call the fucking shots here, not Gizzo."

"So how should I handle Peppy?"

"You're a college graduate. Be smart." Then he turned quickly and went back to join Baldy.

With the door closed, Carol and I were left in the dark with Blacula. I put a protective arm around her shoulders, threw an "up yours" glance at the stiff, and sauntered back to the bar. I would have run but I didn't want to alarm Carol.

CHAPTER 2

The Orestes was one of those Greek diners that features kitschy decor and cholesterol. We'd often stop there after work, unwinding over coffee, eggs, and a peek at tomorrow's entries. Convenient but depressing.

We were almost there when Tommy poked his face between the headrests. He had a nose for turning a buck and his nostrils had been flared from the time we'd left the lounge. "Something's up," he said. "I can smell it, sure as shit."

The only thing I could smell was trouble. That and Carol's Obsession which drifted over to me in nauseating waves. She'd thrown a pair of designer jeans over her tights and wrapped herself up in a fake beaver coat. So far, she hadn't said a word.

Tommy persisted. "Come on, Carol, what's goin' on?"

She snapped her head around. "You'd better mind your own business, Milano."

"Hey, fuck you, eh?" Tommy said. "You think you're hot tit because you spread your legs for the coon?"

"Back off, Tom," I said. "You're steaming up the windshield."

"Hey, fuck you, too. She knows what's happening. If that prick is dealing on the premises, it's our asses too."

He made sense, though I didn't care for his choice of words.

"How about it, Carol?" I said. "Those two guys back there weren't Fuller brush men."

She started to say something, then pulled her collar around her mouth. Orange hair, furry face, the girl belonged on Sesame Street.

"I oughta bang her a shot," Tommy said.

He would have if I hadn't caught his eye in the rear-view mirror. A wink was all it took. We used to pull that when we were bouncing together. If it looked like I had the inside track on a girl, I'd wink him off. No sense in competing for the same fox. Especially when our objectives were different. I'd be after her body while all Tommy ever wanted was her bankbook.

He had a hundred different scams to get money off a girl. Like his famous "line of credit" bit. He'd see a girl for a while, borrow a few dollars—ten, twenty, like that—pay her back within the week to build up his line of credit. Then one day he'd hit her up for five hundred dollars, usually for swag: "I got a truck full of Sonys sitting on the docks. We can buy the whole load for a thousand and dump them for three. Whataya say, babe, fifty-fifty?" Six months later the girl would still be waiting for her first dividend check. "You think it's easy to dump them Jap sets? Takes time. I'm working on it." One girl had the audacity to ask for one of the TVs as a return on her investment. "What you trying to do," Tommy said, "eat up our profits?"

I used to think that Tommy hated his mother just because she happened to be female. But that was speculation.

There was plenty of room in the parking lot. I eased into a slot. Tommy and I stayed put while Carol scampered into the diner. We needed a caucus and I didn't want to do it in subzero weather.

"She won't talk to you," I told Tommy. "Why don't you let me find out what she knows?"

"And what do I do, sit here and pull my johnson? It's fucking cold."

"I'll leave the motor running."

"No way. She'll tell us both or I'll break her legs."

"Don't worry," I said. "I'll find out."

Actually, I wasn't even sure that I wanted to know what Dusty was up to. I'd seen something tonight, something I wasn't supposed to see. Something that for some reason made me think about hospitalization insurance. Carol knew what it was and I figured, with a little effort, I could sweet-talk her into telling me.

Tommy disagreed. "You go home to your wife and let me at her. She'll tell me or—"

"I know," I said. "Or you'll break her legs."

"Fucking right."

"Hey, man, it's not that important. Chill out. We're not involved in whatever Dusty's into, so let's just keep it that way. We didn't see anything. I promised him."

"Don't be an asshole," Tommy said. "If he's gonna shit where we eat, then we got a right to do something about it."

"Like what?"

"Leave it to me."

"You think I'm a moron?" I said. "It's none of my business. You get us involved and we'll both wind up in a car trunk."

"Let me worry about it," Tommy said. Then he jumped out of the car and trotted toward the diner.

I'd seen enough of Tommy's schemes to know that he had one brewing. Problem was that I never knew what they were until the payoff. Whatever this one was, my well-being was taking a back seat to his avarice. I didn't think Carol would talk, so there wasn't much he could do, but I ran after him just to make sure.

15

She'd planted herself in a booth against a fogged window that rattled against the wind. We sat across from her, Tommy on the aisle, me inside. I was in good position to flash eye signals at Carol. Except you had to see Carol to know that it was impossible to make eye contact with her. She was walleyed. One eye kept staring straight out while the other focused on her shoulder bone. Damn disconcerting.

"What'll it be?" The waitress had dark hair, dark skin, and a white uniform that just made the tops of her thighs. Her bored expression told me she wasn't thrilled with her work.

"Three coffees," Tommy said.

"That's it?"

Want to make an enemy? Take a booth and order coffee only.

"That's it," I said courageously. She grimaced and shuffled off to the coffee rack. I checked her ass for panty lines. There weren't any.

We waited for the coffee, then I said, "Dusty told me he might have to split for a few days. He wants us to run the place while he's gone."

Tommy looked surprised. "Me too? Dusty told you that? Why the fuck didn't he tell me?"

"I think it just came up. I told him he'd better check it with your uncle. I don't want Peppy to get his bowels in an uproar."

"Fuck him!"

If Tommy ever took himself literally, he'd be a sure bet for the *Guinness Book of Records*.

Meanwhile, under the table, Carol's hands were doing what her eyes couldn't do: flashing signals. She was squeezing the shit out of my leg.

Her mouth was all twisted up and she was nipping her lips like she wanted to cry. Mascara had wiggled down from the corners of her eyes. The rest of her makeup looked like she'd applied it during a brownout. Still, she was shapely enough to appeal to some men. Hoods, creeps like her

16

husband Leo, and slickies like Dusty Sands. I felt sorry for her.

I pointed to a pile of newspapers next to the cash register. "Get me a *Times,* will you, Tommy?" I figured thirty seconds alone with Carol was better than no time at all. Tommy wasn't fooled but he got up anyway.

"New York Times," he said. "The guy can't even fold it and he wants to read it."

As soon as he was out of range, Carol said, "If Dusty ain't back in a week, he wants you to go see Barney Rubbles."

Barney Reuben, nicknamed "Rubbles," was Dusty's accountant. I had a dozen questions to toss at Carol but Tommy had the *Times* and was on his way back.

"He doesn't trust him," Carol said, hurriedly. "Dusty's in trouble. That's all I can say."

"Those two dudes at the lounge," I said. "Who are they?"

She shrugged. Tommy was back.

"Answer him," he said, sliding in.

She looked at her watch. "It's late. I have to go."

Tommy snatched her wrist. "You ain't going home yet."

"Ouch!" He was squeezing so hard that Carol was doing a little jig in her seat like she had to take a leak. "Let—let me go, you fuck."

"Hey, Tommy, for Chrissake," I said. I grabbed his wrist and we looked like three Apache warriors performing a religious handshake.

"I'll make her tell us," Tommy said.

"Not here."

He glanced around. The owner, a burly Greek, came bounding over to us. "Watch what you do in my place. You go out. Wrestle outside. Not in my place. No wrestling in my place."

So much for the inquisition.

We drove back to the Skyview to pick up their cars. The ride took three minutes and Tommy used every second to badger Carol into telling what she knew about Dusty's private business. She said nothing, though I could see Tommy was getting to her. Tears were welling up in the corners of her eyes.

I turned the corner, then jerked to a stop, double-parking alongside Carol's Chevy. I was surprised to see Dusty's El Dorado still parked just behind her car. The street was poorly lit, bordered by spindly trees. On our right was a row of clapboard houses separated by black slivers: driveways too narrow for cars, perfect for muggers. Across the street was the fire door through which I assumed Baldy and Blacula had gained access to Dusty's office. There were no windows in the back of the building so I couldn't tell if he was still entertaining. Everything outside seemed quiet in an eerie sort of way.

Carol said, "Call me tomorrow, Frankie." She leaned over and pecked my cheek. The tip of her nose was cold as a puppy's.

I waited for her to pull out. She hit her lights, waved and eased ahead slowly in a trail of white smoke. The radio said it was fifteen degrees. I followed until I reached Tommy's Buick, about forty yards farther down. He had already climbed into the front seat.

"We gotta talk," he said.

"Come on, man, I'm beat."

"One cigarette."

I knew Tommy's routine. One cigarette meant he was wired and needed time to come down. Usually, he'd reminisce through half a pack of Kool 100's.

"Okay, but make it quick, eh." I pulled in behind his car and opened the window. I don't smoke and it drives me crazy when anyone does it in my car. He reached over and turned off the motor.

"Remember Flossie?" he said.

Regrettably, I did. She was a homely chick he'd found one night in some after-hours joint over in Sunnyside. She had a pencil-like body and a long bony face with a wide mouth. Smiling she resembled a skull impaled on a spear. I couldn't see the attraction until Tommy introduced us. "Meet my partner," he'd said. I grimaced. "No shit," he went on, Flossie beside him, grinning her grisly grin. "Remember that hair shop I told you about? Well, me and Floss are takin' it."

Of course I had no idea what he was talking about.

"I'm a widow," Flossie said with a hint of pride. "My husband fell off of a ladder putting up Christmas lights."

"Broke his neck," Tommy added. "I told her she oughta do something with the insurance money." He winked and I got the picture. "I mean you can't sit home on your ass feeling sorry for yourself, right, babe?"

"It's only five thousand but Tommy says that's enough."

He squeezed her tightly. "With my contacts? You bet your sweet ass it is."

I never asked if Flossie had any kids. Though I often wondered.

"I can't believe that bitch never gave me the bread," Tommy said, lighting his first Kool.

"She gave you a grand, down payment. What more do you want?"

"Why settle for a piece when you can eat the whole fuckin' pie? Yeah," he said, drawing deeply, "I bet one of her douche bag girlfriends ratted me out."

"I guess they didn't know a good deal when they saw one. Now what do you say we leave memory lane and call it a night?"

He looked across the street at the lounge. "This shit tonight," he said. "You think my uncle and Dusty are in it together?"

"Why don't you ask your uncle?"

He winced. "Because my uncle's a scumbag." He blew a stream of smoke in my face. "You know, I don't think Dusty's got the balls to deal drugs on his own. I'll bet my uncle's behind him. I betcha Peppy knows about it, too. We're the only assholes don't know nothin'."

"First of all," I said, wearily, "Dusty was dealing on

his own long before he got into the Skyview. So why can't he be doing a solo now? Second, even if Uncle Charlie is in with him, what difference does it make to us? We've got nothing to gain by poking around. If they wanted us to know, they would have told us."

He shook his head. "Can't understand why my uncle won't trust me. I could be a big help to him by just keeping an eye on Dusty."

"That's Peppy's job."

"Another scumbag."

This conversation was going nowhere. Like Carol, I'd had enough of Tommy Milano for one night. I was thinking how stupid it was to waste any more time talking about Dusty when we heard the fire door slam shut.

"Hey, there he is," Tommy said. "Get down!"

Instinctively, I slid down in my seat. Tommy turned around, was peering over the headrest out the back window. I adjusted the side mirror until I caught sight of Dusty trotting toward the El Dorado.

"What are we hiding for?" I said.

"Shut up!"

Dusty had reached his car door. I could see him fumbling with his keys when from the corner a car turned slowly toward us. The driver flicked his brights over Dusty who froze like a startled cat. The car glided closer. I couldn't make out the model in the glaring headlights, nor could I make out the driver. I spun around for a better look.

Now the limo was right next to Dusty. The window on the passenger side seemed to slide down by itself. Dusty leaned over to say something to the driver and from the gestures, I could tell they knew each other.

"I can't hear," Tommy said.

"Shhh."

We were peeking over the headrests like two kids at a horror movie. They were too far away to pick up the conversation. What we did hear was Dusty's tone, a whining pitch that might come from a man denying guilt or begging forgiveness.

Squinting against the headlamps, I could see only an outline of the driver's head. A man's head. He was hatless and appeared to have a long hook nose, though that may have been shadows playing tricks. Something terrible was about to happen. I could feel it as sure as I'd felt a foreboding when I'd first glimpsed Blacula. Dusty, I realized, wasn't denying or begging. He was pleading for his life.

I heard a thud, like the pop of a Dwight Gooden fastball. Dusty jumped back. He grunted, clutched his throat and fell against the car door. He hung suspended for an instant. Then a second thud spun him around. He grabbed the door handle and then slithered lower and lower until all I could see was his hand. He groaned and the hand dropped out of sight.

"Jesus Christ," Tommy whispered.

I said nothing. I couldn't. My stomach had kicked up a coffee–bile potion that burned out my vocal cords.

"Down!" Tommy said. "Get down!"

For a second I thought the shooter had spotted us. His car lurched forward and the lights seemed to jump at us. We threw ourselves across the console between the seats, Tommy first, me on top pressing my face against his back. We heard wheels spinning. He must have fishtailed because his lights swept across my car at a crazy angle as though he was coming at us broadside. A loud screech. Wind whipped over my back as he raced by, peeling rubber all the way.

Get the plates, I thought. I sat up quickly but not soon enough to make out the number. Jersey plates was all I saw.

"Did you see him?" I asked Tommy.

He didn't answer. Instead, he scrambled out and I thought he was going to check on Dusty. Before I had a chance to follow, Tommy was already climbing into his car. He turned back to me and said calmly, "Follow me. We gotta talk." He was so cool that he astonished me.

I stuck my head out the window and looked at Dusty Sands. He was lying face down in the street, arms at his side, head toward his car. He looked like he was checking a faulty muffler. Blood was pouring out from under his chin, a stream that glistened in the light of a distant streetlamp.

I didn't have to get any nearer to know he was dead. Still, I felt guilty for not going to him. I'd known him well enough, and I'd liked the guy. Yet there he was, murdered right before my eyes, and all I could do was sit like shit on a cobblestone. I pictured myself rolling him over, seeing a bloody pulp where his face used to be, staring into lifeless eyes that said, "Where the fuck were you when I needed you?"

Tommy's Buick was purring. He pulled out and I followed. In the mirror, I watched Dusty's body shrink with distance. He reminded me of a run-over dog you might see lying on the roadside on your way to work. By nightfall the carcass is gone and you wonder what poor shlunk earns his keep carting away dead dogs. How long would Dusty have to lay there before someone carted him away?

Like two cars in tow we rolled slowly onto the Grand Central. I wasn't about to lose Tommy and from his rate of speed I was sure he didn't want to lose me. With irritating caution he cruised along while I impatiently flashed my brights. Now that I'd run away I wanted to put distance between myself and the remains of my ex-boss. The more I flashed the slower Tommy went.

"We gotta talk," I repeated facetiously. So much composure from a maniac who rips cable boxes out of TV sets. It was demoralizing to think that Tommy Milano was cooler under pressure than I was. But I guess you never really know about a fellow until you've witnessed a murder with him.

Sure, we had to talk. We had to get our stories straight. We could never admit to being eyewitnesses to murder, especially one that had all the earmarks of a professional hit. Not if we wanted to stay alive. Still, the police would know we were the last to see Dusty alive, and so we'd be the first ones questioned. Headline: BARTENDERS HELD IN DISCO DEATH. Beautiful.

We zipped past the Long Island Expressway at thirty miles an hour and I wondered if we'd rendezvous before dawn. I was developing a fondness for the dark—the first phase, I assumed, of my new role as suspect-fugitive. I wondered what was in store for me in the next few days. Questions? Cops grilling me? The smoke-filled room? Disembodied voices behind blinding lights: "All right, Fontana, let's go over it one more time."

One slip, one minor contradiction and I'd be cooked. Obstructing justice, accessory to murder, conspiracy, and who knew what other charges they might throw at me. In the span of fifteen minutes I'd become inextricably involved in a mess that to me meant permanent disaster.

As I drove, my priorities began realigning themselves. All positions changed, except of course, for number one— self-preservation—the instinct mightier now than ever before. Self-preservation would depend, however, upon my ability to lie. Simple enough, I thought. As a bartender, I'd learned to wear more phony faces than Lon Chaney, Sr. Lying was part of my job and I'd spent the last four years behind a bar sharpening my skills. The question was: Were my skills sharp enough to keep me from spending the next five years behind bars?

Tommy finally signaled us off the parkway. At Northern Boulevard and Main Street, he pulled over, cut his engine, and ran back to join me. It was still too early for traffic. For the first time in years I envied the nine-to-fivers safely ensconced in their banal world of purchase-money mortgages and deferred compensation plans.

"Frank, we're in trouble," Tommy said. He hopped in beside me, still puffing from the short run.

"No shit," I said. "Took you all this time to figure that out?"

He lit a Kool and I opened the window. "It don't matter if we saw the guy or not," he said. "They put our names in the paper and we're fucked. We left the diner ten minutes before it happened. That's something they can check. It's certifiable."

So are you, I wanted to say. Instead, I said, "Tell me something I don't already know, will you?"

He snorted smoke from his nose. "Hey, man, guys get blown away for shit like this."

"Shut up, will you?"

"Okay, what we have to do is work out our stories. Times, locations, everything."

"Okay," I said. "They can't prove what time he was killed. Not to the minute. We can tell them exactly what we did but leave out what we saw."

"That'll put us right on the scene, man."

"So what. His car was still there when we dropped Carol off. She can back that. She must have seen it."

"I don't know," Tommy said.

"Look, if we start changing things around we're bound to get tripped up. Besides, we don't have time to program Carol."

"I guess so. Hey, turn the heat on, I'm freezing."

I turned up the heat but it didn't stop me from shaking.

"So we're straight on what happened?" I asked.

"We got no choice." He took a deep drag. "Who do you figure it was?"

"Better we don't think about it," I said. Not that I wasn't curious, I was just afraid I'd come up with the answer.

"You think my uncle had something to do with it? With Dusty whacked, he gets the whole joint. What do you think?"

I studied him for a moment. His face had lit up like a three-way bulb. I could almost see the thing over his head: idea, good idea, great idea. He squinted at me as though I'd read his mind. Then he shook his head and answered his own question. "Nah, I don't think it was Uncle Charlie. You gotta figure some clown from the Bronx. A head maybe, or some low-life pusher."

"You going to tell your uncle what happened? The real story, I mean."

24

"Fuck no. We don't relate as it is. Besides, I don't owe that prick any favors."

"I know that," I said. Yet I couldn't help thinking about how it might go down. Candy Gizzo packed some heavy clout and I wondered whether he'd use any of it to protect his nephew. True, he had no use for Tommy, but the fact remained, they were related. Which meant that Tommy might get out of this. But what about me? My uncle lived in Akron.

"You know, Tommy," I said, "the law's going to be all over us like ugly on an ape."

"Cocksuckers."

"Yeah. But don't let them bug you."

"Motherfuckers."

"Better cool it, Tom. You get crazy with those guys and we're both up shit creek."

"Take care of your own end," he said, staring out the windshield.

He was deep in thought, the three-way over his head going crazy. I didn't like it. He glared at me like I'd suddenly become his enemy.

"I'm gonna turn this around," he said.

"What?"

He opened the door, got out, then leaned back in. "Just watch your ass, Frankie. Watch it good 'cause I gotta be watching out for my own."

CHAPTER 3

I didn't need a degree in accounting to know what Tommy meant. Still, old habits are hard to break. I'd been trained to think like an accountant, to resolve problems in a precise and orderly fashion. Determine the problem, sort and analyze the facts, then record what you find. It worked well in legitimate enterprise. Of course, murder and drugs were not your classic examples of legitimate enterprises, but it was a way to begin. So I did.

As to the problem, easy enough: How much trouble had I bought by witnessing Dusty's murder? What could I do to get out of it?

I analyzed the facts, sorted them into pluses and minuses. Like plus number one: I hadn't actually seen the killer's face and as far as I knew he hadn't seen mine. On the minus side, the gunman might be the black dude. In which case he'd know I could pick him out of a lineup. And so could Carol. He'd then have to kill us both to be sure we'd never talk.

A minus that size had me way out of balance, so I

quickly threw in another plus: the killer's profile. It wasn't even close to Blacula's. The nose I'd seen in the getaway car might not have been as pronounced as I'd imagined, but it certainly didn't fit any black I'd ever seen.

I needed one more plus to balance out, and I found it fast. There were two of us who could place Blacula at the scene of the murder around the time of commission. Chances were that both he and his bald companion had police records, that if they *were* committing premeditated murder they would do so with more discretion.

Having balanced that part of the ledger I moved to the next entry: Dusty. His life had been filled with dark corners infested with vermin like Blacula and Baldy. Through investigation, the police were bound to turn on the light that would send those grimy bastards scurrying for cover. Those with protection would survive, the rest would be squashed. And if evidence proved too sparse, then maybe they'd put the wood to a few little guys just to make it look good. Little guys like Frankie Fontana.

Tommy was next. I thought about the way he'd handle the police. He wasn't the brightest guy in the world but he was streetwise, and I didn't think he'd let himself be goaded into blowing our story. As to myself, however, I had many doubts.

Another item that nagged me was that gleam I'd seen in Tommy's eyes when he told me to watch my ass. It was more a warning than a friendly caution. But why? I figured he was planning to take another shot at Carol, to use what she knew to get himself in good with his uncle Charlie. It was a dangerous business and one I wanted no part of. Yet I couldn't shake the feeling Tommy was at this very moment working on a scam that was bound to get me involved.

I rolled out onto the main drag and headed home. Beside sleep, what I wanted now was to put time between the past hour and the future. A buffer. Like coming out of a nightmare whose chilling effects linger for a while and then wane as the day goes on. Funny, but the closer to home I got, the more I felt that I was driving toward trouble and not away from it.

I live in East Glendale, a quiet residential community sandwiched between a half-dozen cemeteries and some acreage laughingly called Forest Park. Moving from Akron, I'd originally planned on taking a sweet little bachelor apartment in the City. On the Upper East Side maybe, or down in Murray Hill. Then I discovered that the only people who could afford the rent were arbitragers, call girls, and members of the Board of the Chase Manhattan Bank. So, thanks to a realtor, I wound up in East Glendale in four rooms on the top floor of a two-family red brick.

The apartment was about a thirty-minute drive from where I'd left Tommy. I made it in twenty. I took my usual parking spot—the only one ever available by the time I got home—in front of a fire plug, stepped out of the car, and looked around. Dawn wasn't far away, stars dissolving into a gray sky. It looked like snow was coming, or sleet. Something foul. I checked both ways before crossing the street. No hit man. No cops. Nothing except a mangy mutt sniffing garbage cans. I hurried up the cement stairs to the front door. I unlocked the door, stepped into the vestibule, and, by habit, quietly closed the door behind me.

My landlady lived alone, a widow who spooked easily. And though she was used to my crazy hours, I still made it my business to come and go as quietly as possible. On my income, I couldn't afford to alienate the owner.

As for the family upstairs, well, that would be Jackie and me. Not exactly a family, more like two displaced swingers. Which was why Jackie despised living here. She'd been "shanghaied to the boonies," a misdemeanor I was still paying for.

When I met her, she was a whore. Or so Tommy Milano had implied. That was the first time I'd ever set eyes on her. Decked out like the cover of *Vogue,* she'd come strutting into the Skyview on the arm of a high roller named Seymour, a blowhard who measured class by the number of rings a person wore. Seymour owned a Caddy dealership in Bay Ridge.

I'd cleared a place for them the way I always did when I sensed a big tip or a broad on the make. I placed two cocktail napkins on the bar but when I looked up they had already settled into a spot at Tommy's station. It seemed that Tommy knew Jackie from the City. I had no right to be jealous, but I was. In fact, I was seething.

And Tommy knew it. He was all smiles as he turned his back to the bar so no one could see the way he was driving a finger into a loose fist. The signal was clear: this gorgeous woman, this green-eyed goddess, was nothing more than a two-bit whore.

What wasn't clear was whether Tommy had ever balled her. I knew he wanted me to think he had. Even though I wouldn't have believed him no matter what he'd told me, I just had to press him. Until one day when he said, "What kind of guy would *you* be if you fell for a chick *I* fucked?"

He laughed, knowing he'd pegged me right. It was true. I was falling for her. Then, a few nights later, it was late, just before closing. We'd already announced "last call." I was bending over the sink rinsing glasses and didn't see her come in.

"Hi, Frankie."

I didn't look up. "Where's the pasha tonight?" I said, feigning more interest in dirty glasses than her flirtatious smile.

"Seymour? Home with his wife. It's Saturday night. You know how it is."

I kept polishing an already spotless glass.

"Ever hear a song called 'Saturday Night Is the Loneliest Night of the Week'? Well, that's the 'other woman's national anthem.' "

She shrugged. "Kismet. Who cares? I don't want Seymour anymore than his wife does. She wants a divorce."

"He's rich."

"Aren't you?"

"Only in mind and body. I'm a barman, or haven't you noticed?"

"Tommy tells me you went to college. What are you doing here, slumming?"

"I'm learning about life," I said. "Learning and looking."

"For what?"

"Excitement. You ever date an accountant?"

She laughed. I felt my skin tingle.

She said, "I see what you mean."

"Tommy's not here tonight," I said.

"I didn't come here to see Tommy. I like bearded men."

I ran a hand over my beard. "Most women I know don't care for it. Chafes their thighs."

"That's because they don't know where to put their legs."

I placed the glass on the bar. "Let's cut the small talk."

"Fine," she said. "How soon can you leave?"

"Depends how horny you are."

"I've been thinking about you."

"Twenty minutes," I said. "But don't think I'm always this easy. I'm making an exception because it's Saturday night and you've got the lonelies."

"I may decide to hold you over to Monday. Think you can handle it?"

"If you promise not to bore me."

"Yes," she said. "I do believe you can handle it."

She held me over to Tuesday. For two and a half days we lived on passion and pizza. I played it like I was totally indifferent, the laid back, bearded Don Juan. Three days later we were aboard an Eastern jet bound for Jamaica.

Weekly trysts followed. Room 20 of the Briny Breezes, a raunchy Brooklyn motel that came equipped with quivering beds, mirrored walls, and X-rated flicks on closed cable. I must admit that when we checked in I never dreamed it would end in cohabitation. I was thirty-three, a confirmed bachelor with a strong aversion toward parenthood. I just couldn't see myself rolling in at five A.M. to the wailing of a piss-ass infant. My brother James used to tell me I'd feel differently when I had my own kids, when I became a father. To which I replied that the only way I'd become a father was by getting ordained.

Before I met Jackie I was content. Women fell in love with me and that satisfied my ego. In turn, I was absolutely honest with them about my views toward marriage, offering such honesty solely to allay the guilt I'd feel when it came time to say good-bye. It was a self-serving arrangement; I liked it that way. Until Jackie.

Jackie was the kind of woman that very few men could handle. Carnal knowledge embodied in five-and-a-half feet of pure sensuality. Legs like Bianca Jagger, waist no wider than a hand span, and breasts that pouted. Her silky black hair accentuated almond-shaped eyes, eyes the color of Caribbean water, and her high cheekbones framing her face, and those lips you remembered days after they touched you—wherever they touched you.

Her looks had a lot to do with my asking her to marry me. It's one of the shortfalls of the male libido. But what attracted me most was that she was unlike anyone I'd ever encountered. I could never figure out where she was coming from. She was just so exciting.

Never having been married, I could only rely on what I'd been told by scores of divorcees—that marriage was a fucking drag, a bore. No excitement. So there was Jackie, who was everything but a bore. I decided to jump at it. "Let's do it, babe, and see what happens."

Someone once said you can't experience total bliss unless you've suffered complete despair. That's the way it was with us—peaks and valleys, except the peaks never quite reached the previous high and the valleys were breaking records on each dip. A volatile fucking relationship.

She'd bat her eyes and fuss over me, then turn child-like and act all kinds of insecure. As though being loved by me was all she had ever wanted out of life. It was bullshit but she'd make me believe that she'd never found what

31

she'd been looking for until I came along. And so she'd draw me into feeling as though I had to protect her from herself. It was during those peaks that I would feel more a man than at any time in my life.

On our honeymoon, about four in the morning one moonlit night on a Caribbean beach behind the El San Juan Hotel, having just closed the casino, we were too hyped to jump into the sack.

"It's so nice out," Jackie said. "Let's walk the beach."

It wasn't that great a night, really. Oh, the sky was cloudless and a billion stars were winking. But it was close to ninety degrees and the air felt like wet cobwebs. Me, I was so mesmerized by her beauty, I could have marched on the waves to Miami.

We strolled a few hundred yards down the beach, not saying a word, just listening to the gentle swish of the tide. Jackie stopped and looked back. The hotel was a long way off and the beach was desolate.

"Far enough," she said. She tugged at a few strings and the evening dress fell away, a blue rumple on the white sand. "Come on!" And off she ran into the water, her skin turning blue-peach in the moonlight. Except for her ass which was marvelously white in contrast.

I tore off my three-hundred-dollar suit, not caring about buttons, creases, stains. She had a forty-yard lead and I ran after her, hitting the water in a shallow dive. I felt like Johnny Weissmuller, the way he used to chase Jane into the lagoon after she'd playfully bounced a coconut off his head. She knew where to run, Jane did. I mean the lagoon was the one place Tarzan was sure to catch her.

I caught Jackie by the ankles and flipped her over backward. She came up sputtering, dipped back under, and came up spouting water at me like a fountain statue. It went that way for a time, Jackie and I alone in the warm sea, splashing and giggling like a pair of bare-ass country kids.

Finally I caught Jackie in a grip she couldn't wiggle out of. Not that she wanted to. I had her arms behind her back, pressing her body against mine. She could feel me getting aroused and started grinding into me. Releasing her arms, I grabbed her buttocks and lifted her onto me. She wrapped her legs around my waist, threw back her head, and howled. It was wild.

Collapsed on the sand next to our clothes, I remember gazing up at the stars, thinking how I had the world by the short-hairs. I'd married a beautiful and sensuous woman who was flaky enough to keep me on my toes, but sharp enough to know when and how to act straight. Perfect, I thought.

I turned to look at her lying naked on the sand. Cheekbones. Lips. Glistening hair. And then I saw the tears. How sweet, I thought: weeping with joy, choked up by romance.

"What's the matter, babe?" I asked, expecting her to say "nothing," to give me a kiss, and tell me how much she loved me. What I got was *True Confessions*.

She said, "I was just thinking about my mother." She'd moved into the crook of my arm. She wasn't seeing anything except the scene her mind was replaying: "My father ran out on us when I was five. I can't even remember what he looked like—my mother threw out all his pictures—but I remember he was a handsome sonofabitch, green eyes like mine."

"Uh-huh," I said dreamily.

"We'd come home from my aunt's house one night and all my father's clothes were gone. No note, nothing. My mother went berserk, wrecked the house, and then beat the hell out of me. Broke two of my ribs. For days I was black and blue. The bitch!" She practically snarled.

"You know she actually blamed me for what happened. I can still hear her: 'You! Ever since you were born I started losing him.' "

I said, "Some men just can't take kids," knowing I was referring to myself and feeling like a shit because of it.

"That wasn't it," Jackie said. "He never mistreated me. He just couldn't take *her* anymore. He took off with a woman eighteen years older than he was."

"Where is he now?"

"Who knows?"

"Must have been rough."

"It got worse. It took my mother seven years to find another guy. Her Mr. Right. You know, it's funny but all that time I couldn't wait for her to remarry. I figured once she had a steady man things would get better. You wouldn't believe the way we lived, her and me. We never sat together, ate together; she wouldn't even talk to me except to scream orders and tell me how much of a cunt I was getting to be. Like *I* was the one putting out for favors. Shit, she was fucking just to get the phone paid. It was a goddam revolving door, one turkey after another. I'd find them in bed the next morning. The faces were different but nothing else ever changed.

"And then came Mr. Right—Jerry Evans. The shithead. He had his own insurance agency. A slimy bastard with hair all over his back. Ugly. Ugliest man I ever met; breath always smelled like he'd gargled with sewer water. I hated him."

"I can see why."

"No you can't. His charms were only a part of it. It's what he used to do to me."

"Oh," I said. I drew her closer.

"Yes," she said. "While the cat was away the rat was fucking the kitten. I was twelve years old."

"Jesus." I could feel the rage inside me. "The fuck! Did you tell your mother about him?"

A sardonic chuckle. She reached for her clothes and started to get up. "Hey," I said. "Finish it. How did your mother react when you told her about Evans?"

Her eyes seemed glazed. "She said, 'You better get to like it, honey. That's your job for as long as you live here.' "

"What?"

"Yeah, it was all part of the deal. An arrangement. Jerry would pay her each time. Beatings were extra." Softly she said, "Double for sodomy. My mother got to be a rich lady because of me."

"Holy shit!" That was the best I could come up with. Unless you count what I did. Which was to pick her up in my arms and carry her all the way back to our cabana. "It's all right now," I told her. "I love you. I'll love you enough to make up for it."

That was the closest I got to Jackie. Our Everest, peak of peaks. From then on it was downhill, because the other side, the side she didn't reveal until after we'd settled down in East Glendale, was the stone bitch.

Tantrums, sudden and unprovoked, during which she'd profess to hate all men, particularly me, for having "trapped her." Nothing would appease her. She'd simply shut me out with that indifferent air. It drove me nuts.

It was the indifference that wrecked me. No talk, just depression that turned to fits of screaming if I came near her. For days we'd go on that way. Two strangers moping around the apartment without saying a word to each other. Me, bursting; Jackie morose.

I suppose a shrink would have blamed it on Jackie's upbringing. I mean any girl who endured what she had would naturally feel her brains had scrambled a little. I tried to see her that way, to live with it, but it got rougher still. Especially when she started going out while I was working nights. It usually happened when she was at her lowest. Those nights, I'd make it my business to get home as late as possible: five, maybe six in the morning. Sometimes she'd be in bed when I arrived, sometimes not. When she did finally roll in, her mood would be changed, the funk dissipated. She'd be that sweet girlchild, hungry for love, vulnerable.

And we'd make love. For a whole day we'd make love, desperate and fitful, like we were both trying to punish each other for letting it happen in the first place. I'd force myself not to think about what she had done the night before. Why should I? I'd tell myself. She's back now and maybe the bitch that walked out last night will never show her face again.

One of the more unnerving features about being

married to Jackie was that I never knew for sure in the morning if I would still be married by nightfall. With Mrs. Fontana, a good-bye kiss was never just casual farewell. It seemed more like the partnership was being dissolved.

It hadn't bothered me that much at the beginning. I'd been living from day to day anyway, and marrying Jackie was merely an extension of the irregularity I'd become accustomed to. Lately though, I'd found myself wanting a hell of a lot more from our marriage. Permanence. A cornerstone for the future. I tried explaining that to Jackie. She laughed. "I've been called many things, but never a cornerstone." Then she became serious. "What's wrong with you anyway? We didn't get married to have kids or a house in the country."

"I know," I said. "But we're in limbo here. We live like we're waiting for a Manhattan express. What's wrong with wanting some stability in our lives?"

"Stability? Cornerstones? Plans for the future? Who ever gets what they plan for? I look at tomorrow to see what I don't have that I want right now."

"And what do you want?"

"Whatever it is, it will take more money than you'll ever have. I want a high roller."

"Then why did you marry me?"

She thought about that for a while. I remember the way she looked, like she was really struggling for the words, a real zinger to bury me with. "Consider it a layover," she said. "But it doesn't have to be like that, hon."

"How do you figure?" I said.

"Because something's going to happen. I've always had the feeling that one day something's going to fall in my lap. And I care enough about you to share it. Listen, I can't get what I want by saving nickels and dimes. Do you think Dusty Sands ever lived that way? Or Charlie Gizzo? Or the other regulars at the Skyview?"

"You can't compare them to me."

"That's too bad," she said.

"They don't make their money legally."

"If something is illegal, does that make it wrong?"

"Usually."

"Is it wrong to get even, Frankie? Is it wrong to steal from those who stole from you? That's what happens when you cheat on your taxes, or lie to the insurance companies."

"It's not the same."

As I walked into our apartment, I nearly swooned from the heat. Jackie, the sun goddess, hated winter so she'd create summer by upping the thermostat to eighty-five. Fuck the utility bills.

Our apartment door opens to the kitchen. I went to the sink where I dug out a small pot from a pile of large pots submerged in yesterday's suds. I filled the pot with water and set it to boil. For the last few days, Jackie had been between moods, which meant she'd talk, though just barely. I figured we could chat over a cup of instant coffee.

The bedroom was even hotter than the kitchen, yet there was Jackie coiled in a fetal position under a layer of quilt.

I shook her. "Jackie. Jackie, get up."

"Mmmmm," she said dreamily.

"Come on, wake up. I'm in trouble."

"Go away!"

I yanked the quilt off her. She was naked and her rump curved deliciously in my direction. "For Chrissake, will you get your ass out of bed."

She rolled over, opened an eye. "What time is it?"

I sat down on the bed. "Time to bake a cake with a file in it."

"Wha'?"

"Dusty's dead. Murdered."

She came out of it slowly. An amazing broad. Nothing ever grabbed her. She was stoic about everything except sex and money. Especially money.

Money. She could talk for hours about money. But murder? Well . . .

Now, with her eyes still closed she was sitting Indian style on the bed. The quilt lay across her legs and her body glistened with sweat. Droplets slid down between her breasts.

"Somebody shot Dusty," I said.

"Dusty? Who did it?"

"I don't know."

"So?"

"*Jesus Christ,*" I shouted. I could feel my face getting red. "Don't you give a fuck about anything?"

She shrugged.

"Let me spell it out for you. Tommy and I were in my car when it happened. Not more than thirty feet away. We saw him get it. Do you understand?"

"So?"

"So! Sew fucking buttons!" I snapped.

"Well, you said you don't know who did it. What else is there to say?"

"Nothing much," I gesticulated. "Nothing much except if the cops find out I'm a witness, they'll blab it to the papers. Then the shooter thinks I saw him and he comes after me. How's that for starters?" I was hitting high C and she was just sitting there with her boobs sticking out, a blank look on her face.

She covered her ears. "I've got a hangover."

"Show some concern, for Christ's sake. I didn't wake you up to say the dogs knocked over our garbage can."

She yawned, ran a hand through her hair. Three hours at Mr. Godfrey had changed raven silk into a headful of scorched worms. A new punk cut. But she was gorgeous no matter what she did to her hair.

"You want some coffee?" I said. A domestic tack.

She sighed, "yes," and her breath floated to me, slightly sour but still kissable.

"Come on, babe," I said. "Get up."

CHAPTER 4

We talked over coffee. Husband and wife rapping about their respective days. How was work? Oh, fine, except my boss was shot twice in the face by an unknown assailant. And how was your day? I see you had your hair done.

I filled her in on everything that happened, including the cryptic conversations I'd had with Carol and later with Tommy. She seemed vaguely interested. Despite the heat, she'd slipped into a velvet robe that clung to her curves. A high-neck job with long slits up the sides of her legs.

"Well," she said, examining her fingernails. She'd painted them a weird brown color that reminded me of dried blood. "I don't think you have anything to worry about. What can the police do to you? Just stick to your story. You didn't see anything and you don't know anything about Dusty's drug thing. Jesus, but you're twitchy."

"Maybe you're right." I felt somewhat relieved but I still wanted to talk to Carol.

"So call her," Jackie said. "I'm going back to bed."

"Simple as that, eh? How am I supposed to sleep?"

"I said *I* was going to bed. You can stay up if you want."

"Well, I can't sleep. Not until this is straightened out."

"Then you'd better make some more coffee," she said over her shoulder. "You might be up for a long time."

I followed her into the bedroom where I dialed Carol. She picked up on the first ring. "Frankie?" She sounded like she hadn't slept either.

"Jeez, Frank, did you hear?"

"Hear what?" I said. I didn't want her to know I'd seen anything until I heard what she had to say about it. Besides, I wanted to practice my story. If I couldn't convince Carol that I didn't know anything, what chance would I have with the police?

"They killed him," she said. "Dusty's dead."

I wanted to say "so?" But I said, "What happened?" as if shocked by the news. "Gunned down? . . . Where? . . . No shit." I was doing fine until she told me the cops had already talked to her.

"I told them you dropped me off about four o'clock," she said. "I didn't see anything, didn't even know he was still inside. They're on their way to talk to you and Tommy."

"Why do you think they went to you first?" I asked.

"I don't know. Because of Leo, I guess. Ever since I married that bastard the cops have been in and out of here like it's Manhattan South."

"Did you say anything about those two guys?"

"What guys?" She sounded defensive. "I never saw no guys."

Nice game, I thought. Ma Bell's version of liars' poker.

"Come on, Carol," I said, trying to stay calm. "You're talking to *me* now. We both saw them, one was black and ugly, the other was bald and white. Remember?"

"Listen to me, Frankie. I don't know what you saw but I didn't see nothing. Nobody. Nowhere."

There I was with a full house and she was bluffing me right out of my drawers. Liars' poker, hell, this was two-handed cutthroat and if I wasn't careful she'd skin me and toss my bones to the wolves.

"All right, all right," I said. "Don't get your nose out of joint. Just tell me why Dusty wanted me to call Barney. The real reason, Carol. No bullshit."

"I already told you it's something about his books." Her tone now was downright testy. "Frankie, I swear if you get me involved in this I'll tell Leo."

"And what can he do?" I said confidently. "Fuck up my license plates? Remember, Carol, I'm not the one who was putting out for Dusty."

She went silent for a while. No doubt she was considering the ramifications of her extracurricular activity. I'd never met Leo, but from what I'd gleaned from Tommy, Carol's hubby had already made his bones when most of us were still playing with blocks. Dishonoring Leo might have proved fatal for Carol even if Dusty had lived. Without him, she had no one.

At last she said, "You're a moron, Fontana. You and your friend, Milano. Two morons."

"Come on, Carol, I'm no good at this. We're on the same side so be honest with me, okay?"

"I got my own problems."

"Carol, please—"

"Good-bye, Frankie."

She hung up. "Whore!" I said into the dead phone and slammed down the receiver.

Jackie was propped up on one arm. She'd heard my side of the conversation and was shaking her head. "Dumb," she said.

"Who's dumb?"

"You are. Seems to me you need all the help you can get. Carol's on your side, isn't she?"

"Carol's on her own side. Every man for himself."

"Dumb," Jackie said.

"Tell it to her, not me." I dropped wearily onto the

41

bed. "God, Jack, I can feel it all crashing in on me. I've got a sick feeling about all this. Jesus, you should have seen it tonight."

"You worry too much. Take a shower and get some sleep. You'll feel better later."

She was precious, my wife. If she couldn't screw it or spend it, she'd sleep on it. And either way, wasn't it better than worrying?

"How the hell can I sleep? The police are on their way over right now."

"So stay up and wait," she said. "I'm going to sleep. I was dreaming about Las Vegas." She slipped under the covers, placed her hands in a praying position and tucked them under her cheek.

"I can't handle this alone. What should I do, for Chrissake?"

She sighed. "Don't be such a wimp. You got balls; use them."

I'd already accepted the fact that Jackie was the laziest woman in the world, that she was self-centered and that she undoubtedly had had a number of discreet romps in the hay since our marriage. But damned if I'd sit still while she attacked my masculinity.

"If you feel that way, why don't you get out?"

She rolled over, looked up at me. "I've been meaning to talk to you about that."

Just what I need. "This isn't the time," I said. "Let's put it on hold until I get out of this mess."

"Then why threaten me?"

"I'm nervous."

"It's not only now. You're always pushing me. I can't live like this."

"Then leave." I said it roughly but inside I was groveling.

"Maybe I will."

"Don't let the door hit you in the ass on your way out."

She smiled sardonically, and with her eyes locked onto mine she sort of slid across the bed to where I was sitting.

She reached up and pulled me to her, mashing her breasts against my chest. She cupped my crotch with her left hand and with her right hand rubbed my lips, lightly, playfully.

"I'll leave when I'm ready," she whispered. "When I say."

"Bitch," I said, wrapping her in my arms.

I squeezed her, kissed her as cruelly as I knew how, biting her lower lip. She showed no sign of pain, seemed instead to encourage me, squeezing me with her left hand. "Come on, honey," she cooed. "Do nice to Jackie."

I did the best I could. Unfortunately, my mind and body were at odds. Oh, I was hot enough, what with Jackie bucking and squirming and the room temperature tropical. But my head wouldn't stop replaying the grisly scene I'd witnessed earlier, a distraction worse than the damned digital clock calibrating impotence with every click: 7:03 . . . 7:09.

"You really are uptight," Jackie said.

I rolled over, hardly surprised by her perception. "That goddamn clock," I said.

"What clock?"

"Never mind."

I got up and padded naked to the bathroom leaving Jackie to the second best thing she knew how to do: sleep. Avoiding the cabinet mirror, I turned on the shower and stepped under an icy blast. One minute cold, one minute hot. Back again. If that didn't sharpen my wits it might just cause a heart attack. Not a bad alternative.

I guess nonsmokers do have stronger hearts because I survived the intermittent shocks. Feeling sharper, I towel-dried and glanced boldly in the mirror. I shouldn't have. I looked like I had leeches under my eyes. Dark crescents that made me look twenty years older.

I'd grown a beard some time ago, right after a love affair that had ended abruptly, hysterically. When I told Tommy that I thought my luck was turning sour, he said, "You're in a slump. Go bang a nigger, that'll change your luck." I didn't take his advice, I grew a beard instead. A month later I met Jackie and shaved it off.

"Frankie, Frankie!" Jackie was calling me from the bedroom. "Answer the phone." The damn thing was within arms' reach of the bed and *I* had to go answer it.

I dropped the razor, stomped to the kitchen, and snatched the wall phone. It was Tommy, and he was madder than a place-kicker with corns. "That black bastard, I hope the worms eat his balls off."

"What's the matter?"

"Everything. No wonder the cocksucker got snuffed. The sonofabitch was dealing right under our noses. The frigging narcs had the whole joint under surveillance. They got doziers on all of us. You, me, Carol, Peppy, even my uncle. The whole fucking bunch of us all in their doz—doz—"

"Dossiers."

Narcs. They were mostly young turks, humorless and plenty tough. They'd be harder to lie to than the cops from homicide.

"Tell me what they asked you."

"I ain't gettin' rung out on no drug rap. They tried to pressure me, the pricks. They're all pricks. But they can't prove nothing. I don't know from nothing about drugs."

"What do you think they'll do?"

"You'll find out."

"Hey, Tom, cut the shit. We have to help each other out here."

"Help yourself. Just stick to your story and they can't do zilch."

Help yourself. Carol was doing all right and I guessed that Tommy was working on it. What was I doing? Shaving.

"Listen, Tommy, I have to see you. I guess we're closed tonight, eh?"

"No way. I called Peppy. Business as usual. Shows you how fucking important Dusty was."

"Well, I want to talk to you before work," I said. "Meet me in the diner . . . about six, okay?"

"That ain't too bright. They're gonna be watching every little fart."

"I don't care."

"I do."

"Hey, man, I don't know if I can handle these guys."

He laughed. "You better learn, Frankie. I mean it. You fuck me up and I swear I'll—"

"Don't say it," I snapped. "I've already been threatened once today."

"Then wise up."

"Meet me at the diner at six o'clock," I said firmly.

"All right. But no more phone calls after this. See ya."

Wire taps? Murder, narcotics. I was tempted to wake up Jackie just to tell her what an exciting man she'd married.

I got dressed and went into the spare room, a second bedroom which I used to escape the pressures of married life by sealing myself in a make-believe world of recorded fiction.

I had a record collection, horror stories narrated by Vincent Price, Peter Lorre, Basil Rathbone, and their ilk. Four years of acid rock and disco had just about destroyed my ear for music. I slipped the earphones over my head and settled down to Rathbone's mesmerizing narration of "A Cask of Amontillado."

A rotten choice. I realized it when I began picturing myself as the unfortunate Fortunato, chained to the wall of a dank catacomb, being entombed by a madman. Row by row the bricks were laid and with every row I could feel myself drawing closer to suffocation.

I stayed with it, though, and I was actually beginning to relax when Jackie walked in, thighs flashing out of the slits in her robe. Her lips were moving but it was Basil's voice I heard—deep, soothing, soporific. Bemused by the pantomime, I watched for a second or two, then reluctantly removed the earphones.

". . . hear a damn thing with those on," she was saying. "So get up, they're here."

CHAPTER 5

She didn't have to tell me who "they" were. I checked my watch: nine-fifteen. It had taken them four hours to get to me, and now that they were here, I wished it had taken four more.

I went to the kitchen, expecting to see two men in overcoats standing by the door. I saw no one. "Where are they?"

"Downstairs," Jackie said. "You buzz them up, I'm going back to bed."

"Great," I moaned. "Let them freeze their asses off. Alienate the bastards."

I pressed the intercom. "Who is it?" As if I didn't know.

"Lieutenant . . . Detective . . . th precinct . . . to talk with . . ."

I pressed the buzzer to release the outside door and went out on the landing to watch them come up.

The one in the lead was thickset, bulky topcoat and outsized fedora. I couldn't see his face under the brim but I could hear him wheezing as he climbed the stairs. He moved as though this was the only exercise he'd had since his days on the beat, maybe twenty years ago judging by his hat.

The other cop was tall, lean, and black. For a chilling moment I thought Baldy and Blacula had come back to haunt me. I took a closer look and breathed easier. The older one had hair.

Hat in hand, he made the introductions. "Lieutenant Ryan," he said, waving his ID. He buried his wallet and, in the same motion, produced a well-used handkerchief just in time to catch a bone-jarring sneeze. "Excuse me," he said in a soft nasal voice. "Rotten cold, can't shake it." Then he waved an arm toward his partner. "This is Detective Grimm."

Grimm nodded, eyeing me with the cold, penetrating glare of a drill sergeant.

"We're with homicide," Ryan said. "Hunred'n twelfth. Your name is Francis Fontana?"

"Yes," I said. "Come on in."

Jackie's curiosity must have gotten the best of her, because she had settled herself at the kitchen table where she was busy filing her nails. The room was suddenly crowded but Jackie never looked up, just kept sawing away at an already perfectly shaped nail.

I pulled two chairs away from the table. "Have a seat."

"Thanks," Grimm said, and plopped so hard into the wicker that I thought he'd go clear through. It would take more than a flight of stairs to tire this steely-eyed bastard.

"We'd like to ask you some questions," Ryan said. He sniffled. "Damn cold." Out came the hanky. And a thick black pad that cops use to scare the shit out of suspects. "You're a bartender at the Skyview Lounge on Parkway Road?"

"That's right."

"You work for Mr. Horatio Sands?"

Jackie chuckled. "Horatio? Why do blacks have such crazy names?"

I looked at Grimm who was looking disdainfully at Jackie. She'd crossed her legs and had swung around so she was facing the door. With the slit in her robe, I could just imagine the show she was putting on for Mr. Grimm. He didn't seem to care though; either that, or he wasn't a leg man, because he turned back to me without so much as a glimmer of lust. And I know about glimmers of lust.

"I'm sorry, lady," Ryan said. "But I'm afraid this is very serious. Mr. Sands was murdered at approximately four-fifteen this morning."

Four-thirty-five, I said to myself.

"You don't seem surprised," Ryan said to me.

"Well . . ." Had I blown it already? In the first five minutes? And these boys weren't even narcs. "I . . . I . . . talked to one of our waitresses this morning. She told me you'd been there to see her."

"Who else did you talk to this morning?"

"Tommy," I said. "Tommy Milano. We work together." I wanted to bite my tongue when that came out. "I mean we're both bartenders. He told me you'd been there, too."

Ryan seemed puzzled. He looked at Grimm who show-ed some life by making a sound through his teeth like he had something lodged between them.

"Lawson?" Ryan asked him.

Grimm nodded.

I was confused for a moment. Then I remembered that the cops Tommy had talked to were narcs. Two different divisions were investigating the same case. It could mean dissension in the ranks. I didn't know the effect it would have on me but the way things were going it had to spell trouble.

"This waitress," Ryan said. "Would that be Carol Antonucci?"

"That's her."

He scribbled something in his book. "How long have you been working for Sands?"

"Four years."

"What did you do before that?"

"Isn't that written down in your book?"

"Just answer the man," Grimm said. For a second I thought it was Ryan talking; Grimm's lips never moved.

"I was an internal auditor for Lester Morris, Inc. of Chase Manhattan Plaza."

"What happened, you get fired?"

"More or less. Hated the job. I mean some of those guys had been tied to the same desk for fifteen years."

"So you gave it up to pump beer," Ryan said.

"I was single, spending all my time and money in singles bars anyway. I figured I'd mix work with pleasure. You'd be surprised," I said. "You can score better from behind the bar than in front of it." I laughed but no one else did.

"Modest, isn't he?" Jackie said.

"What do you know about Charlie Gizzo?"

"I know he's Dusty's partner."

"What else?"

"That's it."

"You don't know Gizzo is connected with organized crime?"

"I've been told that," I said. "But half the guys that come into our place are supposed to be connected. I don't ask questions."

I was doing fine, watching my ass as advised. The questions continued and every answer was a concise lie or a verbose exaggeration. The affable Mr. Ryan wrote everything down while Mr. Grimm scowled. They were performing the good-cop/bad-cop routine to perfection and though I knew it was an act, I couldn't stop myself cozying up to Ryan. Ever since the saga of Rudolph, I've been a sucker for creatures with bright red noses.

I gave them my life story. Born on Long Island in 1952, moved to Akron in '66, Army '71 to '74. Graduated in '78 from the University of Cincinnati. Father, dead in '82, mother presently living in Akron with her eldest, most sober-minded son, James.

Whatever the narcs had in my dossier, they were keeping it to themselves, because Ryan showed a keen interest, copying it all down. Grimm, on the other hand, just stood there motionless, a window dummy with a flat nose and a fixed stare designed to unnerve the guilty and intimidate the innocent.

"Now about last night," Ryan said and my stomach did two and a half twists. "Did you see anything unusual? Anyone hanging around that might be considered . . . suspicious?"

I thought, how about a black guy with red eyes who sucks blood and turns into a bat? I said, "No, the place was dead."

"Cute," Grimm said. "A punster."

Ryan ignored it. "Anybody ask for Sands? Anybody talk to him while you were on duty?"

"I don't know. His office is in the back. Someone could have gone right in without my knowing." I liked that one.

"Uh-huh." A sneeze, then, "Okay, that'll do for now." He closed his book. "You might have to come in for a statement but we'll let you know. Meanwhile, try not to go on any unannounced trips. We'd like to know where you are . . . for a while, anyway."

"Sure," I said, relaxing. "I'll cooperate."

As they started for the door, Grimm suddenly turned and pointed a finger at me. "You set him up, didn't you?"

I looked to Ryan for help but he had his nose buried in his hanky. My eyes went to Jackie whose prime concern appeared to be an invisible cuticle.

"What do you mean?" I said.

"I mean you fingered Sands." Grimm spoke calmly. "You called him out into the street so someone else could kill him."

"No, I didn't. Why should I?"

Grimm shrugged. "Maybe you had no choice. Maybe it was a question of helping the wrong people or being wasted. It's happened before."

"But not this time," I said. "I told you I'll cooperate, but I'm not going to let you scare me into saying something that isn't true."

"You oughta know about that."

"What does that mean?"

He glanced at Ryan who was still busy with his nose. "This man's got a comprehension problem." To me, he said, "I'll tell you what I think. I think you're lying through your molars. Somebody put the fear in you long before we got here. Enough fear to make you an accomplice. I've seen too many like you, Fontana. Suckhole a few wiseguys and right away you're part of the scene. Instant bigshot. Until they ask a favor you can't refuse. Sound familiar?"

"Hey, look—"

"No, you look. Punks like you are worse than guys like Gizzo. They have guts, at least. Well, I'll tell you something. It's not them you have to fear, it's me. I'm gonna nail your ass to a plank and float it up the river."

Ryan was at last finished wiping his nose. "Come on, Detective Grimm. Give him a chance to think on it." He took a card from his wallet, handed it to me. "Here, if you remember anything else, give me a call. Good-bye, Mrs. Fontana. See you soon, Frank."

Ryan was halfway down the stairs and Grimm was still standing there. "Remember," he said. "I'll have your ass on a plank or I'm Snow White."

"I told you I didn't see anything."

"Then get your eyes checked," he said. "Maybe you'll have a different story for us next time."

"Don't hurry back on my account," I said, slamming the door behind him.

I turned to Jackie. "You know something? Tommy was right. They're all pricks."

Close encounters of the worst kind. Detectives Ryan and Grimm had done little to relax me. I felt certain that they knew I'd lied. And if their plan was to give me time to worry, it was effective.

The way I saw it, I had two choices: continue to lie and take my chances with the police. Or tell the truth and take my chances with the killer.

I was sure that telling the truth would bring the killer down on me. Word would leak out that I was cooperating with the authorities and some bright reporter would translate that into an eyewitness. A five-year prison term, though a horrifying thought, was better than body-surfing in Jamaica Bay.

I had never spent a single day in jail or even seen the inside of a cell except in the movies. How easy it is in the movies. The hero clears himself by becoming a junior crime fighter. He tracks down the killer, single-handedly overpowers him, and turns him over to the police. End of story. Except that this story wouldn't end with a collar for Ryan and kudos for me. Because I'd be branded an informer, and snitches aren't allowed to walk off into the sunset.

I was breaking out in a cold sweat, my stomach churning. If by some miracle I escaped both jail and bullets, I was sure to spend the rest of my life nursing the largest ulcer ever known to the medical profession.

I stood there for a moment while Jackie closed up her manicuring kit.

"You look like you're ready to throw up," she said.

"I am," I said. "And the smell of that polish remover doesn't help."

"What happens now?" she said.

"I don't know. Wait, I guess."

"You're not very good at that. Why don't you do what they do in the movies? Find the murderer yourself."

I grimaced. For all our differences, we did occasionally think alike. It scared me.

"Spare me," I said.

"Okay. But if I were you I'd want to know *why* Dusty was killed. If you knew why, then you could figure out who, and if you knew that, you might be able to help yourself."

For all its faults, this was turning into a banner day. Jackie was actually showing interest in someone other than herself. It made me fear that my situation was more desperate than I had imagined, even if what she said made sense. I wasn't sure how I could help myself even if I knew why Dusty was killed or who pulled the trigger; but if I didn't know, and people thought I did, I was in deep shit. At least, if I knew, I'd know who to hide from.

"In college I'd get these gigantic accounting assignments," I said. "I swear it used to take a half-hour just to read the damn things. I used to go crazy until I figured out the secret."

"Sounds exciting." Her interest was rapidly waning.

"Can I finish?"

"Yeah."

"The secret was in knowing that you weren't faced with one big problem but a series of smaller ones. Once you solved the smaller problems you had the answer to the main question."

"Wonderful," she said. "I think I'll take a shower."

She left me sitting alone in the kitchen. But I didn't care. I was onto something and I didn't want to lose the thought. I kept talking as if she'd never left.

"The main problem is to clear myself."

"Take a physic," she called from the bedroom.

"To clear myself I have to prove to the cops that I'm not involved and at the same time convince the ones that are involved that I can't hurt them. Simple!" I rolled my eyes.

She was on her way to the bathroom. "Clear as mud," she said.

While Jackie was in the shower, I set to analyzing. A hired gun doesn't waste time rapping with his victim. The killer, then, might be anyone who'd ever had business with Dusty. Which meant half the Bronx, where Dusty was evidently still connected, or Candy Gizzo, the guy Dusty might have been fronting for.

I was betting on the Bronx though I hoped that Gizzo was my man. I knew nothing about Dusty's drug operation and had no stomach for nosing around the ghettos asking black men about a black man. On the other hand, Gizzo was someone I knew about and could reach, if and when I had something to use on my behalf. Tommy must have worked that out hours ago, which was why he felt so sure he could help himself. I would talk to Tommy about that tonight. But right now, I had to speak to Barney Reuben. I was anxious to find out how and where the accountant fit into this.

I checked the Queens directory for Barney's number, found it, and wrote it down with his business address. I wanted to call him right away but paranoia stopped me from using my phone. I was sure they had it tapped by now. I headed for the bathroom to tell Jackie I was leaving when she came out wearing a terry cloth beehive on her head and nothing else.

"Forgot my underwear," she said, brushing past me.

I watched her glide into the bedroom. I knew that if I went in there it would be an hour before I called Barney. "I'm going out," I said.

"Bring something home for dinner," she said. "I'm not cooking."

"What else is new?" I said. "Don't you care where I'm going?"

"Why? I've got my own car and a few dollars in my bag. I'll be all right."

I'd positioned myself outside the bedroom door beyond arms reach. "I know you'll be all right. I didn't mean that. I was hoping you'd stop thinking about yourself for five minutes—just long enough to worry about *me*."

She was rifling her dresser drawer, weeding out panties and tossing them on the bed. "Stop feeling sorry for yourself," she said.

I was on her in a flash, grabbed her shoulders and spun her around. The beehive slipped comically over her eyes but the humor was lost in my rage. I let go and shoved her aside. "Shit."

"Go on."

I had never struck a woman in my life but at that moment my record was in jeopardy. She was staring at me as though I had just crawled out of a swamp. How, I asked myself, could she stand there bare-assed and still look so fucking invulnerable? God only knew why I loved this inscrutable bitch.

"I've got enough trouble," I said. "Can't we call a truce until this is over?"

"You're gutless, do you know?"

I made a quick move toward her, then stopped. She really wanted me to slap her. Which was why I didn't. She smirked as she set the towel back on her head.

I grabbed my coat and stormed out.

I was trembling by the time I got outside. I inhaled deeply and let it out slowly. Stay cool. Time for her later.

The temperature was down to twenty; the sky, gunmetal gray. The neighbors had already left for work and my illegally parked car looked audacious by itself. Some conscientious cop must have thought the same thing because there was a ticket slapped across the windshield. I got into my car wondering if anyone had ever plea-bargained accessory-to-murder into a thirty-day sentence for being a scofflaw.

A block away I found a phone booth. I'd calmed down somewhat, but my hand was still shaking when I dialed Barney's office.

"Mr. Reuben's office," a woman said in a switchboard drone that seemed out of place for the one-man practice Barney professed to have.

"Mr. Fontana for Mr. Reuben, please."

"One moment."

It felt more like ten before Barney picked up. "Who is this?" he said sharply.

"Barney, it's Frank Fontana. I've got a message for you from Dusty."

Barney changed his tone in a hurry. It's not every day that a man gets a message from beyond. "Hey, Frankie, how you doing, kid? Damn shame about Dusty. Heard about it on the news this morning."

"You know what they say about bad news. The cops have already been around to see me."

"That's normal," he said. "Nothing to worry about."

"That's easy for you to say. They think I had something to do with it."

"I can see why they might, I mean you worked for the guy. But they have a job to do, you understand. You know the way I felt about Dusty. If there was anything I could do to help the police, I'd do it. You ought to look at it the same way."

This didn't sound like the Barney I knew. The man had no use for the cops and made no bones about it. True, he was a CPA but those initials might just as well have meant Cleaning, Pressing, and Alterations. He hadn't practiced any real accounting since he'd been drummed out of Price Waterhouse for noncompliance with professional ethics.

I had to assume that like me, he was worried about a phone tap. If the Skyview was under surveillance then the narcs probably had a wire on everyone connected to Dusty. I reminded myself to be more careful about the way I used the telephone. "So how about it, Barney? You interested in Dusty's message?"

Hesitation. "Sure, sure I am, Frank. But I was just on my way to see a client."

Client, my ass. Barney was hooked on the horses. He'd even borrowed money from Candy Gizzo to cover his losses. It was close to twelve o'clock now and Barney's "client" was undoubtedly a ten-to-one shot in the first race at the Big A.

"I'm coming over," I said.

"Well, all right. Can you make it here by twelve-thirty?"

"Don't worry, Barn, you'll make the double."

It was no surprise that Barney's office was in Jamaica, less than five minutes from Aqueduct. I pictured him sneaking out to the track each afternoon, returning by six to down a pastrami on rye before rushing off to Roosevelt or Yonkers or wherever the trotters were running that night. Not what you would call generally accepted practice for an accountant, but it certainly fit the bill for a certified degenerate gambler.

CHAPTER 6

Barney Rubbles had a small office in a professional building on Jamaica Avenue; one of those rectangular, one-story brick buildings sporting a pole out front from which hung the names of the resident pros, much like a sharpshooter's medal on a soldier's uniform. This sign boasted two dentists, a podiatrist, and Barney Reuben.

His office door was the first on the left. A solid wooden door that had a button and a typed card tacked to it: "wait for buzzer."

I followed instructions and pressed. The buzzer worked and in I went. As I entered, I glimpsed the back of a tall and skinny middle-aged woman going into Barney's private office. Nothing to do but wait. I paced around the reception area, a small windowless room dominated by an L-shaped desk that seemed to be running interference for the boss. An old Remington sat on the wing with a half-typed letter curling out. There was a corner table, a pair of straight back chairs, a pile of magazines. I drifted over. The one on top was a year-old *Fortune*.

His secretary came out.

"Mr. Fontana?"

"Yes."

"Mr. Reuben will see you now."

I followed her in and she closed the door behind us. Barney's office was just about what I'd expected. A pigsty with an antique electric adding machine, cement block walls painted beige, unmatched file cabinets of chipped walnut veneer, a tremendous black metal desk covered with manila folders, ledgers, staplers, spreadsheets. High up on one wall was a casement window masked by venetian blinds that hung askew. Some daylight filtered in but hardly enough to spike the glare from the overhead fluorescent.

Barney didn't rise to shake my hand. He may have wanted to but the simple processes of standing and sitting were monumental efforts for a man his size, and most of it was hanging over his belt as though he'd swallowed a medicine ball. His face had the flush of a man with high blood pressure.

I took a chair even though Barney hadn't offered one. His secretary gave me the once-over. "Should I stay?" she asked.

"It's all right, Clara. You go on to lunch. Have the answering service take the calls."

"Will you be back today?"

"I don't think so."

"You have an appointment with the IRS at three."

"For Christ's sake, Clara, will you just go to lunch and let me worry about the Internal Revenue."

I couldn't have said it better myself.

I waited for Clara to leave. Although the office was far from warm, Barney was sweating profusely, and I wasn't sure if it was because of me or his physical condition.

"Barney," I said.

He placed a stubby finger over pursed lips. "Shhh."

He sat that way until we heard the office door close. With Clara off to lunch, I watched his face go from red to purple, and thought surely he was about to have a stroke. Then he exploded.

"What the fuck's wrong with you? Are you nuts? You trying to bring the law down on me? Jesus Christ, what an asshole."

There was a wire basket full of papers on the corner of his desk. In one motion, I jumped up, sent the basket flying, and slapped both hands on the desk. He lurched back, nearly falling over in his chair. He was surprised and clearly frightened, because his face lost its purple hue and settled somewhere between gray and white.

"Take it easy," Barney said.

"I will as soon as you stop wailing and tell me what's going on."

He looked quizzically at me. "You don't know? Dusty didn't tell you?"

I sat down. He had information I wanted, something he thought I already knew. I rocked back in my chair.

"I was told to look you up in case he had to leave town and couldn't make it back. Well, he's not coming back so I guess I'm where I'm supposed to be."

"That's all he said?"

"Stop jerking my chain."

"All right, take it easy." Barney Reuben was collecting himself, leaning reflectively on the desk with his hands steepled under his chins. "You were an accountant once, weren't you, Frank?"

"That's right."

He nodded and stared off into midspace. A few seconds went by. "Must be the books," he said.

"Sure," I lied. "The books. What about them?"

An oily grin spread his face. "Who's jerking whose chain, Frank? You know about them or you wouldn't be here."

"You're pissing me off, Barney."

"What the hell do you want?"

"It's what I don't want. Riddles, for instance. Dusty

60

had a reason for sending me here. You say it's the books. That's a start. Now what else?"

"I can see why you gave up accounting," Barney said.

I snatched the metal stapler off his desk, got up slowly, cocked my arm, and said, "You got three seconds to save your bridgework, Barney."

"All *right*," he whined. "Sit down, will you?"

"Do I have to count?"

"The books were protection," Barney rattled quickly.

"Go on."

"You don't wanna hear this."

"I'll chance it."

"Don't say I didn't warn you."

"Protection against what?" I said.

"His partners."

"Gizzo?"

Barney held up his hand. I waited.

"Maybe," he said. "That's the one thing that's not clear. Now sit down, will you please?"

I took the chair but held onto the stapler.

"He kept a separate set of books for himself," Barney went on. "Recorded all of his—let's call them nonreportable transactions. Every deal—dates, names, amounts. All recorded."

"You said names."

"All but his partners. He shows distributions." Barney held up three pudgy fingers. "A three-way split. Profit sharing, you know?"

"But no names."

He shook his head. "The books were insurance, Frankie. They can put a lotta guys out of commission." He gave me a crooked smile. "Or make someone very rich. You can see for yourself when I give them to you."

I'd come in search of threads and I'd found a three-piece suit tailored for the occasion. Barney was right. If the books contained what he said, then there was no question they could make someone rich. So the question was why turn them over to me? Surely he was greasy enough to turn an item like that into quick cash. If he had the balls to try. I took one look at his beady eyes and I had my answer: an unequivocal no.

"Dusty wanted me to have them," I said.

"I guess so. He must have figured you'd know what to do with them in case he got picked up. There's a thousand ways you can use this information, if you get my meaning. If the narcs had arrested him, his partners would have let him rot with no help."

"Why's that?"

"That's the way they operate when you're not connected. But if they knew about the books, you can bet your ass Dusty would get the best legal sharks in the city. Dusty was a lot of things, but a jerk he wasn't."

"Then how come he's dead?"

"Yeah, I know. That's the reason I'm glad to turn them over to you," Barney said, a slight smile on his face. "I haven't slept right since he gave me the damn things. Can't burn them, can't use 'em."

"When was that?"

"Day before yesterday. Guess he knew he was in trouble with somebody."

"But you took the books anyway."

"Just for a few days. I'd already told him to take them back but he said he wanted them out of his office. The narcs were watching him, and what the hell, that was no place to keep something like this, right?"

"Did you know he was keeping a set of books on his own?"

"Hell no. If I knew that, I would have told him to flush them. They're too dangerous." He heaved himself out of his chair.

"Where are these books? I said.

"Not here. I got them put away."

I got up. "Let's get 'em."

"Tomorrow. We'll arrange a meeting tomorrow afternoon."

I threw him my newly found tough-guy look and said, "Today, Rubbles. Right now."

"Don't be a schmuck," he said. "How do you know you weren't followed here? You think I want the cops to see us together?"

"That's your problem."

"But—"

"You don't sound like you're as anxious as you said to get rid of them," I said, glaring. "You're holding, remember?"

"I know. The cops . . ."

"Let's go."

"What do you think you're going to do once you get them?" he said. "If you take them to the police, you'll implicate yourself worse than you already are. Even if you figure out who Dusty's partners are, you can't go to them. They'll kill you as soon as you turn the stuff over. And don't think you can blackmail guys like that. They're stone killers, Frankie. Can you understand that? Killers."

The mere word sent furry moths down my back. But I stood my ground and kept glaring for all I was worth. "I want those fucking books, Barney."

"It's your funeral."

I couldn't have agreed more but my options were limited.

"Thanks for the warning," I said. "But I still want them—today."

"All right. Listen, I'll pick them up. Meet me," he checked his watch, "at the track. The finish line, right after the fifth race."

"Aqueduct?" I said disbelievingly. "You're going to take those things to the *track*?"

"Best place. It's crowded and if we're spotted—well, it's a chance meeting. I don't want to be tied into you in any way. I don't even want to see you again after today. That's okay with you, isn't it, Frankie?"

"I'm not in love with your face either," I said. "But if I

think you can help me, I'll be back. And if I find out you've lied to me, I'll be back sooner."

Over Barney's protest, we left the building together. The afternoon air had turned somber and the ground was dappled with something between rain and sleet. A damp wind set me shivering. As seamen say, it was fixing to make weather.

Barney took a deep breath. "Good," he said, buttoning his carcoat. "There's a couple good mudders on the card today. I've been following them. You don't play the ponies, do you, Frank? They say it's the sport of kings but I call it the sport of schmucks."

"Then why play?"

His face was already brick red and breath steamy. He grinned widely. "You gotta have some action, don't you?"

"Maybe *you* do. Me, I've got all the action I can handle now."

"Well," he said, then he slapped me on the back and pumped my hand like we'd just closed a million-dollar deal. Maybe we had. But my game plan was to take one problem at a time and right now the problem was to get my hands on Dusty's books.

Barney's car was across the street in an all-day lot. I watched him duckwalk to the corner, wait for the light, and start across. Suddenly I was hit with the horrifying thought that if anything should happen to Barney before he'd had a chance to deliver . . .

I was pondering the consequences when I spotted trouble with a capital B. Blacula's bad ass.

He was perched behind the wheel of a bright, yellow Continental. Baldy was riding shotgun. They sped by me without a glance, which came as no surprise. They weren't looking for me. Their target was the fat man crossing the street.

A panel truck came barreling out of the lot just as Blacula zeroed in on Barney's portly frame. It all happened in a blink of an eye. A quick cut to the left, fishtail to the right, and miraculously Blacula missed everything, including Barney. Barney just kept walking as though nothing had happened. And it hadn't.

Were they really trying to kill Barney? Or was I simply suffering the after-effect of what I'd seen last night? But if they weren't after Barney, what were Baldy and his pet rock doing lurking around Barney's office?

I got to my car, made a U-turn, and waited for Barney. I knew he would be followed, which was no great deduction since I could see the big yellow car idling on the opposite corner. Baldy was pointing over and they were both hawking Barney, who was pulling out in a blue Toyota. He rolled into the westbound flow. They followed and I let a few cars go by before joining the parade. Unless Barney realized he was being tailed, he would lead them right to the books. And short of a kamikaze attack, there was no way I could prevent it.

It took only a minute to confirm that we weren't heading for Dusty's books. Not unless Barney had them stashed in a stable at Aqueduct. We were heading straight for the track. I had the gnawing sensation that I'd been conned, that the understanding with Barney had been merely a ruse to get me out of his hair.

But suppose Barney had already auctioned off the books, arranging to meet at the track this very afternoon to make the exchange? It fit. If there was a choice between giving me a freebee or making a score, there was no question which Barney would go for. The big question was how to prevent it.

We reached the track at one o'clock, too late for the daily double but early enough to catch the demolition derby taking place in field number three outside the grandstand. The compulsion gamblers have to lose money is never more evident than in the life-and-death struggle to reach the two-dollar window before the start of the next race.

Several cars shot by me in the lot like launched missiles homing on empty parking slots. A van had cut me off, a VW cut the van off, and by the time I got around them I'd lost both Barney and his admirers. Close to panic, I took the first spot I could find, piled out, and found myself running stride for stride with some man who looked like his wife had just given birth to quints. I knew why he was running, his tout sheet scrolled in his hand like a baton, but where was I rushing to? Sure, I had to find Barney, but where? And what would I do when I found him?

By the time I got inside the track I was out of breath and I was out of answers. The only thing I wasn't out of was perseverance. I'd already decided to go all the way; nothing and no one would stop me. It sounded good, as I began the search for a blimp in a carcoat and a mixed pair of hoods who dealt in drugs and quite possibly murder.

"They're off!"

Something bizarre happens when thoroughbreds race. It's like an atomic blast. People flip out. Judges become irrational, psychiatrists turn into manic screamers. The horse race, like imminent atomization, is the great social equalizer.

From under the grandstand on the main floor, I could see the entire length of sellers' windows and several elevated TV monitors under which ticket holders clustered, shouting at quarter-inch horses gliding effortlessly across the screen. The call of the race was lost amid the tumultuous roar and I could almost feel the bleachers rocking overhead. I wondered if Barney was up there screaming his lungs out or if he was holed up in a secluded corner making his deal with Baldy.

I was close to the hot-food counter and the aroma of steaming clam chowder wafted over, stirring my appetite. A healthy sign, I thought, and ordered a bowl of chowder with a handful of saltines.

The race ended, the crowd began pouring in from outside. These were the guys who liked to mob the finish line so they could curse at the jockey for pulling their horses. It was their way of releasing frustration, blaming the riders. One guy was actually muttering what a bitch Lady Luck was. I couldn't have agreed more.

For some reason, I had trouble swallowing. I left most of the chowder but managed to force down the crackers. I had to get going. The bars I'd check first, then the cafeteria. I started walking when someone grabbed my arm. I spun around expecting the worst.

"Wanna buy a watch?"

He was a rheumy-eyed old geezer in a shabby peacoat. His breath was stronger than the cauldrons of hot chowder.

"No thanks."

"Five bucks," he said. "Whataya say?" He held the watch up close to my face. "Four bucks?"

The crystal was so beat up that I could barely see the hands but the old man held it as though it were a family heirloom. His face was heavily trenched and he smiled proudly at me through a mouthful of jagged teeth. He was repulsive. Still, I couldn't help feeling sorry for the old guy. No man gave up on life without a fight and this dude must have given it his best shot.

"Tell you what," I said. "I'll give you five if you help me find somebody."

"Pay me up front?"

He may have been down but he was far from out.

"Sure," I said. I gave him the five and he lit up like a kid ogling his first girlie magazine.

"Who we lookin' for?" he said, stuffing the bill in his ancient peacoat.

"The fattest guy in the place."

"How's he dressed?"

I told him.

"What do I do when I find him?" Not *if*. *When*. One of us at least had confidence.

"You look upstairs," I said. "When you find him, come down and get me. I'll be looking around down here. Meet me right here in fifteen minutes no matter what."

He looked at the watch, then shook it vigorously before bringing it up to his ear. "Damn thing ain't worked right since I found it." He shrugged as he turned and went. "Ah well. Easy come, easy go."

It took me twenty minutes to search the main floor. I tried the bar, the cafeteria, and the finish line and there was no sign of the three B's. I made my way back to the hot-food counter and there was the old man peddling his watch to some gent who kept backing away as though hard times were some sort of communicable disease. "Five bucks," I heard the old man say.

"I'll take it," I said. They both turned to me, the prospective buyer shaking his head disbelievingly, the old man nodding as if to say, "see, I told ya so."

He shuffled up to me, shoved the watch in my face. "Here ya go, Mack. Five bucks."

This time I took it. "Did you find him?"

"Who?"

"The fat man. Did you find him?"

"Five bucks."

"Christ!" I gave him another five. "You're having a good day, aren't you?"

"Pretty fair," he said, smiling. I was sure that wherever bums go on cold nights, I'd find this one pouring the wine. "The fella you want is upstairs at the bar," he said. "Far end, by the clubhouse."

CHAPTER 7

He was exactly where the old man said. And so was
Baldy, the two of them like old buddies talking real close
and drinking each other's health. I must have been nuts to
think Barney would turn over the books for nothing. How
could I survive in this league? Education and intelligence
were a drawback. What they had was a well-honed instinct I
didn't even understand.

Watching Barney, I wanted to march over there and
jam that shot glass down his throat. Then I saw the black
one. He looked like he had bought his clothes in a hitman's
boutique. Today's outfit boasted the wet look: leather
boots, hat, and three-quarter coat, in which I could see a
slight bulge under his left arm. It looked like a hand-me-
down from the Marquis de Sade. The whole damn getup
must have weighed him down a lot. If I couldn't take him,
at least I could outrun him.

He was coming toward me. I buried my face in a
program and moved closer to the group under the tote
board. "Who do you like in the sixth race?" I said to the guy
next to me.

He was staring up at the numbers flashing on the board. "Don't know. Lemme see your program for a sec."

I gave it to him. He looked at it quickly and then threw it back at me. "You had any winners today?" he asked.

"No." I kept my eyes on Baldy's dusky associate who was coming closer.

"No wonder," said the tout. "I've heard of systems but yours is the worst yet." Blacula was less than ten feet away. "That's yesterday's sheet you're looking at."

"Yeah?" I said. "No wonder I keep losing."

The guy looked at me like I was crazy. Maybe I was. I expected to feel fangs on my neck any second, but nothing happened. He walked right on past me and by the time I turned to look he'd been swallowed by the crowd.

At the bar, Barney and Baldy were still playing he-loves-me-he-loves-me-not. I figured Blacula wouldn't stray too far from his pal so he wouldn't be hard to find. He reappeared alongside his partner. The three split, Baldy heading downstairs, the other two disappearing into the giant men's room. I went in after them through a different door, feeling about as psyched up as I'd ever felt in my life. The place was mobbed.

The black was washing his hands in one of the sinks on the far wall. The men's room attendant, a small black man with leathery skin, was standing beside him holding out a bottle of musk, all arrogance and admiration.

Keeping my head down and parka collar up, I went into a stall and squatted, peering through the door jam.

Blacula spread his hands and the attendant anointed them with musk. The next race was announced and the place emptied totally.

Baldy walked in and stopped at the sink, where his cohort was dousing his face with something that smelled like one of today's entries. He looked over at Baldy. "Ya get it?"

At first I thought he was talking about Dusty's books but I knew enough about ledgers to know that they didn't fit inside your coat pocket.

Baldy tapped his breast. "Right here." And then I thought that maybe I didn't know that much about ledgers after all.

"Problem?" the black guy said.

Baldy said, "Later."

His face, I noted, was predominantly nose. It wasn't hooked, it was flat, a fighter's nose. Abruptly they left. I came out of the stall and quickly washed. Holding my hands up, the soap dripped down my arms. The attendant tossed me a paper towel. No cologne for honkies.

Whatever deal they had made with Barney Reuben I'd find out from Barney himself. I'd ring his chubby neck if I had to, but I'd find out.

I had an hour before my scheduled meeting with Barney but saw no reason to wait. I started back toward the bar.

Barney was there, staring off at something only he could see, a slight smile touching his lips as though reliving a sexual experience. He seemed too pleased with himself. To a man like Barney, there was only one thing that would have caused that cow-eyed leer.

I slid in next to him and placed my hand on his shoulder. "How much did you get?"

He seemed startled but recovered quickly. Being cool means never letting yourself get caught off balance and this sonofabitch had the reflexes of a fat cat.

"Hiya, Frank," he said. "You're early." To the bartender: "Hey, Lou, give us a drink. What are you drinking, Frank?"

"Chivas Regal," I said. "You can afford that, can't you?"

"Today I can buy the joint. Chivas, a pair," he told the barman.

The scotch was rich and thick and burned all the way down. I held the empty glass in my hand. Not because I wanted another drink but because it made a good weapon. Something I'd learned at the Skyview. Slam a shot glass against a man's temple sometime and you'll see what I mean.

"Okay, Barney, we had our drink. Now how about those books?"

"Sure, Frank. Just take it slow, all right?"

His hand was flat on the bar. I held the shot glass like a rubber stamp and notarized the back of his knuckles the way they stamp registration forms down at the Motor Vehicles.

"Ow! Sonofabitch." He was waving his hand as if he'd touched a hot stove. "Whatcha do that for?"

"Because I don't like being jerked off unless the atmosphere's right. Now let's get those books before I plant this glass in your ear."

"For Christ's sake, take it easy. I got what you want."

"You bastard, you had them on you all the while and you've got me schlepping all over Queens."

He shook his head and his jowls flapped. He looked like a bulldog with peanut butter stuck on the roof of his mouth. "Here." He reached in his side pocket and came out with a small, green spiral notebook. Hardly what I'd expected, but then these weren't the books of a corporation listed in the *Fortune 500*.

I took the book and thumbed rapidly through its pages. Lots of dates and amounts preceded by huge dollar signs; and plenty of names, all scrawled in what looked like a review course for speedwriters. I'd need time to make them out but those I could read didn't ring any bells.

"What am I supposed to do with this?" I said.

"Homework."

"Don't get smart."

"You wanted the book, you got it. Now give me a break, Frankie. Disappear."

"All right," I said, putting the book in my pocket.

"All right?"

"All right."

"Then our business is concluded," he said. "I can't say it's been a pleasure, Frank, because it hasn't."

He turned his back to me and ordered another drink. Just one.

"A last item," I said.

He sighed, turned slowly to me. "You know, I never figured you for a troublemaker."

"You ain't seen nothing yet. The deal you made with Baldy, tell me about it."

He glanced around the way you glance around when you're about to say something you don't want anyone else to hear. "You're pushing your luck, Frankie. I mean it."

"So are you. I can lie about where I got this notebook or I can tell anyone interested that you gave it to me. I don't think you'd want that."

"That wouldn't help you."

"No. But it won't do much for you either. I'm halfway down the tubes anyway, so it makes no difference to me." I hated to admit it, but it was the truth.

He nodded, yet didn't appear convinced. There was no twitching around the eyes, no tightening of the lips. No fear. If he had an ace, he'd pull it now.

"Frank, I want to show you something." He tossed a few dollars on the bar. "Come with me."

We walked out side by side without saying a word. The crowd roared as the horses charged into the stretch. The noise followed us but faded, and was only a distant rush as we reached the parking lot. A freezing rain was falling and the cars and pavement were already coated with a thin sheet of ice that crackled under our feet. We headed for his car. I figured the slippery track to be a plus for Barney and a minus for me. In case I had to run. Beside being desperate, the one advantage I had over Barney was swiftness of foot. But what the hell, everyone else was lining up against me, why shouldn't Mother Nature?

As we walked, I fished inside my pockets for a weapon, something to replace the shot glass I'd left on the bar. Anything would do. As long as I could use it to intimidate Barney, who seemed so easily intimidated.

73

Beside the notebook, I had a pack of gum, some loose change, and a well-stacked keyring. Bingo. Make a fist, slip the tip of each key through the slits between your fingers, and what you've got is a nifty set of brass knucks. But don't hold it backwards or you'll give yourself permanent stigmata.

Inside my coat pocket I played with the keyring until all the keys were right side up. They fit nicely between the fingers of my right hand, my power hand, if I had such a thing.

We were well into the parking lot when Barney said, "There's my car." He'd parked his Toyota just two spots away from my car and I hadn't even seen it.

He let himself in while I waited on the passenger side. Sleet whipped against my face and for a while it felt as though stalactites were forming on my eyelashes. I squinted through the windshield and saw Barney reach in the glove compartment for something before he pulled up the button that unlocked my door. Both my hands were out of my pockets. I tapped my power fist against my left palm. Needles. Like the sleet stinging my face. I opened the door and got in.

I don't know much about guns but I do know the difference between an automatic and a revolver. The gun Barney was holding was an automatic. A cute little thing, if you can ever call a gun cute. It looked like an overgrown Derringer that I guessed had a pearl handle. I couldn't see the handle because Barney had his fat little fist wrapped around it.

"I know how to use this, so don't get smart."

"I won't," I said.

"Now you listen to me, you cocksucker." (Amazing what a gun does for a person's character.) "I did you a favor by giving you that book."

"Thanks, Barn."

"You're a pain in the ass, Frank. Worse than that . . . you're dangerous, sticking your nose into everybody's business. But I'm going to do you one more favor."

"Thanks, Barn."

"I'm going to shoot you."

CHAPTER 8

I'll say one thing for Barney, he was being gracious enough about it. He wanted to shoot me for my own benefit.

"Just a little flesh wound," he said. "Something to get you out of the way for a while. Believe me, it's for your own good."

Somehow I couldn't bring myself to thank him.

I wasn't sure if he was bluffing and I wasn't about to call it. How was I going to take the gun away from him? Could I request one last cigarette and then jump him while he lit it? I didn't smoke, Barney knew it.

I was agonizing over what to do when, as so often happens, an option popped up that I hadn't figured on. It was unexpected. A car horn. Someone leaned on one. Barney flinched, I swung.

My right fist caught him flush on the mouth. Against the metal keys, his teeth had as much chance as stemware. It must have hurt like hell because he forgot about the gun, threw his hands up to his face and howled for all he was worth.

Barney was too busy feeling the new edges of his teeth to feel me yank the gun from his lap.

"Here, Barn," I said, handing over a handkerchief. "You'd better cover your mouth."

"Thunofabitch!" he cried. "Watcha do that for? I only wanted to thcare you."

"It worked," I said. I poked the gun at his belly. "Why don't you cut the crap and tell me what's going on?"

"Okay, okay."

His speech was a phonetic disaster and I had to remind him several times to speak clearer, but he finally managed to get it all out. It seemed that in addition to the book I now had in my pocket, Dusty had also prepared a straight-forward list of coke dealers. The list contained the names of suppliers, mostly a group of illegal aliens operating out of Jackson Heights. There were other names on the list, including a bald guy, Phil Carbone, and a huge black stud named Terrance Williams. Barney had laid off the list to them. Dusty had been the middleman, buying coke from the aliens in Jackson Heights and selling it for a substantial profit to Messrs. Carbone and Williams. It sounded big. Too big for an independent entrepreneur like Dusty, but not too big to fit nicely into the consolidated income of one Charles "Candy" Gizzo. The whole deal smelled like mob to me and I told that to Barney.

"Sure ith the thyndicate." Bits of enamel sailed out of his mouth. "Thath why you can't make wavth."

"It didn't stop you from making a few ripples," I said. "Why didn't you turn the list over to Gizzo?"

"And tell him I know whath going on? No thankth."

"Well," I said, "whatever you got for that list, I hope it's enough to live on for the next twenty or thirty years. Because you'll have to hide that long once Gizzo finds out."

"You gonna tell him?"

"Maybe. If it's your ass or mine."

"Shit, Frank, I got a kid—"

"All right. We both have problems. Just make sure your two bozos stay away from me."

"They don't care about you. They don't even know you."

"Good. Let's keep it that way. As long as I stay healthy, you'll be okay."

I thought that was rather charitable of me under the circumstances. He was ready to put a bullet in me and here I was giving him a break.

"Fair enough," he said.

"Thanks, Barn."

Then, for reasons I can't explain, I aimed the baby automatic at the rear seat and fired away. I hadn't fired a pistol since my army days and that was on a firing range using a heavy forty-five. I remember thinking how senseless it seemed then to have to qualify with a pistol when missiles could wipe out New York City in one shot.

Anyway, I banged several rounds into the back seat of Barney's car. I kept squeezing the trigger until the ringing in my ears subsided and all I could hear was the click of the empty magazine. Barney was impressed.

I wiped my fingerprints off the gun and gave it back to him. I thought that a clever thing to do, having seen enough movies where the hero leaves his prints on a gun that later turns out to be a murder weapon.

I left Barney worrying about his future. I didn't like the man before this and I liked him even less for selling that list to Baldy. If I had to take a fall, Barney Reuben was going down right beside me.

It was almost four o'clock by the time I was back in my car and I had a lot to do before meeting Tommy at six. I had to work on Dusty's book.

It wasn't exactly in code, but it was close to it. The army had taught me nothing about codes. It hadn't taught me much of anything really, except the meaning of humility. Being a soldier was much like being a convict, except the pay was slightly higher. They gave you a number, a uniform, and a place to sleep. In exchange, you forfeited your individuality. Was prison going to feel like the army?

I was scaring myself again. My underarms were wet.

My hands, clammy from nerves, slid around the steering wheel as I drove toward the Queens County Courthouse on Sutphin Boulevard. Short of an indictment, I had no intention of setting foot inside that courthouse or any other. What I was looking for was one of those little print shops you find close to municipal buildings, a place where lawyers and bondsmen go when they need a Xerox machine in a hurry.

It cost me two dollars and when I was finished I had a complete copy of Dusty's notebook. Thirty-five pages, which I stuffed in an envelope addressed to my brother in Akron.

My brother James was a lawyer, though I never got too excited about it. His practice was one that didn't lend itself to getting his kid brother out of a jam. Actually, most of my brother's clients were dead. He was a T&E man, Trusts and Estates, and unless they were hearing criminal cases in probate court, I didn't think James could be much help to me.

I had only one ace—the book. I decided to hold it to a four-card draw.

Along with the thirty-five pages, I sent a note with instructions to do nothing except hold the package until I needed it. It was all quite cryptic and I guessed that James would think it was just one more of my idiotic schemes that might eventually cost him a buck or two. Like the time I'd met this girl who worked on Wall Street. She was the personal secretary to some hotshot investment banker. She'd given me the inside track on a few highfliers and I'd passed the information on to James. What are brothers for, right? Well, it worked out fine until the girl realized I wasn't dating her for her personality, or even for her body, which on a scale of one to ten read close to four-point five. So she slipped me a dog named Hydrogyro at twelve dollars a share and I slipped the dog to James. The stock gyroed right off the big board and it cost my brother about twelve thousand. It also earned me the label of "idiot brother."

But this was not a ticket on a highflyer and as I dropped the package into the mailbox I hoped James would intuit its importance.

She wasn't home. As I entered the apartment I tried not to think about what she was doing or with who she was doing it. Instead, I went to my favorite room to see what I could learn from Dusty's book. I put some easy listening on the stereo and stretched out on the couch.

I don't know how long I laid there reading the notebook. I went through it several times and it made less sense each time I read it. Entries were made in separate paragraphs of not more than one or two lines. Each paragraph was preceded by numbers that resembled days of the month: 1227, 0102, like that. Then dollar amounts with names after each entry: $10,000 Jorge, $5,000 Geraldo; first names, mostly, and all of them Hispanic. I didn't find this terribly incriminating. I did, however, agree with Barney's observation that the very existence of the book would be enough to rattle Dusty's partners. Unfortunately, there was nothing to indicate who Dusty's partners were or whether he'd had any partners at all.

I wanted to stay with it but my body had other ideas. I rested the book on my chest and dozed off somewhere in the middle of page five. I couldn't have been asleep more than ten minutes when I heard the kitchen door slam shut. Jackie was home. I was still married.

She was in a foul mood, muttering about the weather and how it had ravaged her new hairdo. She had a phobia about her hair, hated March because the wind blew it all over. She'd spend the entire month walking with her head cocked toward the wind.

She came into the room scowling at me as though I had deliberately set the weather against her.

"Look at this fucking hair," she said. "Thirty dollars and just look at it."

It looked terrific to me. Gone were the scorched worms, in their place was a smooth, seductive wave of black silk that dipped low over one eye. She looked the way Veronica Lake used to look when she wanted something from Alan Ladd.

"You look scrumptious," I said.

"Shit," she said. But she fluffed her hair anyway as if she knew it looked great and just wanted to be told.

"Edible," I said.

She sat next to me on the couch, placed an ice cold hand inside my shirt, and said, "Edible. I like that." Then she kissed me and we both forgot about the silly argument we'd had earlier.

The edible remark had triggered it and it wasn't long before Jackie plunged into her favorite sport. She had a first-you-then-me style of making love; her way of taking charge, I guess. But who cared? Her new, loosely hanging hairdo was playing games with the insides of my thighs and I wasn't about to assert myself until the game was over. As always, it ran its course too quickly. It was my turn to play.

Her clothes were somewhere under my knees. I tossed them aside with my own. She threw herself across the couch and started the litany that was always part of it: commands I knew by heart.

"Deeper. Harder. More, you sonofabitch!"

When it was over she was lying on top of me with her face nestled against my neck. "You know, Fontana," she said, slightly breathless, "for all your faults you do have some redeeming qualities."

"Likewise," I said.

We stayed like that for a moment or two, waiting for our hearts to resume beating the way they were meant to.

Sometimes with Jackie I got to feeling melancholy. My middle-class upbringing. Just once I would have liked to hear her say, "I love you." But I wouldn't ask, and she didn't offer.

I said, "Do you think we could ever have a normal relationship?"

She pushed herself up and stared at me. Seconds ago her eyes had been veiled with passion. Now, I found myself looking at a pair of green darts.

"There he goes again. Who cares about normal

relationships? What we're doing is normal for us. Why are you so worried about what other people are doing?"

"Because those other people represent society."

"And society's all fucked up."

"Maybe, but so are we. At least they know what to expect from one day to the next. A man comes home from work and he knows his wife is going to be there cooking supper for him."

"And that's what you want?"

"Could be."

"Christ!"

Her jeans, blouse, and panties were on the floor where I'd tossed them. She sat up and poked around until she found a pack of Salems. She lit up.

"We got married on a lark," she said. "I still don't know why I did it."

"Because I'm such a charmer."

"At the time—maybe. But not anymore. I'm twenty-eight. There's a lot I want to do."

"You only go around once," I said.

"You're damn right."

"You sound like a fucking commercial."

"Stop the shit. You enjoy living this way as much as I do. You think another woman would let you screw around the way you do?"

"It's only been since you started doing it," I said. "I can do without it."

"Well I can't."

"What the hell are you looking for?"

"It's not a man, that's for sure. That's not even a challenge."

"Then what is it?" I was close to crippling her but I held together.

"I hate when you get like this," she said.

My shoes were on the floor beside the couch. She flicked an ash inside one of them.

"You just can't face it, can you?" I said.

"Can't face what?"

"Honesty."

"Bullshit!" she spat.

"No, honesty."

"You're boring me," she said.

"Then tell me again how you really believe that crap about opportunity falling in your lap."

"You and your ego," she said. "Don't you understand that it's not just you? I'd be the same with any man. I like to get dressed up, to be admired. I want recognition."

"That's about as profound as a soap opera," I said. "And stop dropping ashes in my shoe."

"Listen, Frank, I'm as close to you as I've ever been to any man."

"Thanks."

"Don't try to figure me out," she said. "Just be there."

"Like a statue to be shit on."

"You're a disappointment to me, Frank."

"Likewise."

"You talk about being straight," she said. "Well, I've been straight up with you. I haven't changed. I'm the same now as when you met me."

"Did you ever sleep with Tommy Milano?"

"What does that have to do with anything?"

"You said you're the same as when I met you. If you were fucking him then, are you doing it now?"

"Once a bitch always a bitch," she said.

"That's right."

"And you talk about being honest. You lied to me. You made me think you could handle me."

There were pillows on the couch. She hugged one against her waist.

"You've turned out like the rest," she said.

"Like Tommy?"

"You're not so mellow, Frank. You're far from the swinger you like to think you are. You're more like Saint Francis if you ask me."

"Why? Because I want to be loved?"

"Yes."

There had been so many times in my life when I had played the taker in a one-way relationship. Now, with the roll reversed, I found myself commiserating with the givers of the world.

I had my arm bent over my eyes. "Leave me alone," I said. "Go on, get out of here."

I listened to the swish of her jeans sliding up her legs. It seemed to take forever and by the time she'd zipped up, my stomach was fluttering, my flesh got all prickly.

"There's gotta be a way," I mumbled.

"What did you say?"

"Nothing."

I uncovered my eyes in time to catch her slipping into her blouse. She glanced down and then picked something off the floor. "What's this?"

I'd forgotten all about Dusty's book. Jackie didn't have me running in circles, she had me running backward. "That's my out," I said.

She studied the book for a moment and looked the way I looked the first time I'd read it—puzzled.

"No, really," she said. "What is this?"

"I got it from Barney Rubbles," I said. I told her everything that happened at the track and what I intended to do.

"You're going to give this to the police?" she said.

"Only as a last resort. If I can figure out who Dusty's partners are, I might be able to go to them for help."

"And get yourself mutilated in the process."

"I didn't think you cared," I said.

"If Dusty had partners, you can bet your buns he was cheating them. They're the ones who killed him, Frank. It's as plain as the bulge in your pants."

"Then what am I supposed to do? Sit here until they take me away? Besides homicide, there's the narcotics division to worry about. Maybe even feds. Someone's going to get rapped and I look like the simplest choice."

"Simple, yes."

She grew pensive and I swear I saw her eyes rolling around as though they were chasing an idea. They were. "Listen to me, babe," she said.

Babe! Now I knew I was in deep trouble. "Go on."

"I've got an idea."

"I figured as much."

"But you need balls to pull it off."

"Oh, Jesus."

"Look," she said. "You asked me what I wanted out of life. Well, this could be it, the opportunity I was talking about."

"You want me to go to jail or get killed? Is that your opportunity?"

"Yes and no."

"You're fucking up my head."

"You can go to prison for a price."

"Sounds like the name of a game show."

"Don't be such an ass," she said. "A lot of guys get paid to take a rap. Suppose you went to Dusty's partners and told them you'd confess to being—what do they call it—a fingerman. You can say some guy you never saw before offered you a lot of money to set Dusty up."

"Why?"

"Because Dusty was fooling around with the guy's wife."

"Not that kind of why. Why should I put my ass on the line?"

"Because you might be sent away anyway. This way you can make a score big enough to make it worth while. You protect Dusty's partners and they pay for the service. Neat, eh?"

"Fuck. First of all, they may not even care about Dusty getting snuffed. And if Gizzo's involved, which he probably is, he's got flunkies to take falls."

"I told you you'd need balls. But if you can't handle it, just say so."

"That's not the point," I said.

"That's precisely the point and you know it. It's about having balls," Jackie said.

"As long as you want to talk about balls," I said, "let me tell you a story. There was this kid I knew in grammar school. Now this kid had balls. I mean there wasn't a jock big enough to hold them. Henny Bliss was his name. He didn't have a friend in the entire school. You know why? Because everyone thought he was crazy. That is everyone except me. I figured he was just a wild kid who was acting nutty in order to get attention. I befriended Henny, and for awhile there I'd even considered him my closest buddy. Then one day he gets this idea. There'd been a heavy snowstorm and all the kids had their galoshes in the closet."

"Oh for—"

"Anyway, Henny thought it would be funny if we pissed in their boots. Which we did. Except someone ratted us out. I knew Bliss would be expelled because of his record and all. So I said I did it alone. He got away clean and I got nailed to the cross. Counselors, shrinks, the whole bit.

"When it was over, he called me down. Told me I was an asshole."

"Let's hear it for Henny Bliss," Jackie said.

"Henny said that anyone who'd do what I did for him had to be soft, a chicken at heart. We had a fist fight over it and Henny got expelled anyway. I almost did, too."

"So what's the point?" Jackie said, impatiently.

"The point is that when it comes to the Henny Blisses of the world, I'm completely out of my league. I never found out what made Henny the way he was. The only thing I learned was that unpredictable means crazy.

"Take Gizzo, assuming he's the one I'd be dealing with. We both know he's into murder and drugs. How do you make a deal with a guy like that? Do you think he's just going to shake my hand and turn over a quarter-million dollars?"

"That's funny," Jackie said. "I was thinking half a million myself."

"Forget it!"

"Why? You were ready to trade the book for protection. Why should he honor one agreement and not the other?"

"Because your idea sounds like blackmail."

"So does yours."

"That's not the way I expect to handle it. I'll be trading the book for a favor."

"That's still blackmail."

"That's business," I said. "Besides, I'd give him the book first if I had to."

She got a good laugh out of that, then said, "You're serious?"

"You watch me."

"Don't you know what we can get with a half-million dollars?"

"Yeah," I said. "Very expensive funerals."

"We can spend the rest of our lives in the Caribbean. Together, Frank. We can get a villa . . . live like royalty."

It sounded fantastic. Nothing but Jackie and piña coladas for the rest of my life. Provided there was something left of my life after Gizzo got through with it.

"Get real, Jackie. I doubt if the book's worth anything. And you're forgetting I'm implicated in a murder, to say nothing of a drug racket worth God knows how much. Either one of those charges can land me five to twenty-five."

"You'd be out in five."

"And you'd wait faithfully."

"For that kind of money I'd become a nun."

"All right," I said. "Let's look at it another way. Suppose I did go to prison for five years. With inflation the way it is, a half-million will be worth about $300,000. Over five years that's only $60,000 a year. You may not agree but I think my freedom is worth a helluva lot more."

"Then you won't do it?"

"You're getting the idea."

She got up, looked down her nose at me, and said, "You know, Saint Francis, you really are a crashing disappointment to me."

CHAPTER 9

Shortly after our marriage—actually it was during our honeymoon flight to Puerto Rico—Jackie and I had worked out a number of arrangements designed to eliminate as much domestic drudgery as we could think of. Jackie used to think it was cute the way I'd refer to those arrangements as our "marital nuances." One of those nuances dealt with the nasty business of laundry. As Jackie put it, "The only appliance I know how to use is the refrigerator. So if you expect clean laundry, you'd better get a service."

It had been no great concession since I was already enrolled in something called "bachelor service," a weekly drop-off of dirty shorts that came back smelling like spring. It didn't take long to discover that my laundry bag was the one thing in our apartment that Jackie would never, never touch.

It was there, inside my laundry bag, that I hid Dusty's book. Shrewd Frankie Fontana.

With less than an hour to meet Tommy, I called to make sure he was coming.

"I ain't gonna meetcha," he said.

I knew Tommy well enough to realize he'd been stewing all afternoon and his mind was made up that his best interest would not be served by talking to me now.

Still, I had to talk to him before work. Friday was our busiest night and there'd be no time to get him alone. "I think you'd better come, Tommy," I said. "I've got something to show you."

"Yeah? Like what?"

"I don't want to talk on the phone."

"Fuck it. Tell me what it is or I ain't coming."

"I've got something that belongs to Dusty. It might tell us who killed him."

There was silence for awhile. Then: "What is it? Where'd you get it?"

"Meet me at six."

"All right," he said. "But it just better be fucking good."

Dressing for work while trying to ignore Jackie's tirade was no easy chore. "You're going to *show* the book to Tommy?" she shouted. "Go on, be a moron. What do you think he'd do with it? He wouldn't give it away for a promise." She was screeching at me, I'd never seen her so wild. "You give me that book, Fontana. Do you hear me? Give it to me right now!"

"Up yours."

"You're crude. You're crude, you're stupid, and worse than that, you're a coward."

"I love you too, baby."

I should have guessed what was coming but she still caught me off guard. She was all over me, her nails raking while her Halstons did a tattoo on my shinbone.

I grabbed her wrists and threw her down to the floor.

"You sonofabitch!" she snarled. "You bastard! I hate you."

I couldn't remember how long it had been since I'd left the apartment like a normal person. If I wasn't slamming doors, I'd be punching walls, both of which got me no points with my landlady.

She and her husband had come over from Germany shortly after the war. Childless, they'd run a deli for about thirty years until her husband got himself killed in a holdup. "They kill my Karl for twenty-seven dollars," Mrs. Schimmel had told me ruefully. "All I have left is this house."

I got along well with Mrs. Schimmel. She knew how to mind her own business and never asked questions about the battles taking place upstairs. Except on those occasions when I imagined the din overhead reminded her of the Allied air raids.

She met me at the foot of the stairs, shaking her head disconsolately. I couldn't help noticing that lately she'd stopped looking at me with that old German twinkle in her eyes. She was a deeply religious woman who never missed mass and made novenas for troubled souls like mine.

I apologized for the racket, and she said, "For thirty-five years I live with my Karl. We never had such scenes. You're a nice boy, Frankie. Why don't you talk to a priest?"

I gave her a little hug, thinking that if Karl Schimmel had gotten himself killed with a woman like this praying for him, what the hell chance did I possibly have?

I got to the diner shortly before six. Tommy was in the same booth we'd shared with Carol the night before. He was feeling surly, in no mood for games. Except maybe "Show and Tell."

"Show me what you got," he said.

"I didn't bring it with me. You think I'm crazy?"

"Then what's the idea of us meeting like this?" He tossed a thumb over his shoulder. "Did you catch that black Plymouth outside? That's the law, man. I'm being followed."

I looked out the window. "I don't think I was followed," I said. "But I don't know."

"They're with you, don't worry. Now tell me what you got."

"It's a book that Dusty kept. It's got all his personal business recorded in it. I think that's what Carol was trying to tell me last night. She might have told me more if you'd given me room."

I told him more of Dusty's legacy. About the Jackson Heights connection. I told him about meeting with Barney and about my close call at the track.

He seemed delighted.

"That's great! This could be what I've been looking for. Shit, man, that book's like a pat hand. My uncle will shell out plenty for it." He rubbed his hands together. "Beautiful. Just leave it to me. Go home and get it and bring it down to the Skyview."

"I don't believe you," I said. "We've got some heavy problems here, Tommy. I'm thinking about survival and you want to turn a buck."

"Don't worry, I'll handle it. You won't have to do a damn thing. I'll take care of you." Then he toyed with his walrus mustache. "We're in this together, ain't we?"

"That's a switch," I said. "What happened to every man for himself?"

"You think I'd hang you up? Hey, pal-a-mine, this is Tommy. Didn't I get you the job when you were down? And if it wasn't for me you wouldn't have met your wife."

"I'm trying to forget that part," I said.

"Whatsa matter, she bustin' balls again?"

"Nothing I can't handle," I lied.

"Okay, then. Go get the book and leave the rest to me."

"I can't do it, Tommy. I'm going to play this my way."

It was like I'd hit his funny bone except he wasn't laughing. His hands flew from his coffee cup to my shirt. He grabbed hold and pulled me toward him. "You get me that fuckin' book. You hear what I'm saying?"

"Let go of me, Tommy. I'm warning you."

He glanced around and saw the big Greek who'd

bounced us out the night before. He thought it over for a second, then shoved me back. "Then you're on your own, you cocksucker. And this time I mean it."

He hauled himself up and beat a path to a telephone booth. My buddy.

I left the diner and got into my car thinking that from now on it was going to be tough facing Tommy. As a friend he was ornery, but as an enemy he could be downright diabolic.

Sleet had begun falling again, pelting the Big Apple with chunks of rock candy. I didn't mind it at all. When the weather was bad, so was business. And I wasn't up for a hectic night. Not after the day I'd had.

I slid and skidded the few blocks to the lounge, occasionally checking the rearview for a tail. Whoever he was, he didn't seem too concerned about being noticed. When I stopped for a light, he slid right in behind me, once even tapping my bumper.

I started to wave "Okay," when something stopped me. What if Tommy was wrong? What if this guy wasn't a cop but a paid gun? Don't they usually track their victims, commit their routine to memory?

I could feel the hair rising over the back of my shirt collar. From this position, he could easily blow off the back of my head. I considered getting out and walking over to his car. But then I just might get the front of my head blown away.

I slid lower in the seat, waited for the green and then zipped to the Skyview as fast as belted radials can move on ice.

I couldn't bring myself to park on that dark street behind Dusty's office. I also didn't want to make it easier for my friend who seemed to be hanging back a little more.

I pulled onto the blacktop field in front of the lounge. A few cars were already parked but the only one I recognized belonged to Peppy DeSimone. I guessed that he wasn't too anxious to park on death row either.

Peppy had Thursday nights off so I hadn't seen him

since Wednesday. I was curious about his reaction to Dusty's demise, though I didn't expect to get much out of him. Peppy was an ex-con with a mouth as tight as an oyster's ass. Before his lateral promotion to manager/ bouncer of the Skyview, he'd been Gizzo's personal body-guard. Big enough to guard two bodies, he stood about six-feet-three-inches with the neck and shoulders of a hog and the disposition of a wart.

The two of us, we had an agreement of sorts whereby he would stay on his side of the bar provided I stayed on mine. He would never have gotten my vote as sweetheart of the year, yet he'd observed our understanding.

I scampered across the lot into the lounge, stopping inside the foyer to check on my tail. No sign of him. The inside door was locked as it would be until seven-thirty when we officially opened for the night. I tapped on the glass door and Lisa, the hat-check, let me in. She looked pale as I imagined we all looked.

"Anyone here yet?" I asked.

"Just Peppy and a few of the girls."

"What about Carol?"

"She quit. Called an hour ago. I don't blame her," Lisa said. "It's all so creepy, you know? I mean one day you're full of life and the next you're . . ."

"Yeah," I said. "I know what you mean."

But I was more concerned about Carol. I'd planned on getting the names of Dusty's silent partners tonight.

I gave Lisa my coat and asked, "Where's Peppy?"

At the sound of his name I saw him rise up from behind the bar as though he'd been looking for something. Standing on the serving platform, Peppy appeared a foot taller, which put him a few heads higher than King Kong.

Again I found myself preoccupied with noses. Alas, Peppy DeSimone's was a choice candidate for the hook of the month.

"You're late," he said. "And where's the moron?"

"Tommy's on his way," I said.

I got behind the bar with Peppy so I wouldn't have to keep straining my neck gazing up at him. "What are you looking for?" I said.

He was swarthy, with eyes set so deeply that I never knew if he was looking at me or through me. They seemed to flash now as he checked me out.

"Ain't lookin' for nothin'. I'm trying to make some sense out of all this shit you keep back here. You and the moron keep a pretty sloppy bar, do you know that?"

Peppy didn't know the difference between Kahlua and Pabst. And he certainly wasn't into neatness. "Maybe you should try looking in Dusty's office," I said.

"What the fuck you gettin' at? I told you I ain't lookin', I'm checkin'."

"If you say so."

"You know, I've been down here all afternoon with the cops," he said. "They tore the office apart."

"What were they looking for?"

"You're asking a lot of questions, ain'tcha, Frankie? Since when?"

"Since today. They were up to see me, asking questions about Gizzo."

"Don't let 'em rattle you. Just keep your beak shut. They tried to put it to me too. But my alibi checked out so they backed off."

"That's great," I said. "But what about me? Tommy, Carol, and I saw Dusty right before he got whacked. They're going to fuck with us until one of us pops."

"Stay loose," he said. "You weren't the last to see Dusty alive. Unless you wasted him."

"That's very astute, Peppy."

"Ah, what are you worried about? You're a college boy, ain'tcha?"

"What the hell does that mean?"

"You're squeaky clean. That's why we hired you, to give the joint some respectability." That was the longest word I'd ever heard Peppy use.

"I have to ask you something, Peppy."

94

"That ain't smart. You can't get hurt if you don't know nothin'."

"I realize that, but I have to ask anyway. The narcs went to see Tommy. They've been watching this place for months. Why would they do that unless Dusty was dealing?"

Peppy, who'd been busily rummaging around the cash register, was now bent close to the sliding panel which concealed a gun. It was a licensed revolver, strictly legit. Peppy's hand was against the panel. Suddenly, he spun around, pointed at me with an ominous finger. "You keep your mouth shut. Get it?"

I got it.

He knew about the drug operation, that was clear. Was he a full partner or just a salaried employee? A front for Gizzo maybe. I wondered; I wasn't about to ask. Not with that finger aimed at my heart.

I'd wished for a slow night, instead we had a record turnout. Among the many things I hadn't counted on was the free publicity we'd gotten from the media. The news had carried the murder story all day; the afternoon papers had it on the front page. Dusty's connection with the underworld made big copy. The Skyview was the hottest bar in town.

The place was packed. Rubberneckers had been queued outside since nine-thirty, freezing their asses, for a glimpse of what? What did these morbid bastards expect to see—the ghost of Dusty Sands? A spook in a blue silk shirt and a white three-piece suit breakdancing?

What made it rougher were the no-shows among the hired help: Carol, another girl, the kid who handled the valet parking, and my good buddy Tommy Milano.

I figured three possibilities: the police had him, Gizzo had him, or he was hiding out somewhere hatching some kind of scam. I didn't care for any of the possibilities, least of all the third.

I realized I never should have revealed the existence of Dusty's book. The way Tommy's face lit up—Jesus, did I honestly think he'd react any other way?

The more I thought about it, the more I convinced myself that Tommy was holed up somewhere plotting something devious. But there was nothing he could do without the book and he knew I wasn't going to hand it over. Probably he was just giving me a chance to worry before putting the squeeze on me one more time.

By eleven o'clock I'd had enough different newspapers shoved at me to know I'd become somewhat of a celebrity. According to a police spokesman, I'd been questioned about the Sands case. Although I wasn't officially under suspicion, there was enough between the lines to imply that I was. Swell.

The patrons ate it up and seemed disappointed when by midnight the place hadn't been raided and no one had cuffed me to the bar. Still, they hung in there, three deep, the dance floor overflowing, and every table occupied. Good thing we had the fire inspector in our pocket or we would have been cited for violating the city ordinance against amassing highly combustible swingers in heat.

I'd been on automatic for the past hour. A mechanical mixologist, pouring drinks, running tabs, and occasionally flicking a light toward an unlit cigarette dangling from the mouth of a surprised female. Like the one that had just elbowed herself to the bar.

A cute little blonde with a round face, big bright eyes, and a button nose. She puffed on her cigarette without inhaling and all the while she kept smiling at me, throwing out a warm friendly glow like I'd just given her a candy-gram instead of a light.

I had her pegged for a white wine spritzer but she fooled me: I. W. Harpers straight up. She threw me again with the way she polished it off. The girl had problems. Didn't we all.

The next few hours moved quickly and all the while I continued to play with my new friend. Her staring didn't bother me. I was accustomed to getting the fisheye from women. Not all women, only the cultists who got off on bartenders. I never could understand it. After a time I gave up trying and just took whatever fell in my lap. Why shouldn't I? Living with Jackie had all but annihilated my ego.

But the blonde with the candy smile didn't have that flaky look of a groupie. Her clothes didn't look as though they'd been borrowed from Goodwill. My guess was that she'd shopped at Bloomingdale's, toiling long and hard before making her choice. For tonight, it was a black velvet vest over a white silky blouse that sort of wrapped around her chest so that when she turned a certain way I caught a good glimpse of her breasts.

It was almost three A.M. before the thrill of Dusty's murder began to wear thin on the crowd. My back was aching and my legs felt like they were caught in an undertow.

The blonde, who hadn't budged since she arrived, was beckoning to me. I went to her, moving slower than I had all night.

"You look tired," she said, in a raspy voice barely audible over the blaring music.

"I'm beat."

"What you need is a good rubdown."

"And what you need is a strong cup of black coffee."

She toyed with the empty shot glass. "I can handle it."

"I once said that to someone and I haven't been the same since."

She winked. "I'm okay."

She wasn't slurring so I assumed she knew what she was talking about. "You've been hitting the ice-cream sundaes pretty hard," I told her.

Behind her wistful stare I could sense the wheels spinning. She had plans for tonight and as I'd expected, I was definitely part of them. Any other night I wouldn't have hesitated.

"You picked a bad night," I said.

"For what?"

I was about to tell her when Peppy walked up and cut me short. "Fontana, come on out here. There's some guys wanna see you."

My blood pressure plummeted while my stomach did its usual half-gainer.

I apologized to the blonde, gave her the tab, and went out to follow Peppy across the dance floor. He was heading in the direction of Dusty's office. I had no idea whose music I'd be dancing to. The only thing certain was I'd be dancing alone.

It was Detective Lieutenant Ryan and another cop I hadn't seen before. He was glaring at me like a gunfighter who'd given up robbing trains to fight on the side of the law.

"This is Lieutenant Lawson, Narcotics," Ryan said. His cold sounded worse.

I didn't bother offering my hand to Lawson. It wasn't that type of introduction. I just nodded. I tried glaring back at him but my bloodshot orbs were no match for those black pearls of his.

"We'll talk in the office," Lawson said. "You too, DeSimone."

Peppy and Lawson locked eyes. Now that was a match. Dead even. I felt sure that stepping between those two would mean instant disintegration.

We walked single file into Dusty's office. Lawson closed the door behind us and for awhile we just stood there staring each other down. Then Lawson took Ryan aside for a conference.

While they caucused, I took the time to look over Dusty's office. Jackie could learn much about housekeeping from the NYPD, I thought. The room was immaculate, the junk that Dusty once kept piled on his desk had been cleared away. The mahogany corner bar, Dusty's pride and joy, had been emptied. But the biggest change, the thing that really hit me, was the void created by Dusty's absence. He'd dominated this office. Now he was gone.

It reminded me of the old house in Akron right after we'd buried my father. I'd gone straight to the parlor expecting to find him in his favorite wing chair. No tears for Dusty Sands. Just the realization that he'd been blown away.

The conference was over. Ryan took out his pad and said, "Either of you know anything about a diary Sands was keeping?"

I don't know how Peppy reacted because I was too busy watching Ryan watch me. I knew the blood was rushing to my face but not even Houdini ever learned to control a blush.

"Well," Lawson said. "You heard the man."

"I didn't know he could write," Peppy said.

Lawson nodded at me with his chin. "What about you?"

"I didn't know he could read."

"Shut up," Lawson said. He looked over at Ryan. "What is this guy, some kind of fucking wise-ass?"

"He's just a little confused," Ryan said. "I'll tell you what's happened, Frank," he said to me. "We got a tip that Sands had a diary. We've looked in here and tomorrow we'll tear that bar apart if we have to. If you know anything about it, we'd appreciate your telling us and saving us the trouble. I know you know it's against the law to withhold evidence in a murder case."

Lawson said, "Your boss was a pusher. Did you know that?"

"We don't allow any heads in this place," Peppy said. "We run a straight business here. You check our income taxes."

"We already did," Lawson said. "This place reeks of drugs. I smell it. You DeSimone, you and Sands and Gizzo. You think we're idiots? We know who comes in the back door around here."

Except for last night, I told myself.

"You got proof, use it," Peppy said. "If you don't then go take a flyin' leap through a fuckin' doughnut."

Lawson got redder than Ryan's nose. "I've seen your rapsheet, DeSimone," Lawson said. "One more trip and you'll be a hundred and one before you're back out on the street. I'm going to nail you, you sonofabitch. You and this other weasel. Now get the hell outta here, the both of you."

I hadn't even let go a sigh of relief when Lieutenant Ryan said, "Not you, Frank. I've got some more questions. I'll contact you later, Ed," Ryan called after Lawson who was pushing past DeSimone.

Ryan waited for the door to close. "Lawson's a good cop," he said. "It's just damn frustrating working narc. They make more busts in a day than we do in a month. They bust them and the court lets them go. It's like a revolving door. That's why I like homicide. We don't nail as many, but once we do they stay hammered."

"I understand. It's the permanence you enjoy."

He took out his hanky. He blew hard. "Damn cold. You know, Frankie," Ryan went on, "we've got a lot of unsolved murders on our books. But we'll break this case."

"You're getting it done?"

"Maybe. Do you know where Milano is tonight?"

"No, I honestly don't."

"You were seen with him just before work."

"So it was your guys following us?"

Ignoring the question, he said, "What did you two talk about?"

"Nothing special. We always meet in the diner before work."

"That's a lie. You go there after work, not before. Listen, Frankie, you'd better start realizing how serious this is."

"I'm not stupid," I said.

"Then why don't you let me help you? I know you lied about Sands' diary. I saw it all over your face. Now why don't you let it out once and for all. Whatever you're involved in, I'll see you get consideration. Just cooperate."

With his moon face and red nose he seemed like such a pleasant man that I was truly tempted to level with him. But

I didn't. "I'd like to help you, Lieutenant, believe me."

"And you can believe me when I say I'd like to help you."

I thought for sure we'd be hugging and kissing at any moment. Then it all changed. The moon face turned sour and the red nose flared. "But you're a dumb fuck. You're dumb, Fontana, and you're scared and you're going to wind up in a mess of trouble. Lawson thinks you might have some shit stashed in your apartment. He's ready to pull a warrant to toss your place. If he looks hard enough, I'm sure he'll find something. You get my meaning?"

He was looking more like a cop every minute and I wouldn't have hugged the bastard now if he turned out to be an uncle on my mother's side.

Yet, out of all my options, Ryan still seemed the safest. I decided to play ball on a limited basis. "Would you tell me something?" I said.

"Depends."

"That tip on the diary . . . when and who?"

"A few hours ago. Anonymous caller."

Who? I thought. Not many knew about the book. Although at the rate I was blabbing, half of Queens would know by tomorrow night.

"A man or a woman?" I asked.

"Neither."

"Come on, Lieutenant. You want cooperation, don't you?"

"I shouldn't be telling you . . . It was a kid. Teenager. Probably paid by the one who wanted us to know. We'll never find the kid but that's not important."

"Clever," I said.

"Maybe. Your turn. What have you got?"

"I might be able to lead you to the book."

"Where is it now?"

"I don't know."

"Not good enough."

"I only found out about it last night. Carol Antonucci told me Sands had a book he wanted me to take in case."

"What else did she tell you about the book?"

"Nothing."

"Not good enough."

"So arrest me," I said. I think I would have cried if Ryan had taken me in. As it turned out, he had other ideas.

"I want you out on the street for a while, Frankie. I got a feeling you're in deeper than I thought. You'll screw it up soon enough." He started for the door. "Meanwhile, I think you'd better get me that diary. I'll be back tomorrow night. Try to be here. And I'll expect you to tell me where to find your pal, Milano."

He held the door for me and as I walked out he patted my back. "You're a lamb among wolves, Fontana. For your sake I hope they don't eat you up."

CHAPTER 10

"Last call!" I hollered. "Last call for drinks."

Bright lights flooded the lounge, which meant the players had only fifteen more minutes of game time to score.

The blonde had waited patiently for me all night, leaving the bar only once or twice to go "tinkle." She was only weaving slightly on the bar stool. Not bad after all the Harper's she'd put away.

"I want you tonight," she said. "And you want me too."

More than a pretty face, this girl had psychic power.

I saw no reason to say no. Jackie wasn't home—I'd called. It meant being alone while my mind drifted in and out of perverse visions of Jackie doing somebody.

"I'll get you some coffee," I told the blonde. "I don't want you falling asleep on me."

"Don't worry about me," she said.

I left her and went to join Peppy who was draped over the register wrapping cash in rubber bands. He was stuffing his pockets with receipt money, fifteen thousand dollars by my estimate. Spectacular night. All it took was a murder.

"I'm cutting out," Peppy said. "You lock up. And when you talk to the moron you can tell him he's canned."

"You coming in tomorrow night?" I asked.

"If the pricks don't close us down." He came closer to me and it was like being surrounded. "You know anything about that diary?"

I guess lying is like any other sport: the more you practice the better you get. "What would I know about it?" I said.

"Yeah. Okay, Frankie. Just watch your ass, eh?"

"Hey, Peppy," I said. "Do you think Gizzo would see me?"

A mistake. I knew it by the way Peppy was twisting my wrist. I tried to pull his hand off me but I would have done better just fainting. "Get your fucking paws off me," I said, trying hard to make it sound like I could have stopped him if I really wanted.

He let go and I watched my wrist go from white to red. You didn't question Peppy about Gizzo. I was being paid to run the bar and mind my own business and until yesterday I'd managed both with moderate success.

It didn't seem important anymore; nothing seemed more important than preserving my own ass.

"You got no business with Gizzo," Peppy croaked. "You'll give ideas to the wrong people if you start sucking around the man. You got something to tell him, you tell it to me."

"Then tell him something for me, will you, Peppy? Tell him I want major medical."

I quickly discovered something about Peppy's sense of humor. He didn't have one. The left corner of his mouth turned down as though he'd just taken a shot of Novocain. His ears seemed to snap back against the sides of his head and I swear he looked like a Doberman.

"Fuckin' college asshole," he said, and swaggered away. I turned my attention to other matters.

The blonde's name was Tina Webb. In her late twenties, I guessed, though she may have been younger. Smoke, drinks, and dipshit lovers can take their toll on a girl. I figured Tina had about three or four more good years before her track record caught up to her. But for now, at least, she showed no sign of wear.

Coming around beside her, I said, "How do you feel?"

"Loose," she said.

"All right," I said. "Let's get out of here before you tighten up."

She winked at me again and I began to suspect she might have an affliction. "I'll get my coat," she said, easing off the stool. She walked away with surprising steadiness. If nothing else, Tina knew how to handle bourbon.

I started after her, then stopped. I had the feeling I was forgetting something. Not knowing what it might be, I went back behind the bar for one last look. Then I remembered. The gun.

It shook me a little when I thought of the many times I'd been so close to it. Every time I'd bent under the register my head had been inches away from the barrel.

I slid open the panel, reached into the shelf and felt the cool metal against my fingers. It made me shiver. I drew back my hand.

The feel of Barney's automatic was still fresh in my mind and yet I recoiled from the touch of a gun I couldn't even see. A premonition? Perhaps. Or maybe I knew my next target would be an object more animated than a car seat.

The gun was a snub-nosed revolver. A thirty-two or a thirty-eight, I wasn't sure. It felt heavy and I had to think for a moment about where to carry it. I tried jamming it behind my belt, then reconsidered. If it should accidentally go off—well. There weren't many dumber ways to go.

I decided on my coat pocket, buried it deep inside and went out to join Tina. She already had her coat on, a black knee-length suede with a fur collar pulled up around her face.

"You don't seem very anxious," she said.

I held the door for her, we stepped out, and I looked up. "Had to check on something," I said. "Do you have a car?"

"I came by cab. I never have trouble getting a lift home."

"I wouldn't think so."

In the parking field my car sat frozen under a solid sheet of ice, glistening like a piece of rock candy. We walked gingerly with our heads down against the wind. I kept Tina on my left so my right hand would be free for a quick draw. The wind was doing a job on my eyes. I couldn't see through the tears. Everything seemed wavy, the streetlamps, the buildings—a dark sedan.

The only other car in the lot, it was parked near the exit, smoke purring from its exhaust. Police, I thought, but with Tina on my arm I couldn't gamble.

"Quick!" I said, running ahead. I prayed the lock wasn't frozen as I fumbled with the keys, found the right one, and forced it into the hole. The button popped up. "Thank you, God."

Tina was in no rush, moving nonchalantly to my side. "Get in," I told her. She took a deep breath but didn't move. "Get in, for Pete's sake."

She was halfway in when I shoved her the rest of the way. I locked the door and ran around the other side keeping a blurry eye on the sedan. It hadn't budged.

"Open the fucking door," I yelled. Tina hesitated, then raised the button, and I scrambled in.

"God," she said. "I was only kidding about your not being anxious."

I spun the starter for a moment before it caught. "Let's hear it for Sears," I said.

"You're crazy," Tina said. "Do you know you're crazy?"

I let the motor heat up, turned to her, and said, "If I'm crazy, what does that make you? Don't you know what's going on here?"

"Sure. I picked you up and now you're taking me home. It's been done before. You're a sexy-looking man and I—"

"Where the hell have you been for the past twenty-four hours? In case you haven't heard there was a man killed here last night. The cops think I'm involved."

"I know," she said, casually. "That's what drew me out here tonight."

"And you think *I'm* crazy," I said, shaking my head.

"You are."

"Listen to me for a minute, will you? I know you've had a lot to drink but try to follow this. I'm being tailed."

She turned around. "Really? God, that's exciting. Where? Over there?" She pointed at the sedan. "Is that him? Wow."

I pulled down her arm. *"Don't* point."

"You think he's the murderer?" She had an idiotic grin on her pretty face and her blue eyes were wide with excitement. She was actually enjoying it. Jesus.

"I don't believe this," I said. "Aren't you afraid?"

"You've got a gun, haven't you?"

Instinctively, I grabbed my pocket and felt the gun.

"So?" she said. "What are we worried about? Let's go."

I waited for the ice to melt off the front and rear windows, then I floored the accelerator, and away we went, skidding a little before the tires caught pavement. The sedan took off after us.

"Wheee!" Tina squealed.

"Shit," I said.

Even with the extra liters and compression, I couldn't shake him. After a few frustrating miles I quit trying.

Tina was disappointed. "What are we slowing down for?"

"If we're going to get killed," I said, "I don't want it to be in a one-car accident. Besides, he's not trying to catch us."

That mollified her somewhat but she kept turning

around until finally she gave herself a pain in the neck. That made two of us.

She lived in an area known as Hollywood East, a hot section of real estate between the borders of Astoria and Long Island City. There were film studios nearby and rumor was that Woody Allen had used one to shoot his latest flick.

"Just a few more blocks," she said, and started looking over her shoulder again. "You didn't lose him."

"I know. And turn around!"

"That's the place," she said, pointing to an apartment building.

I pulled up in front of a clean white high-rise that couldn't have been more than five years old. Light from an ultramodern lobby spilled out onto a freshly shoveled side-walk. Behind the plate-glass entrance a doorman was eye-ing us. Red uniform, gold braid, he looked like an Elton John fan.

I leaned across Tina and opened the door. "Run inside as fast as you can. Understand?"

"I'm semi-intelligent," she said. "But I'm not leaving you alone. I said I wanted you and I meant it."

Of all nights, I had to pick this one to hook up with a whackjob named Tina Webb. I was trying to protect her body and she wanted it violated.

"Good night, sweetheart," I said.

She slammed the door shut. "I'm staying with you." She looked back. "He's gone anyway. Why don't you just park and come upstairs."

From the side mirror I could see that the sedan wasn't gone. It was a half block back, double-parked.

"He's still with us," I said. "Now will you get out of the car?"

"Forget it." She sat back in her seat and folded her arms defiantly. "If you don't come up with me I'm going to open the window and call them over here."

Before I could say a word, she had the window down and was shouting: "Hey! Hey you! Take a hike, creep." The girl had enough balls for the two of us.

"Get in here," I said. I tried pulling her in but she fought me. The doorman must have thought I was molesting her because he came charging out of the lobby like Rambo.

"I saw you, I saw you," the doorman hollered. He wrapped his arms around Tina and tried yanking her out of the front seat. "Let go of her, you degenerate," he shouted at me. He kept tugging at her. The door popped open. His face got redder. He had to be close to seventy. I decided I'd hang onto Tina until the color of his face matched his coat.

"Goddamnit," Tina said, "will you both let go of me." We let go at the same time and Tina went toppling out.

She was lying on her back when I looked down at her. "You all right?"

"You're crazy," she said, as I stood over her.

"You want me to call a cop, Miss Webb?" the doorman puffed.

"You don't have to." A man's voice. Familiar. My tail. He'd pulled alongside us.

It was too dark to see his face but that profile appeared vaguely familiar. He leaned out and I breathed a sigh of relief.

"Christ," I muttered.

"Having fun, Mr. Fontana?" said Detective Grimm.

"A regular romp," I said.

"So I see." He got out of his car.

"Who the hell are you?" the doorman said.

"Police." Grimm jerked a thumb toward the lobby. "Inside, old man."

"I'm fine, Frederick," Tina said.

The old timer tipped his cap to Tina and headed back to his post.

Tina was on her feet wiping ice chips off her coat. "You okay, Miss?" Grimm said.

"Are you the voyeur who's been following us? You know you scared this poor guy half to death?" She looked at me and nodded. "Right?"

"You know this man?" Grimm said.

Cops have their own way of answering questions. Ask

one how to get to Forty-second and Broadway and he's likely to come back with, "Who you looking for?"

Tina gave him an exasperated look. "Would I be with him if I didn't? Go bust somebody or something."

Go get him Tina, I said to myself.

Grimm seemed puzzled. He started to say something to her, then gave up. Turning to easier prey, he said, "Come over here, Fontana." I followed him to the back of my car. "Your time's running out," he said.

"What do you mean?"

"Which word didn't you understand?"

"That's cute," I said.

"Ryan wants me to stay with you. His gut feeling is that you're okay. Mine tells me something else."

"That's a helluva way to communicate," I said.

He pushed me over the trunk. One hand held me down while the other became a fist pressed against my cheek. "I think you've been lying to us. If it was up to me, I'd screw you into the ground until you uncorked."

It wasn't exactly a punch but it was damn close to it. Kind of a shove that caught my tongue between my teeth. He sauntered back to his car. As he was getting in, I said, "Why don't you say it?"

He looked back. "Say what?"

I spit some blood into the street. "How about 'watch your ass, Fontana'?"

His face cracked into a thin smile. "Won't matter if you do, kid. You're going down."

We elevatored to the sixth floor accompanied by the Boston Pops. Tina's apartment was a short, silent walk down a shamrock-colored hall adorned with bright mosaic sunbursts. Not what you'd call a retirement home motif but just as tacky.

She unlocked the door to her apartment, hit a rheostat, and the whole place lit up.

"Make yourself at home," she said, disappearing behind a closet door.

I took two paces inside and had to sidestep the bed, which was actually a couch that folded out. It was disappointing. I'd envisioned a penthouse with a panoramic view of Manhattan, a three-thousand-a-month apartment. The kind of place a kept woman lived in. This was a room and a half-efficiency not much larger than a walk-in closet. If efficiency meant that Tina could cook without getting out of bed, then this place was efficient. Tina wasn't being kept, she was being taken.

"Take off your coat, for heaven's sake," she said.

Remembering the gun in my pocket, I laid my coat on the floor next to the bed. "I'd better leave this here."

"Oh no," she said, snatching up the coat. "You're not pulling any hit and run with me. You're in for the night." She hung the coat in the closet and came back with some tissues. "Here, you're dripping blood on the sheets."

"Thanks." I dabbed at my lip.

"He doesn't like you too much, does he?" Tina said. "That cop, I mean."

"No."

She was next to me on the bed pulling off her boots. "Why's that?"

"I guess he doesn't think I'm scared enough. If he only knew."

"What's he want?"

"My ass. Him and a few more like him."

"I can see that," she said. "It *is* sort of appealing." But, hey, why don't you tell them what they want to know and get them off your case?"

"Tell them what? The only thing that would get them off is a confession."

She'd slipped out of her blouse so nonchalantly that a few seconds went by before I realized.

Dropping back on the bed, I said, "Man, I'm tired."

111

"How tired?" She kissed me gently on my bleeding mouth.

"Mmmm. More."

"Let me get out of these clothes," she said. I closed my eyes and when I opened them again she was naked except for a pair of pink bikinis.

"How about a drink?" she said.

"No thanks." Since becoming a bartender I'd cut down considerably on my drinking. For some reason it seemed redundant.

"Some dope? A couple of lines?"

"No, thanks."

She undressed me, rolled me under the covers, and slid in very close beside me. Her body felt like a cool compress to my aching bones. I relaxed. Most of me relaxed.

"Oh, that's nice," Tina said, reaching down for the one part of my body that wasn't screaming for sleep. I could almost hear my brain flashing a bulletin to the rest of me: "Up, up! Everybody up!"

One thing I was still learning about women is that they never give what you expect—especially in bed. Tina was no exception.

I'd picked up the classic flake, the nutsy blonde with a penchant for kicks. Quick, shallow, and perverted. What you'd expect from a chick who does dope and falls out of car windows. What I got was something else. I sensed it the moment we kissed. Where was the frenzy? The prelude to kinky sex?

Her lips were soft and her tongue probed tentatively, as if she were testing me. There was a message in that first kiss that belied the one-night stand and all that I knew about Tina Webb.

"I had to get you here," she whispered.

I remained silent, replaying her words in my head. She should have sounded desperate. She didn't.

I studied her for a long moment, searching hard for the giveaway. If this was a lie, I would see it. "Why?" I said.

Jackie would have shrugged to a question like that. Tina smiled. "I trust my instincts."

"What if they're wrong?"

Her hands were under the sheets. She wriggled around for a second or two and came out with her panties. "Let's find out," she said.

Suddenly, I was wide awake and pain-free. My lip had been healed by the kiss. I rolled on top of her.

She loosened the sheet and placed it over my back. "Just for a while," she said. "Till we warm up."

I was used to a turbulent kind of sex that came and went in a blur. Vindictive sex designed to punish. Tina seemed to sense what I was about and let me run the course I knew.

When I was through, she pulled me to her, held me tightly and said, "I wasn't going anywhere, Frank. I'll understand if you want to sleep. But I'd like to try this again. My way, if that's all right."

I turned onto my back and Tina showed me the way it would have been. She kissed me. Lips, neck, ears; every other place I'd been kissed before. So why did it feel different?

I was too weary to analyze. About all I could do was lie back and enjoy it.

Wait till tomorrow, I thought. Figure it out in the morning.

CHAPTER 11

I awoke to the aroma of fresh coffee and the sound of Tina warbling a Madonna tune. A soothing way to start what I hoped would be an uneventful day provided the events didn't include threats of bodily harm. Wishful thinking, I mused. Reserved for men with nothing better to do on Saturday than polish golf clubs.

I yawned, stretched, and did all the things you do when you don't want to get your ass out of bed.

In the midday light, Tina's apartment looked bright and cheery. TV and stereo components rested on walnut veneer shelves. The floor was done in dark blue shag and a pair of white lacquer Parsons tables topped with reading lamps sat on each side of the convertible sofa—our bed. An efficiency apartment, as advertised.

What I hadn't noticed the night before was the accumulation of artwork. Oils, watercolors, pastels. Still life paintings of fruit, flowers with dew drops glistening on their petals, country landscapes. Beautifully and professionally done and all with the same signature scrawled in the lower right: Tina Webb.

She'd pulled the drapes back from a picture window. I had to squint against the sun, the light of which bounced off the sash as bright as burning magnesium. I sat up slowly, Lazarus rising. "Hey, kill that light, will you?"

Tina peeked out from behind the open refrigerator. " 'Tis a fine day out, lad."

"Let's keep it outside, okay?"

"Humbug," she said, breaking into a chorus of Billy Joel's latest.

I groaned.

"How's your lip?" she said.

"Sore."

"How do you like your eggs?"

"Laid. I like everything laid."

"Men," she said. "That's all they ever think about."

I checked my watch. "What do you want on three hours sleep?"

She walked the four steps from the kitchen to the bed. I peered up blinking life into my eyes. She was wearing jeans and a cherry-red, man-tailored blouse. She'd scrubbed the rouge and lipstick off her face and her skin had a fresh, pink glow. She'd also performed some magic on her hair, an upsweep that looked more captivating than casual. I decided that if I hadn't been hooked on Jackie, and if I wasn't hopelessly enmeshed in a small nightmare, I would have found waking up to Tina Webb a delight.

"Poor baby," she said. "A cup of coffee and some scrambled eggs will make you feel better." She went back to the kitchen and started clanging some pans around. "There's a toothbrush in the bathroom," she said. "I don't keep a supply of jockey shorts in the house but if you want to leave yours here I'll launder and mail them to you."

I laughed. "There's a devil in you, Tina Webb."

"Why? I'm just trying to be domestic, the perfect blend of whore and housewife. You don't approve?"

"Oh, I approve. But I doubt if my wife will. She's not exactly faithful. Far from it. But I doubt she'd appreciate having my drawers arrive special delivery."

"You sound like you care more than you want to admit."

"The only thing I care about is self-preservation. She taught me that."

"At least you've learned something from your marriage. I got married when I was eighteen and divorced before I was twenty. I never learned a damn thing from that clown. No," she said. "That's not true. I did learn about one of the fundamental building blocks of life."

"What's that?"

"Oral sex. Now go take a shower while I whip these eggs into shape."

I dragged myself out of bed. "You do great work. The paintings. They're great, really."

"I've taken a few courses. I don't spend my whole life picking up men in bars."

"How do you get by? This place, it's got to cost."

"Too much," she said angrily. She was beating the hell out of a bowl of eggs. "*I* pay the rent. Don't worry, I don't intend to ask you for anything. What is there about a woman living alone? Right away men get ideas. Nobody pays my bills but me and that's the way I want to keep it. You think a woman can't afford to live as good as a man? Bullshit!"

"Hey," I said. "Take it easy. You're fighting with yourself."

"Oh, go take your shower before I really get mad."

I spent the next half hour in the think bin. When I don't have gothic horror to stir my mind, I like to seal myself off from the world and let a needle spray stimulate my thought waves. I've made some monumental decisions in the shower. Like should I use premium or regular, when to break out my summer wardrobe. And more mundane decisions like how much abuse I should take from Jackie before calling it quits.

I didn't want to think about my wife. Not in Tina's

shower. But Jackie's face kept appearing before me, an apparition that seemed to rise out of the steam. She was haunting me like she always did and I hated her for it. And I hated myself for allowing it to happen.

If Grimm was right, I didn't have much time before the police would begin applying heavy pressure.

Who tipped the cops to Dusty's book? I went over the candidates: some of the most proficient liars I knew. I'd never be able to read the kind of shit they could sell, bald lies told straight-faced without a modicum of guilt. In the art of deception, I was a mere novice, an on-the-job trainee.

Still, I had to start somewhere. I figured Barney to be the least likely to make the anonymous tip. The one thing he didn't want was to stir up muck. He was already choking in it, and with *his* playmates, the sooner the Sands case dropped back to page twenty, the better off he'd be.

That narrowed the field.

Jackie? No. She was flaky enough. Her mind had more nooks and crannies than a toasted English, but it didn't add up. Tommy either.

Would Gizzo believe I had nothing to do with it? Would Ryan? Christ on a bar stool!

The heat from the shower was making me weak. I felt light-headed. I slid down the tile wall and slumped into a corner. Thoughts. Imagination. All so dreamlike. Newspapers relate stories about crime, bullet-riddled bodies found in cars. Unreal. The other guy, not me. How would I react when actually faced with someone whose purpose was to kill me? Would I grovel, plead for mercy? Was it really coming down to that?

"Frankie? Frank, are you all right?" The shower door slid open and Tina looked down at me huddled in the corner, hugging my knees, head on my arms. "What the hell are you doing down there?"

"What do you think it feels like to die?" I asked.

"Oh, God. Come up here! Get up and come here to me." She was holding open a large, lavender bath towel.

I got up unsteadily and wobbled toward her. She

bundled me up and began a gentle, soothing massage. "Tell me about it, Frankie. Maybe I can help."

"I'm afraid of what's going to happen," I said. "At first it was all in my mind—make-believe. But these are real characters. Killers, pushers, blackmailers."

"Blackmailers?"

"It's a fucking mess," I said.

She handed over my pants. "Here, put these on and come inside. I've got breakfast ready. We'll talk."

I took her advice—dressed and ate. She had the TV going.

"Feeling better?"

"Yeah, thanks."

"What are you involved in, Frankie? I want to know, please."

Why not? We were on the same wavelength. I told her everything right down to last night.

"Your wife sounds like a winner," she said. "Why do you take it?"

"Sex. I'm a sexual prisoner."

"I can't believe you're that shallow. You don't have trouble getting women. So come on, what is it? What makes you stay?"

It was a question I'd asked myself a thousand times. I was hung up on her; the whys and hows didn't mean a hill of shit.

"Frank?"

"These eggs are delicious."

"Tell me," she said.

"I don't know. She's the most selfish individual I've ever known. And yet I keep thinking she's not really that way. She won't let anyone near her. It's like she's constantly denying herself any honest emotion. As though sincerity would weaken her resolve to be a stone bitch.

"She wants total independence, not just financially—though that's a large part of her game plan. What she wants is total human detachment. The only time she relents is when she wants something from someone."

"Sounds like she belongs on a desert island," Tina said.

"I'd agree, except that she thrives on admiration. Guys get blown out when they see her and she eats it up. Except when they try to put the hand on her. Then they have to watch their balls."

"What are you doing around all these characters?" she asked. "You've got a decent background, you seem straight. Tommy Milano, Sands, Gizzo—there's no common denominator between you and them. Why do you waste your time with low-lifes like that? They're one percent of the world, Frankie. Misfits, all of them."

"I know. But their motivation is so fucking warped that I'm intrigued by it. Crazy, eh?"

"Suicidal is more the word. So now what are you going to do?"

"For starters, I'll have another talk with Jackie. See if I can dissuade her from getting us both killed. I promised Ryan I'd get him the book. I'm toying with the idea of just turning it over and letting him do his thing."

"Do it, Frank. Don't dawdle. Just get rid of that book. The accountant—Reuben?—he was right. It's dangerous." She poured some more coffee.

"Why can't they all be like you?" I said.

"You mean women in general? Or one-night stands?"

"Not feeling guilty are you?"

"Please," she said. "Spare me. Just for the record, that wasn't my mind you penetrated last night." She shook her pretty blonde head. "You're such a moron."

"You're right."

"Don't be so goddamn condescending."

"I'd like to stay here with you," I said.

"And they say women are the romantics." She gulped her coffee. "Tell me," she said. "What makes you think I'm that much different than your wife?"

I picked up my cup and drifted over to the window. We weren't far from the Roosevelt Island Bridge. I said, "For one thing, you're an artist. Artists have feeling for life, for people."

"Artists can be just as cynical as the next person. I'm not deceiving myself about you, Mr. Fontana. You're no rose garden. Tina Webb can be just as phony. But when the time comes to make a commitment, I can do it."

"That explains the change," I said.

"What change?"

I turned. "You. Last night you came on like Tina Dipshit and today you sound like the *Playboy* Advisor. Or is this just the same line of horseshit you lay on all your one-nighters?"

"You bastard!"

"I'm a bastard 'cause I want to know more about you? Last night: 'Some dope? A couple of lines?' What the fuck was that? If you're a head, I don't need it. If you're not, you really are a phony. Or confused. If that's the case I got one at home that's more fucked up than you ever dreamed of being."

"Maybe you're the one that's fucked up," she said, crossing over to me. Her face was an unhealthy red. "You don't learn about a woman by calling her a liar and a tramp. Sure, I've been around the block once or twice. But only once or twice. I'm selective, Frank."

"Yeah," I said. "You follow your instincts."

She winced. "I think you better leave."

It would have made good sense to just get my coat and get the hell out. I didn't.

"Listen, Tina, I'm in a knot, you know? What I'm saying here is uncalled for. I'm sorry." I reached out for her. She backed away like I had hooks attached to my wrists.

"Thanks for the eggs," I said. I started to walk around her.

She grabbed my hand. "Wait. Don't go yet."

She smiled, looking up at me. "You know, Frank, the one thing I demand is honesty."

"Like last night in the car?"

She flushed. "I was drunk."

"I know when someone's drunk and when they're putting it on."

"All right," she said. "So I wasn't that drunk. I thought you were playing. I didn't realize how serious it is. I'm going to help. I want to."

"Okay," I said. "The first thing is find out who shot Dusty. Convince the maniac that I don't know who he is or why he did it. Then get Lieutenant Ryan and make him believe I know nothing about Dusty's affairs or Uncle Gizzo's. Get them to put it in writing, have it notarized, and bring it to me in twenty-four hours."

"How much do you really know?" she said.

"Too much to live happily ever after."

CHAPTER 12

I told Tina to keep the coffee hot. "I'll be back," I said. She looked troubled. "When?"

"Sooner than you think."

"Leave the gun," she said. "I'll feel better."

Sound advice. I had to stay out of the slam and breaking the Sullivan Law was no way to do it.

I gave Tina the gun, along with a big kiss, took my coat, and left. I was going to Maspeth, where Leo Antonucci's wife was reaping one of the benefits of their marriage: an all-expense-paid one-family Cape, compliments of the Mob. The house was the least they could do for Carol. Although I'd heard Leo's paychecks were still rolling in during his absence. An allotment, I guess you'd call it. In Leo's case, about ten years' worth.

Carol lived close to the commercial district, in a section called Polack Alley. It was about midway between my home and the Skyview Lounge. She'd had car trouble a while back and I had given her a lift to work. I remembered the house.

I kept checking the mirror for a tail. There was none that I could see but I took an indirect route just in case. Like the neighborhood, the Antonucci house was quiet. I could hear the gong from the steps. I gave her a few seconds to answer, watching the curtains while I waited. She would usually check before opening.

I tried again. No answer. A walkway alongside the house led to the back door. I jumped the steps and hustled to the back. It was a wooden door with a diamond shape glass that accessed an alcove. She only locked it when she went out. And it was open.

Carol's fake fur was hanging on a hook; her boots lay flat in front of the kitchen door, a glass door with flimsy curtains. I knocked once, cupped my eyes, and looked in.

"Carol," I called. "It's Frankie."

There wasn't much to see inside: a round oak table on a tile floor, fridge, sink. No Carol. She could have been upstairs.

I knocked harder, yelled louder. Nothing. I tried the door and went in. "Carol? You upstairs? It's Fontana." A few steps to the dining room. Beyond that the parlor. And Carol.

She was lying on her back, her face outlined by a red puddle. The front of her hair was matted with something that shimmered as it ran slowly down the side of one temple.

I wanted a closer look but the slime bore an uncanny resemblance to this morning's eggs. My stomach slammed into reverse. I spun on my heels and raced into the kitchen. A chair toppled in my wake. I made the sink.

I'd been sicker once: in Nam, when I poked my face into a certain ditch on my way to headquarters. What I saw might have been human once, but at the time it was hard to tell.

I rinsed the sink, splashed water on my face, and waited for the bright flashes to disappear from my eyes. If I had any nerve I'd go back inside, look around, check her pulse. Who was I kidding? It was all I could do to stagger out of there. Being a private sleuth was never meant for the faint-hearted.

I'm not sure how long I drove before I realized I wasn't stopping for lights or yielding at intersections, I heard brakes squeal, a horn, and a gush of words I hadn't heard since Tommy cracked his shin against the slop sink. I offered a lame apology, got the finger, and kept going.

Apparently my subconscious mind had its own notion of self-preservation because I wasn't driving toward Glendale. Instead, I found myself heading straight for Tina Webb, where safe harbor and a weapon were at my disposal.

With the initial shock behind me, the implications of Carol's death were beginning to sink in. I figured she'd been offed for one of two reasons: she could finger Dusty's killer, or she had information the killer wanted. Either way, she'd been brutally slain for something she knew. What I knew could fit inside a squirrel's jock. Sure, I had the book. But the list that Barney sold seemed more incriminating. Unless the book and the list were tied together somehow. In which case the next victim would be Barney Rubbles. Or yours truly. This was one race I definitely wanted to lose.

My face must have been paler than the faded-gray smock Tina wore when she let me in. The smock was blotched with globs of paint. Wet paint, orange and red— like the top of Carol's head.

"Jesus, Frank, you look awful," Tina said.

I mumbled something, brushed her aside, and beat a path to the bathroom. By the time Tina caught up I was on my knees in front of the bowl, retching miserably. She tried to comfort me by massaging the back of my neck.

"Easy, easy," she kept saying.

"That's easy for you to say," I replied between spasms.

I think she chuckled. More importantly, she kept right on rubbing. Eventually, it worked.

"Try to stand," she said. I took her arm. Hoisting me to

my feet, she led me inside and gingerly planted me onto the couch.

Sighing, I looked around. She had an easel in front of the window, a high stool alongside with a palette and brushes on the seat. I hadn't noticed before, but from here she had a damn nice view of Manhattan.

"All right," she said, sitting beside me. "Tell me what's going on. What happened?"

Her brow was furrowed, her forehead creased. There was concern here, genuine, if I read it right. "Carol's been murdered," I said.

"Carol," she repeated. "Dusty's girl?"

I nodded. "She was the one person who could have shed light on this. I figured if I got her alone—" a deep breath— "I could get her to open up. She was pretty sore on the phone yesterday. But face to face, you know . . . I'd go easy at first. Then shake her up if I had to."

"I know," Tina said. "And someone else had the same idea. Except they shook a little too hard. She must have been involved. The Mob doesn't kill without a reason."

I shook my head. "I don't think it was them. Wasn't their style. I mean her head was bashed."

"You sure it wasn't a bullet?"

I closed my eyes. "Don't remind me."

"Even so," Tina went on, "you can't rule them out." She leaned over and kissed my eyelids. Her lips felt soft and doughy.

She said, "You need help, Frank. I think you better go to the police right now. Tell them what they want to know. They'll help you."

"Sure they will. Come off it, Tina. Once the press finds out I'm talking, my name would go right from page one to the obituary. No thanks. Besides, I don't know what the hell's going on any more than they do. I mean it."

"I believe you."

"Somehow, I don't think that's enough."

"We'll work it out."

"What's wrong with you?"

"I want to help."

"Join the Peace Corps."

"I can take care of myself, Frank. I can take care of you, too. If you give me the chance."

There were so many things I wanted to do. Like getting home, locating Tommy. Unpleasant things that required more energy than I possessed at the moment. I looked at Tina and saw refuge. She wanted me now and I knew it. Why not, I thought. A little rest, a little love. What better way to charge my batteries?

There was a certain tenderness in Tina's lovemaking, a confirmation of the sensitivity I had gleaned since meeting her. Sex was serious business with Tina, but it wasn't desperate or demanding. It usually takes a number of sessions before I can pick up on a woman's style. Sometimes it's never quite right and I know it never will be. That afternoon on Tina's couch convinced me that I had found someone special.

We said nothing to each other. We didn't have to, our minds were more closely coupled than our bodies. Every move, every nuance was anticipated: tacit reminders of what we had now and what we could have going for us in the future. If, indeed, I had a future.

Without even trying we peaked at precisely the right moment. Tina shuddered and I sighed mightily, pressing her buttocks into me in that final instant.

I could have slept a few hours, a few days, really. I'd made love to Tina looking to tap an energy source. Instead, I felt enervated, completely spent. It was nice, in a dreamy sort of way.

"What are you thinking about?" Tina said, bumping aside the reverie.

"You know as well as I. Feast or fucking famine."

"What do we do about it?"

I pointed my chin toward the easel. "You paint. Me?" I shrugged. "Run, I guess."

She put her arm around my waist. "Not without me, you don't."

We stayed that way for a while, about as safe and serene as two bears in hibernation. I tried to block out all that had happened in the last few days. But I kept hearing Carol, and Dusty. "Get up, you horse's ass," they were saying. " 'Less you wanna join us."

I stirred. Tina groaned. "I have to make a call," I said.

"Later."

"Now!"

She sat up. "In the kitchen." She indicated a wall phone next to the refrigerator. "Who are you calling?"

"My loving wife. I want to see what we're having for dinner."

The phone rang about ten times before Jackie picked it up.

"Hello," she said curtly as though I'd interrupted something important—like packing her bags for instance.

"It's me," I said.

"Really. Are you finished whoring around for the night? Make it fast because I was just leaving." Her voice shot through the line like venom.

"Just park your ass," I said. "I'll be home in fifteen minutes."

"You don't understand, love. I'm leaving you. I told you I would when I was ready. Well. I'm ready."

"You fucking bitch!"

"Flatterer."

"Wait there for fifteen minutes," I said, trying not to whine. "It's important."

"I doubt it."

"Carol's dead." I paused for effect. "Her head was beaten to a bloody pulp. So are you going to wait for me or what?"

"Good-bye, Fontana."

Her voice was too smug. *Jesus. She had found the book.*

"Wait!" Visions flashed through my mind. A cop in the back of a panel truck, adjusting dials on a recorder, taping every word. "I don't want to talk on the phone. I've got to see you."

"Why? It's over. You had your chance. Besides, if I see you now I might want to hang around for one last hump . . . for old time's sake. You're a great fuck, did I ever tell you that?"

"Not often enough. Look," I said, "the cops told me they got a tip about a book Dusty was keeping. You wouldn't know anything about that, would you? . . . Would you? . . . Jackie? Jackie, answer me."

"Bye-bye, love."

I slammed the receiver and turned to Tina, who, with more than casual interest, had watched me squirm under Jackie's assault. It was fucking degrading. "Where's my coat?"

"What's wrong?"

"Everything. Jackie's leaving and taking something important. Get my coat, will you?"

She came back with two coats, hers and mine. "I'm going with you."

I slipped into mine. "Where do you think you're going? My apartment?"

"If that's where you're heading."

"No way. Listen," I said, trying hard to compose myself, "were you serious about helping me?"

"Of course."

"Then stay here by the phone. I'll get back to you in an hour or so."

"You're lying."

"You can't come and that's final."

I left Tina holding her coat, with a look on her face that was neither anger nor pain but a combination of fear and concern. Anxiety, I think. It made me feel rotten though I wasn't sure why.

CHAPTER 13

The drive to East Glendale should have given me time to decide what I should do with Jackie. But by the time I reached our apartment I wasn't any closer to a decision than when I'd left Tina. Had I driven to San Diego, eight hours a day with nights off at Holiday Inns, there still would not have been enough time. It just wasn't the type of decision a man could mull over, pros and cons carefully weighed, logic strictly adhered to. No. Whatever I did to Jackie needed to be spontaneous. "Believe me, Your Honor," I'd tell the judge, "it wasn't premeditated. She pissed me off so I broke her neck."

I took my usual spot in front of the hydrant, got out, and started across the street. I didn't see Jackie's car but that didn't mean she wasn't home. Sometimes she'd park so far from the apartment, I'd have to drive her to her car.

Weird what anger can do to you. The remorse I'd felt for Carol Antonucci was now all but forgotten, consumed by my compulsion to get at Jackie.

Instead of moving cautiously, I became careless,

forgetting it was open season on asses, and mine was ticketed for some brute's trophy case. Like the monster who intercepted me.

"Fontana?" he said, blocking my path.

He was one of those guys who looked like he was born without a neck. Short and stocky with a square jaw and a large head that would have looked right at home under a football helmet. I would have been more intimidated except I was so pumped up over Jackie I felt charged with bravado. Which was why I said, "What about it?"

His eyes shifted toward a new Caddie Seville parked right beside us. "Get in the car, Fontana," someone said from inside the car. I bent down and saw Nunze, Gizzo's man. He was wedged between the front seat and the steering wheel like a huge granite block.

They were killers, yes, but were these two behemoths working or just selling tickets for the annual "Get to know your Don" dinner-dance?

I looked around. What was the hurry? Across the street a blue-haired old lady carrying a full bag of groceries eyed us curiously between a loaf of Italian bread and some celery stalks. Down the block a teenager with a ghetto blaster was bopping toward us. Eyewitnesses, I thought. Poor bastards.

"Okay," I said warily.

"Okay," Nunze said. "Just get in the car and every-thing'll be cool." I felt like a guy whose doctor just told him it's malignant but don't worry, we'll get you a second opinion.

I'm not a religious man. Still, I always believed there had to be something more than what's here on earth. Call it heaven, call it anything you want, but even a non-practicing Catholic knows that you can't get there unless you're buried in consecrated ground. Which does not include the marsh-lands of Jamaica Bay. So let them kill me here and now. That way at least I'll wind up in St. Somebody's Cemetery with a shot at eternal happiness.

"I have a gun," I said, reaching in my pocket. No-Neck stepped back, looking quizzical while I groped for the gun. It was gone! I had given it to Tina.

No-Neck was grinning from ear to ear. "You ain't the fastest draw I ever seen," he said, staring at my empty hand. "Now get in the fuckin' car!"

"Sure, sure," I said. "But just one thing."

"Yeah?"

"I want to leave a note for my wife."

"Hey!"

"Yeah, I know," I said. "Get in the fuckin' car."

I wasn't exactly stuck between a rock and a hard place, but jammed between those two goons in the front seat of that Seville was as close as you can come without being laminated. My knees were pressed against the dash and I had to hug myself to keep my shoulders out from under theirs. If that wasn't enough, the smoke from their guinea stinkers was making me woozy.

Anyway, I could barely breathe, so I said, "Would you mind cracking a window?"

"Why?" said No-Neck. "You gonna jump?" A little gangland humor. He laughed and a chunk of cigar ash dropped to his lap. He ignored it.

"Where are we going?" I said.

"Long Beach," Nunze said. "You asked to see the man so we're taking you to him."

I flashed to last night's conversation with Peppy DeSimone. He'd gotten so out-of-joint when I'd asked to see Gizzo that I never figured he'd pass it on. Wrong again.

Sure, I wanted to see Gizzo but I would have preferred waiting until I was ready. I hadn't even thought about what to tell him and here I was on my way to meet him. Or was I?

Did Gizzo live in Long Beach? I tried to recall if Tommy had ever talked about his uncle's house. I couldn't remember. I couldn't remember anything. It was so hot in the car that my brain felt like it was melting, oozing right through my forehead.

Nunze paid the toll and we rumbled over the Cross Bay

Bridge, over cold murky water that swelled toward a bleak horizon like an immense shroud.

"Nice day for a swim," No-Neck said.

"For you, maybe" I said. "I didn't bring my trunks."

"This guy's a riot," No-Neck said between guttural noises which might have been a laugh.

"Yeah," Nunze said. "I'm in stitches."

We turned off at Beach Channel Drive and headed east under an El past gloomy streets pointing toward the sea. Any one of those streets would have been a dandy place to drop me off—permanently. I kept waiting for Nunze to hook a sudden right, stop next to an open field and drag me out of the car. But as we got closer to Long Beach, I began to believe they were actually taking me to Gizzo.

Smoothly, silently we continued east on a tarmac road, the yellow line whizzing by, the hum of snow tires hypnotic.

I'd always had difficulty keeping quiet. I mean, who ever heard of a barman that didn't like to talk? Ironic to have wound up in the Skyview, a lounge frequented by a society sworn in blood to eternal secrecy. Along with their other faults, the wise guys were a taciturn, brooding bunch of sadists who wouldn't holler "shit" if they stepped in it.

I'd seen enough of them at the lounge, drinking hour after hour, listening to me babble, nodding or shaking "no"; occasionally glaring if I got too close to "business." They all had the same thing in common: lockjaw.

"I hope you still feel like swimming after the man gets through with you," No-Neck said, bringing me back.

"Shut up, Al," Nunze said.

"Just drop me off at the corner," I said.

"Relax," Nunze said. "We're almost there."

The order could have come down already and this meeting might be nothing more than a work-over before the actual hit. "Let's see what he knows before we kill him." One of those numbers.

Detective Grimm, I thought. Where the fuck was he

now? Or Ryan. Goddamn cops are never around when you need them. But it gave me an idea.

"You know," I said, "the police have been on me since yesterday."

No comment.

"How do you know they're not following us right now?"

Zero.

"I don't have to tell you what—"

"Ain't nobody followin'," Nunze said.

"Are you sure? How do you know? They're pretty slick."

No-Neck laughed like that was the funniest thing he'd ever heard. "Them fuckin' gabrones. Pretty slick. My fuckin' ass is slick."

We were on Park Street. The Lido Beach sign was just ahead when Nunze turned right onto a typical suburban street: one-family homes separated by squares of grass, short and neat. At the end of the block was a large house surrounded by a wall covered with ivy. The wall and the house were flamingo pink stucco. It was an eyesore but it was private, a regular fortress.

Nunze parked in front of a two-car garage, which, except for the doors, was on the verge of being swallowed by ivy. We got out and they took me through a squeaky wrought-iron gate, which opened to a concrete walk that swung around the side of the house to a renaissance-style patio of multiple arches. A rusting barbecue sat in a corner, listing to port. Gizzo may have had money coming out of his ears, but he sure as hell wasn't flaunting it. Not on his home, anyway.

The side door was open and they hustled me down a short, narrow flight of stairs to another door, which was locked. Nunze opened it with a key and stepped in ahead of me.

"Inside," No-Neck said. He was a few steps above me.

I walked into the room which not only shocked me by its spaciousness but by its contents. It was a tremendous game room that ran the length of the house. In the middle was an eight-foot pool table. Along one wall a full-length shuffleboard. Several large poker tables with cards scattered across them. A few pinball machines, dart boards, and on the far wall a Bally slot machine. With its red wall-to-wall carpet, the place looked like a screwy blend of Caesar's Palace and the playroom of a condo for senior citizens.

"Have a seat," Nunze told me.

He went back upstairs while No-Neck took a stance like he was guarding the Tomb of the Unknown Soldier. I took off my coat, pulled a chair out from under a card table, and sat down to wait for Gizzo. What else could I do?

A candy machine was set between two pinball games. I fished a quarter from my pocket and started to get up. "Sit down!" No-Neck said.

"I just want a piece of candy."

"Whataya think, you're in a fuckin' candy store? Now sit down."

They came down the stairs in no particular hurry. Gizzo came in first, looking surprisingly frail compared to a month ago when he'd harpooned Tommy with the swizzle stick. He stood about five-feet-four-inches with platforms and he couldn't have weighed more than a hundred-twenty pounds. His hair was pure white and kind of wispy. Except for the tan, the most formidable thing about Candy Gizzo was his reputation.

Maybe because he was smiling. I hadn't expected a smile. Down at the Skyview he'd always looked like he was pissed off at the world. You'd look at him and if he caught your eye you could almost hear him thinking: what the fuck are you staring at, you turd?

But here he was, smiling, his thin lips tightly drawn over crocodile teeth. He looked like a middle-aged astronaut returning from the planet Mongo.

He walked toward me. I got up, stuck out my hand, and said, "Mr. Gizzo," like he was the President or something.

He waved me down without a word, then turned to Nunze and said, "It's all right. Wait upstairs."

It wasn't really a voice but a reverberation preceded by a "gulp" and a mechanical "brrr." A voice box, the kind surgeons implant when removing vocal chords riddled with cancer. So the rumors were true, Gizzo was fighting an enemy that no amount of money or power could conquer.

So I heard, *gulp—brr* and, "Frank Fontana, right?"

"Yes, sir."

"Peppy tells me . . . you're a good man with the . . . sticks." He moved his hands back and forth as if pouring beer through imaginary taps.

"I like my job," I said.

"That's good. A man should enjoy his work. I enjoy what I do." So did Hitler, I thought. "Except when things don't run smooth," he said. "Like now."

The smile was beginning to wane. I fidgeted.

"Relax," he said. "How about a drink? You want a drink?"

"No thanks."

"Candy bar? I've got a sweet tooth, you know?"

"No thanks," I said, glancing appreciatively at the vending machine.

"All right then, let's talk business. Tell me what you know about Sands."

My kind of guy, I thought. Straight to the point.

I told him I knew about their partnership in the Sky-view and that even though Dusty had a reputation for being a prick, he'd always been square with me. I said I thought he was pimping off some of our girls, but it was none of my business and I never cared about it.

"The cops," I said, "think he was involved in drugs, but I don't know anything about that."

He looked skeptical. "Uh-huh. And you were working . . . the night Sands . . . got it?"

"Yeah, me and Tommy."

"Tommy," he said, grimacing. "That little bastard. My sister-in-law called me . . . from Miami. She says she can't reach him. Peppy says he didn't show last night. It don't look good for him to take off at a time like this."

I searched Gizzo's face for a lie. For all I knew he could have had his nephew stashed some place, or whacked. But all I discerned was a benign smile.

"I was surprised he didn't come in," I said. "I met him for coffee just before work and he never said a word about not showing up."

"You and Tommy are pretty tight, ain't you?"

"I guess so."

"He got you the job, didn't he?"

I nodded.

"What did you guys talk about last night?"

I figured he was baiting me. He knew about Dusty's book, would have gotten the whole story from Peppy, including my lie that I knew nothing of its existence. I was still clinging to the hope that I had nothing to fear from Gizzo, that the police would soon get off my back, and that I'd never have to trade the book for protection. And if it didn't work . . . well, then I'd have to tell Gizzo I had it. But for now I resolved not to reveal anything, at least until I knew where this conversation was going.

Gulp—brrr. "Well? What'd he have to . . . say?"

"We talked about Dusty. I was uptight because the police had been up to see me. I knew they'd already talked to Tommy and I wanted to know how he'd handled it."

"And what did he say?"

"He said they were cocksuckers."

"Yeah, that sounds like Tommy. What'd he tell them?"

"The same thing I told them—nothing. Neither of us know anything about what happened to Dusty."

"Tell me something?" Gizzo said as if I had a choice. "You think I'm responsible . . . for knocking him off?"

"No," I said, wishing it were true.

"Why?"

"Too sloppy. I mean the man was killed right behind the lounge. That's too close to home, you know?"

Gizzo's smile broadened. Apparently he liked my answer and in all modesty so did I. Not that I believed it.

"Too close to home," he said. "That's all right. So then you feel safe, here in my home?"

"I don't know, I guess so. Any reason why I shouldn't?"

He looked pensively at me and began tugging his upper lip. He gulped, brrrd, and said, "You know what I think? I think you and my scumbag nephew saw something last night, something that scared the shit out of the two of you. I think Tommy took off" —brrr— "because he's a punk. And because he's never faced anything in his life. But he should have come . . . to me about it."

"We didn't see anything." I could feel my face turning red, the way it did when I'd lied to Ryan about the book.

"Uh-huh," Gizzo said. He went to the stairs where he rapped his bony knuckles on the wall. His boys came thundering down the steps like two Saint Bernards to their master. They huddled for a few moments, then Nunze went back upstairs. Turning to me, Gizzo said, "I heard they found Leo's wife today. What's her name?"

"Carol."

"Yeah, Carol. Was Tommy fooling around with her?"

"No. She was one of Dusty's girls."

"That wouldn't have stopped me when I was Tommy's age," Gizzo said with little humor.

A moment later Nunze was back. He handed an envelope to Gizzo, and along with No-Neck the three of them approached me like they were stalking someone fierce. All I could think of was Gary Cooper in *High Noon*. I mean I didn't see any six-guns but I knew they were around somewhere.

Nunze got me from behind. With his beefy forearm under my neck, he squeezed, and squeezed some more until my eyes saw nothing but starbursts, explosions that blasted away the hope I'd had about not having to fear Gizzo. Everything began to spin—Gizzo, the candy machines, the whole damn room zipping around like I was riding one of those Coney Island loops that makes you want to throw up just watching it.

I was seconds away from blacking out and almost looking forward to it, when from far away I heard Gizzo: *Gulp—brrr*.

"Enough."

CHAPTER 14

Nunze let go. I gagged and felt for my Adam's apple. A few seconds more and my voice would have sounded worse than Gizzo's.

"I don't want to see you roughed up," Gizzo said. "But I will if I have to." He showed me the envelope. Western Union. "Now what's all this?"

I opened the telegram and read, "I have what you want. $500,000 gets it for you. See F. F. for details. Signed, A Friend."

Some friend. F. F. could have meant Friggin' Fool but I knew it meant me and that was the same thing. Jackie had been a very busy girl since last night. She'd found the book and had beaten me to Gizzo. It had to be her, the $500,000 asking price was just too coincidental.

"Okay, F. F.," Gizzo said. "Speak."

Now what? Sure, I had a copy of the book but I couldn't offer that to Gizzo. He'd want to know how many other copies I'd made and even then he'd never be sure I hadn't spread it all over town. I was starting to realize how ridiculous my idea really was. The book for protection. Shit! He'd never let me go even if he believed I didn't know what the contents of the book meant.

I had to stall, hand him the same crock of shit I'd fed Ryan and Lawson. I knew I'd have to be more convincing this time. And maybe I could if I sweetened it a bit.

"I swear I didn't send you that telegram," I said. Nunze grabbed me again but Gizzo shook him off. "No," he said. "Let him talk."

"I don't know who sent it," I continued and damned if my voice didn't sound a little like Gizzo's. "But I think I know what it's about."

"I'm listening."

"The night Dusty was killed Carol Antonucci told me about a book. Like a journal, you know? A diary?"

"The one Lawson was asking about last night?"

"Yeah. Dusty had all his private business recorded in this book."

"How did Carol know about that?" Gizzo asked. "Dusty tell her about it?"

"No. Actually she didn't know what the book said. Only that Dusty kept one, and he wanted me to have it in case . . . in case he had to go away unexpectedly."

It wasn't hard to see the concern on Gizzo's face. His eyes were pinching in and his mouth was forming words you see scribbled on the walls of public toilets. I hurried on. "She told me I was supposed to contact Barney Reuben."

Gulp—brr. "Rubbles? Where the fuck does he come in?"

"He was holding the book for Dusty."

Gizzo bristled. "Rubbles has it now?"

"I'm not sure. He may have sent it to me. You see I called Barney yesterday. He admitted to having the book and said he'd be glad to get rid of it. I told him Dusty wanted me to have it and he said he'd send it to me right away."

"Did Rubbles tell you what the book said?"

"He couldn't figure it out. Didn't think anyone else could either."

"That don't sound like the Rubbles I know," Gizzo said. "He's too much of a fucking weasel to get caught up in this." Gizzo was pacing the floor. He stopped at a candy machine, dropped a coin, and pulled the handle. An Almond Joy fell out. He opened it and popped one in his mouth. "Why would Dusty want to give this book over to you? A fucking bartender?"

"I couldn't figure that out either. But then I thought it over."

Gizzo swallowed the last of the Almond Joy and tossed the wrapper to No-Neck, who backhanded it as if he'd spent years catching them. "So?"

"I used to be an accountant," I said. "I went to school for it. Maybe Dusty figured I'd be the only one who could understand the financial entries. I don't know. It's just a guess."

"And you figured he didn't trust Rubbles, right?"

"Something like that. Except I still don't understand what he expected me to do with the damn thing. I guess I'll never know."

"Yeah," Gizzo said. "We'll see." He waved the telegram at me. "So this F. F. shit, that's not your doing?"

"No way. I'd have to be crazy to try something like that. Listen, Mr. Gizzo, I've been straight all my life. You'd have to know me to realize I'd never pull a stunt like this." The only honest statement I'd made since I arrived.

"Maybe I *will* get to know you, F. F. We'll see." He waved at No-Neck. "For now I want you to go home with Al here, get the book, and bring it to me. There's a lot that doesn't make sense. Barney's an accountant and if you can understand the book, why shouldn't he?"

"Look, I don't know what Dusty had in mind," I said.

"Well, we'll find out," Gizzo said. "Now go with Al and bring me that book."

"What if Barney hasn't sent it yet?"

"What if he hasn't sent it? Simple, you lied. And then

I'll get to know you better. Hey, Nunze, show him how I get to know people better."

There was a fraction of a second between the time Gizzo finished brring and the instant Nunze's fist caught my solar plexus. I gasped, doubled over, and hit the floor.

"That's how I do it, F. F.," Gizzo said.

Like a limp doll they heaved me up and back on the chair. "Who sent the telegram?"

"Ba . . . Ba . . . Ba . . ." It sounded like a nursery rhyme but that was all I could get out. When I finally managed to talk my voice wasn't just raspy, I had the gulps to go with it. "Ba— Barney Rubbles. Ha— had to be him. Who . . . who else?"

No one said anything for a few moments. I welcomed the silence because I'd used all my strength on the last phrase. Then Gizzo broke it. "I'll talk to Rubbles. Meanwhile you take a ride home with Al." He turned his back to me and headed toward the staircase. When he reached the first step, he turned, "And you'd better not come back empty-handed." He started up the stairs and I could hear him muttering, "Nothing runs smooth. Nothing ever runs fucking smooth."

Tell me about it, Candy, I told myself.

Al and I had nothing to say to each other on the return trip. His face was veiled in tranquility; mine, twisted in anguish. In a way I envied the palooka. Nothing to do but run errands, act tough, and rough up a few punks now and then. Being on their side had definite advantages.

I kept thinking about that little spiral notebook I'd tucked away in my dirty laundry not more than twenty-four hours ago. In that time I'd been threatened by Ryan, Grimm, Lawson, and Peppy. I'd been consoled by an all-night nurse named Tina Webb. Carol Antonucci had been murdered. Gizzo had me on the goddamn ropes. Tommy had disappeared. And Jackie had walked out on me, taking everything of value including my fucking laundry bag probably. Still, it wasn't the past twenty-four hours that had me worried—that was behind me and I was still breathing. But

142

what about tomorrow at this time? One thing for sure, No-Neck wasn't worried about it.

I was rehearsing what to tell him when the time came to produce the book. Somehow nothing sounded right: "Sorry, big fella, but you see my wife had it laundered by mistake." It seemed that nothing I could dream up would prevent my being bashed by Gizzo. It was becoming more evident that what I needed now was a plan of escape. Oh, I needed a lot more than that but unless I got away from No-Neck there'd be little need for anything except a priest.

I fished out my key ring. Why not? Wasn't I one-for-one in front seat fisticuffs? Of course Barney wasn't built like No-Neck, but I did have that all-important element of surprise. Fine, but what if I clobbered Al only to discover that the book was still where I'd left it? Maybe I had Jackie all wrong? Maybe she hadn't sent the telegram?

There were only a few blocks to go and I was rapidly convincing myself to do nothing, to sweat it out and pray for a break. And damned if I didn't get one.

We had just turned the corner leading to my apartment when Al suddenly pulled over. "Cops!" he said.

In front of my house I saw what looked like a raid on a Times Square porn shop. Warning lights flashed angrily from the tops of several squad cars. A plainclothes dick near an unmarked car barked orders at uniforms dashing in and out my front door. Neighbors lined the sidewalk gaping at the action. One guy was pointing at my illegally parked car. He looked pleased, as though at last I was getting what I deserved.

Meanwhile, No-Neck was in a quandary. Clearly, decisions weren't his thing. So I helped him. "I better see what they want," I said.

"Wait a min—" Too late. I was already out of the car, jogging toward my apartment. Let him explain that one to Gizzo. I would have some explaining of my own to worry about but if I could find that book I'd think of something.

I ran past the detective and bounded up the front steps. Inside the foyer, a patrolman was talking to Mrs.

Schimmel. She seemed relieved as soon as she saw me. "Oh, Frank," she said, obviously upset, "I'm so glad you're here. I couldn't stop them. They had a warrant and—"

"That's all right," I said.

Now the cop came to life. "Hey," he said, "you're him. Wait!" He called upstairs. "Lieutenant! Hey, Lieutenant, I got him. I got him!" Like I was Dillinger, for Christ's sake. He ushered me upstairs. Behind us I could hear Mrs. Schimmel clicking her tongue. "Such a shame. A nice boy like that."

"Come on in, Fontana," said Lieutenant Lawson. I stepped into the kitchen. Thanks to Lawson's wrecking crew the whole place resembled the South Bronx. "Where were you?" Lawson said. He was seated at the kitchen table writing in one of those ubiquitous black books.

"Visiting." I waved at the mess: upturned chairs, opened cabinets, pots and pans, silverware, dishes, towels all over the floor. "Was this necessary?" I said.

"Sit down!"

I righted a chair thinking that no one seemed to enjoy talking on their feet anymore. "Did you find anything?" I figured if Jackie hadn't pilfered the book then Lawson surely had it. With everything turned inside out there seemed little chance he'd have missed my laundry bag.

"What's the matter, got something to hide?"

"Don't you need a warrant to destroy someone's home?" He showed me something that looked official but I was too nervous to read it.

"Hey, Bill," Lawson said, slipping the warrant back in his pocket.

From the bedroom, a young guy appeared in dungarees, sneakers, and a warm-up jacket. "Yes, sir."

"Show him what we found," Lawson said.

I expected Officer Bill to produce Dusty's book but instead he pulled a small plastic bag out of his jacket. The bag contained a white powder that I knew wasn't baking soda.

"Cocaine," Lawson said. "Tell him where you found it, Bill."

I figured for sure Bill would say "his laundry bag."

"In his dresser drawer."

The one thing I knew now was that Lawson had not found the book. Which meant Jackie had sent Gizzo the telegram. It also meant that she'd tipped the police last night. But why? It wasn't easy but I tried to think like Jackie. Maybe she was trying to drive up the price by making the police aware of the book? The more people who wanted the book, the higher its value. Supply and demand and all that stuff. Could be.

"Read him his rights," Lawson said.

"That's a plant and you know it," I said.

But the Miranda card came out and Bill sang the refrain that begins: "You have the right." I could have named that tune after one note. Halfway through, we heard, "Hold it, Ed!"

Ryan. Detective Lieutenant Ryan, my guardian angel. And like any respectable angel he'd appeared at just the right moment.

"Stay out of this, Ryan," Lawson said. He seemed more annoyed than surprised at Ryan's sudden materialization. "We're handling this."

"It's still a homicide case," Ryan replied in a hoarse voice.

Lawson said, "Show him, Bill." Bill held up the bag. "That's coke," Lawson said. "And that's my department. Now butt out or somebody downtown will hear about it."

"It's a set-up," I said feebly.

"Can we talk alone?" Ryan said. I was ready to walk out but it wasn't me Ryan wanted gone, it was Bill.

"It's all right, Bill," Lawson said. "You can take off. Leave the stuff here." The young narc left, probably on his way to quarterback a game of touch-tackle down at the schoolyard.

With Bill gone, Lawson said, "I'm taking him in."

Ryan pulled up a chair. Another one with tired brains.

"Come on, Ed, we can work something out. Frank's not exactly a babe in the woods, but he's no pusher."

"Listen, Ryan, I'm gonna bust somebody. If he's all I got then that's it. Comprende?"

"I think that's a mistake," Ryan said.

"I second that," I said.

They both gave me a dirty look. Ryan went on. "He can be useful to both of us. Isn't that right, Frank?"

"I'm trying."

"See that, Lieutenant, he's trying."

"He's trying my fucking patience, is what he's trying. But go ahead, tell me how he can help us."

"Go ahead, Frank," Ryan said. "Explain it to the lieutenant."

Silence.

"Let me help," Ryan said. "You see Frank's got that book we've been looking for. He's agreed to give it over without any strings. He's cooperating with our people and I'm sure he'll do what he can to help you. Right so far, Frank?"

Silence.

"Right, Frank?"

I nodded imperceptibly.

"See that, Ed? It doesn't make any sense to lock up our only lead."

"It's no good, Ryan. I'm getting a faceful of flack from the DA. He wants some asses and he wants them now. I've got one to give him and I'm not about to let it go. Besides," Lawson said, "there's no guarantee that there's anything in that damn book that's worth a shit."

"Yes there is," I said.

I'd struck a nerve with that one. They both edged forward in their chairs. "Well," Lawson said.

Silence.

Lawson jumped off his chair. "Oh, fuck this. I don't need this. Come on, Fontana, let's go."

"Hold it," Ryan said, then sneezed.

"Bless you," I said.

"Thanks," Ryan said.

"Oh, bullshit," Lawson said.

Ryan shook his head. "Listen, Frank, why don't you just give me the book now."

"I don't have it."

Lawson yanked my arm. "That's it. Let's go!"

Ryan said, "Just a minute. What do you mean, Frank? Where is it?"

"I mailed it to someone to hold for me. For insurance."

"But you can get it back, right?"

"Of course."

"Okay," Lawson said, releasing my arm. He sat down. "I want to know what's in the book."

You and how many others, I told myself.

I figured he'd have a breakdown if I told him I'd read it but hadn't the vaguest clue as to what it meant. So I let my imagination take over. "According to the book, Dusty had some partners."

"We know about Gizzo," Lawson said.

"No, I don't mean in the lounge. I'm talking about Dusty's other interests."

"Drugs?"

"I'd say so."

"Can we tie Gizzo into it from what's in the book?"

"I don't think so."

Lawson looked the way I must have looked when Nunze slammed me in the stomach. "Why not for Chrissake?"

"Because Dusty didn't name anyone. You see," I said carefully, "the book records the transactions, sales, dates, the split between partners. But no names."

"It's no good to me without names," Lawson said.

"That's what I'm working on. But with you guys hounding me all the time I'm not getting anywhere. I've got a theory."

"I don't need your theories," Lawson said. "I need names."

Ryan said, "Let him talk, Lieutenant. It can't hurt."

It seemed agreeable to Lawson, so I went on.

"I think Dusty was skimming the profits. His partners must have found out and one or both of them dissolved the partnership."

"It's too pat," Lawson said. "Sands knew we had his place under surveillance. If he knew, so did his partners. They wouldn't have killed him then. Not until they were sure that Sands couldn't hurt them. There's too much at stake here."

"I thought about that," I said. Actually I hadn't considered it until that moment. But listening to Lawson had given me an idea. "Suppose there wasn't any partnership at all. What if Dusty wasn't a partner but only working for someone—on salary, say, or commissions. He sees all that money rolling in. Even handles it. He's got his own list of dealers so he decides to strike out on his own. Instead of buying ten kilos of shit, he goes for fifteen. Then he sells it and pockets his own share plus his salary."

"I don't think so," Ryan said.

"Why not?" said an anxious Lawson.

"Because Sands would never keep a record of it. If his book ever fell into the wrong hands it would finish him. No. He kept that book for an ace. But so far I can't make the connection."

Lawson said, "So much for your theory, Fontana."

But I had another supposition that I kept to myself. Because if I was right, it meant I'd be running for the rest of my life.

"Who do you think tipped us off about the book?" Ryan said.

"Carol Antonucci," I said. There'd be no rebuttal, not from Carol anyway. "She had a thing with Dusty. Knew a lot about his business."

Ryan nodded. "Too much, I'd say. I just came from her place. Somebody clipped her."

I had a feeling this was coming. *Shock the Suspect* was a game these guys played well, and often. This time I was ready. Let them stare all they want. Stone-face Fontana wasn't giving an inch.

"Maybe you didn't hear him," Lawson said.

"He heard me," Ryan said with a crooked grin. "He's learning, that's all."

"All right," Lawson said. "I'll leave him on the street for a couple days. But I want that book."

I looked at Ryan. "It's okay, Frank. We're working for the same company. Getting me the book is the same as getting it for him."

"You've got a man on him?" Lawson asked Ryan.

"Grimm."

"Was he on me today?" I asked. If he was, I thought, then Ryan knew I'd talked to Gizzo. But why wasn't he saying anything about it?

"No. He's been outside all morning. That's how I knew about this." He indicated the kitchen.

"You mean Fontana's been on his own?" Lawson said.

"I had someone else on him. Like I told you, Ed, we have to take care of him."

"Like you took care of Carol Antonucci? And what about Milano? You got that under control, too?"

"Come on," Ryan said. "We had Antonucci's apartment covered."

"Not well enough, I'd say."

Ryan flushed. "We missed him, okay? All right? As for Milano, you scared him off before we had a chance to talk to him." Ryan turned to me. "You don't happen to know where he's hiding, do you, Frank?"

"Why don't you ask his uncle?"

Ryan looked at me suspiciously. "We've already checked."

I wanted to bring the conversation back to Gizzo. It didn't figure that Ryan would let me walk in and out of that house in Long Beach without questioning me about what went on inside. But Ryan wasn't biting. He was playing another game called monkey in the middle, with him and Lawson on the ends and me, the monkey, in between.

149

Lawson said, "I suppose your boy has an alibi for the Antonucci thing."

"Yeah," Ryan said. "Grimm had him shacked up all night with some lady he met at the lounge."

"Uh-huh," Lawson said. "Never too busy to knock off a piece, eh? What time was she killed?" he asked Ryan.

"Between four and five A.M. Frankie never left the lady's apartment house."

"And DeSimone?"

"Not sure. He shook us off last night after he left work. But knowing Peppy, he'll produce someone to back him up."

"You and Grimm should have stayed in Organized Crime," Lawson said derisively. "You weren't solving anything over there either."

"Don't worry," Ryan replied calmly. "We'll break this one."

Lawson was getting up, putting on his coat. "Well, one of us better do something and damn soon. You, Fontana, you're free as long as you play ball. Fuck up and we'll look for more party favors on your premises." He opened the door to the hallway, stopped, and turned to me. "You know, with Milano missing and that waitress dead, it seems to me you might be the next one they take out."

CHAPTER 15

After Lawson left, Ryan started walking around the apartment, picking up overturned chairs, replacing lamps. I followed him from room to room wondering if he planned on asking for the vacuum cleaner.

"Man, what a mess," he said.

"In more ways than one."

"I know. But Ed Lawson's very effective."

"Is that what you call it? To me he's as bad as the people he's after. He was getting ready to frame me before you showed up. That's illegal, isn't it?"

"Sure," Ryan said. "But putting on the squeeze is very effective."

We walked back in the kitchen. "Say," Ryan said, "do you have any tea in this place? A cup of hot tea would go good right now."

Everything Ryan said and did was designed to unnerve me. I understood why he was doing it, but I resented the oblique manner in which he did it. And after Gizzo, who fired head-on with both barrels, dealing with Ryan was like dodging Frisbees.

"What do you want from me, Lieutenant?"

He lowered himself gingerly into a kitchen chair. "A few things," he said. "But mostly I want a cup of tea. You wouldn't happen to have some of that Chinese stuff, would you?"

"Lipton."

"That'll be fine."

So there we were, sipping hot tea like we were on a fifteen-minute office break. He smacked his lips. "Ah, that hits the spot. By the way, where's your missus?"

Here it comes, I thought. "She does her thing and I do mine," I said.

"An open marriage? You know I never met anyone that actually practiced that sort of thing. How do you manage it?"

"It's got some advantages."

He shook his head. "I can imagine. You know if I ever stayed out the way you did last night my wife would have her lawyer all over me. Her brother's a lawyer. Makes it tough to fool around."

"My brother's a lawyer, too."

"That right? Where does he practice? I might be able to throw him some business."

"Akron," I said. "But don't bother. He's in trusts and estates. Most of his clients are dead."

Ryan chuckled. "I could get him a lot of business if he practiced in New York."

"You know, Lieutenant, I watch Cagney and Lacey, too. If you've got something to say, why don't you just get on with it?"

He smiled. "All right. Let's talk about the book. I know you've seen it. I don't know if you still have it, but you've read it. Now why don't you stop playing around? Can't you understand I might be your only friend?"

"I wish I could believe that," I said.

"You can trust me, kid. Just give me the book. I'll work it out with Lawson."

"I told you, I don't have it anymore."

"Then tell me where it is."

"I can't. I don't want to drag innocent people into this. It's bad enough as it is."

"You're being stupid, Frank. I could pull you in if I wanted. It's against the law to withhold information." He gestured toward his empty tea cup. "How about a refill? Tea's the best remedy for a cold, you know that?"

I poured out another cup. "I'm not withholding any information," I said. "How can I withhold something I don't have?"

"But you had the book and you gave it to someone else. It's the same thing. And this bull about no names— Jesus, you think Lawson's a moron? You could have dreamed up a better story than that."

"I looked at the book for ten minutes. It didn't mean a damn thing to me."

"Tell me how you got it."

I told him about Carol leading me to Barney.

"So after you left Reuben," said Ryan, "you mailed the book to someone for safekeeping. Is that it?"

"That's it. I was afraid to give it to the police because I didn't want my name in the papers. I figured Dusty's killer wouldn't appreciate it too much if he found out I was cooperating with the law."

Ryan nodded as if he agreed. "There's still one thing I don't understand. If you didn't want us to know about the book, why did you tip us off?"

Time to dip into my well of lies. "I told you, I didn't want to go public on this. But I didn't want to withhold the information altogether, so I had some kid call it in."

"Why didn't you just give the book to the kid and have him deliver it to me?"

"I didn't have it anymore. I told you that."

"Ah, Frankie, Frankie, you're all messed up. Your whole story's messed up. Now come on, you can't walk a line on this. You're either on my side or you're not."

"Well what would you have done? Your boy Grimm was threatening me, accusing me of fingering Dusty. And then I find out about the narcs. Would you be able to think straight in a situation like that?"

Ryan sniffled over his cup. "You know what I do when I have a problem I can't work out by myself? I talk it over with my wife, that's what. You must have discussed this with your wife—what's her name?"

"Jackie."

"Yeah, Jackie. What did she have to say about all this?"

"Nothing. Like I said, we go our own way."

"You poor bastard," Ryan said, and I couldn't tell if he was sincere. "You can't get out of this. We've talked to Gizzo. He knows about the book. It won't take him long to track it to you. What are you going to do then, run? You'll just get yourself killed if you try to run. I hate to admit it but men like Gizzo are much better at finding people than we are. By the time we find them, they're dead."

He must have read my thoughts because at that instant the idea of running had just streaked across my mind. Of course, I had no idea where to go. Even if Jackie hadn't already cleaned out our joint account, how long would I last on the few hundred dollars we had in it?

"No," I told Ryan. "I won't run. Being a fugitive is almost as bad as being in prison. Besides, I'm broke. I couldn't get any farther than . . ." Suddenly I knew where I'd go. A place to hide. And it wasn't more than twenty minutes from where I was sitting.

"You're scheming, Frank," Ryan said. "I can read it all over your face. Don't be stupid."

"Excuse me, Lieutenant, but I've got some things to do. And I'm all out of tea, so if you don't mind . . ."

He sighed and got to his feet. "All right. But I'll be close by if you need me. There's only one thing I want you to do for me before I go."

"Come on, Ryan, give me a break."

"I want you to call the person you sent the book to. Call right now and have it sent back to you. Do it, Frankie.

154

Do it now or I won't run interference with Lawson anymore."

"Sounds like blackmail."

He winked.

"All right," I said. "But can I ask you something first?"

He nodded.

"Lawson said that you and Grimm should have stayed in Organized Crime. What did he mean?"

"What is this, Frankie? A fishing expedition?"

I returned the wink.

He chuckled. "Why not? Grimm and I were assigned to the unit a few years back. Lawson's group was close to a bust. A big one. Out here in Queens, as a matter of fact. They had a snitch on the inside. Except this one was working for us at the same time and Lawson didn't know it."

"Did you?"

"Maybe. Anyway, it was our job to protect the guy. It didn't work out."

"And the bust?"

Ryan sighed.

"I see," I said. "He won't let you forget it, will he?"

"Lawson's all right. Just hates to lose, that's all. Like most of us. Now," Ryan said, "that call."

"Okay," I said. "Just remember, this person has nothing at all to do with this."

I went to the telephone and dialed. I had to get Ryan out of my hair and this was the only way to do it.

After several rings, I heard, "Hello."

"It's me," I said.

"God, I was worried. Why didn't you call sooner. I was just on my way—"

"Listen to me. That package I sent you."

"What package? What are you talking about?"

"Yeah, that's it," I said. "Mail it back to me, will you?

"Frank? Frank, are you all right? Where are you?"

"That's right," I said. "Do it right away." I hung up

before Tina had a chance to ask any more logical questions. Turning to Ryan, I said, "Okay?"

"You have my card," Ryan said, donning his huge fedora. "Tomorrow's Sunday. If I don't have the book by Tuesday afternoon I'm calling Lawson and he can do what he wants with you." He started out, then stopped. "Oh, thanks for the tea. I feel much better."

Ryan shut the door behind him. I listened as he retreated down the stairs and out the front door.

I was alone now, alone and dejected. Staggering a little, I made my way to the playroom where I flopped heavily onto the couch. The sudden absence of confusion had created a void so serene that within seconds I felt myself dozing off. Outside, kids were shouting in a game of street hockey, their voices barely audible over the high-pitched ringing in my ears. I used to think of the ringing as a noise hangover. I'd come home feeling like there was a radio turned on inside my head; several stations in a simultaneous broadcast of blaring music and indiscriminate chatter. And overriding all of the noise was the familiar ringing.

Ringing . . .

I couldn't have been asleep for more than ten minutes when a ring of a different sort brought me back. Telephone.

I hauled myself off the couch and went to the bedroom. Somewhere on the floor, under a mess of shirts and underwear, the little Princess was madly ringing. I waded through the clothing. Lawson's men had done a thorough job in this room, too. The bedding had been torn down and the mattress hung off its boxspring. It was enough to drive any respectable housewife to nervous collapse.

"Hi, hon," Jackie said as I placed the receiver to my ear. Speaking of housewives.

" 'Hi, hon' your ass," I snapped. "Where the hell are you? What's going on?"

"I miss you already," she said. "That's something, isn't it?"

"Then why aren't you here?"

She was silent for a few seconds. "I want to see you first," she said.

"Correct me if I'm wrong, but didn't I ask you to wait here for me? What are you up to?"

She laughed her playful laugh which I knew was designed to make me think she was just a cute kid and that the havoc she'd caused had been nothing but whimsy. I decided to play along. "So where are you?"

"The Briny," she said. "You remember the Briny Breezes, don't you?"

As if I could ever forget those giddy nights at the Briny. The mirrored walls, the blue movies, the waterbed undulating beneath our sweaty bodies.

"I remember," I said.

"I'm in room 133."

"I'll be there in twenty minutes."

I hung up. I didn't want to hear any more. Whatever else she might have said would only have reinforced my feeling that I was being taken for another ride. But what could I do? She had the book and she had my head and I needed them both to survive.

On with a fresh shirt and Levis. There'd be no work tonight. Not this night or any other night. I was giving up my tenuous career at the Skyview. From now on I wouldn't pour the booze, I'd drink it. Lots of it.

I threw a few slices of Kraft's American cheese into a folded piece of white bread, then I dashed out the door taking the stairs three at a time. Mrs. Schimmel must have been waiting for this because she opened her apartment door and caught me as I reached the ground floor.

She was toying with her apron, her forehead lined with concern, eyes slightly downcast. "Frankie," she said. "Frankie, I've always thought you were a good tenant. You know that, don't you?"

"Sure I do, Mrs. Schimmel, but I'm in a big hurry now so if we could talk later—"

"I'm afraid not," she said, looking at me for the first time. I could see her eyes watering up. "I'm going to have to ask you to find another place. I'm sorry, but I can't take all this. Ever since you married that girl . . .''

I touched her arm and she broke down, sobbing into the apron she held over her face. "That's all right, Mrs. Schimmel," I said. "It's okay, I understand. I'll look for another apartment as soon as I can."

"Oh, I'm so sorry," she wailed. "Really, I am. But . . . you and your wife . . . I wish I could . . .'' Then she waved the apron as if to shoo away the funk. "I'm sorry." She backed into her apartment and closed the door on me.

"I'm sorry, too," I said, to no one.

Sure I was sorry. But not because she'd asked me to leave. I'd already decided to get out, to lay low until I had a better feel for what lay ahead—like whether I'd be living in an apartment, a cellblock, or not at all.

Grimm was outside waiting for me, parked a few doors away in a beige Plymouth instead of the dark sedan he'd used last night. Just like Grimm to use a dark car at night and a light one during the day. Camouflage and concealment à la NYPD.

I couldn't stand the guy but I was still glad to see him. By now our relationship was becoming symbiotic. I was the host and Grimm the parasite. Which was all right because as long as Grimm stayed on my back there was little chance that bigger, more deadly parasites would get at me. In my mind's eye I could see Grimm doing battle with Nunze and No-Neck Al. And doing it all for me.

Yet Grimm had taken it upon himself to walk off the job last night after our tussle. Why hadn't I been followed to Gizzo's this morning?

I couldn't help thinking that I was the key to Ryan's investigation, that if I didn't produce Dusty's book he would have a lot to answer for. Ryan must have been less than thrilled with Grimm's dalliance, because here was Grimm right back on the job.

I saluted him as I trotted across the street to my car. He was watching me all the way and I could almost feel his eyes punching holes in my back. It's okay, I told myself, you don't have to like me as long as you come through when the time comes. And the time, I felt, was rapidly approaching.

I headed for the Belt Parkway, toward Sheepshead Bay and the Briny Breezes where my wife awaited me with open arms and closed mind. I knew Grimm had to be baffled by this mid-afternoon rendezvous. He'd also be suspicious, being a detective and all. But I was prepared for him. This was how Jackie and I put zing into our marriage. You ought to try it, Grimm, you'd be amazed at what a waterbed can do for your sex life. I could hardly wait to see his frozen face when I laid that one on him.

Yet, as I drew closer to the Briny, I found myself thinking less about Grimm and more about Jackie. We hadn't utilized the facilities for some time but the memories were right up there in the front of my mind. The hours we'd spent rolling around on waterbeds, floating on a wave of carnal pleasure, rocking in unison toward a summit that blocked out everything except the sensation of flesh against flesh. It was sexual delirium, plain and simple. How do you forget something like that?

It wasn't difficult to see why Jackie had chosen the Briny to set up shop. There weren't too many places nearby that were better suited for seduction. Her moods may have been unpredictable but when it came to getting what she wanted from me, she'd consistently relied on sex. And why not? As a persuader her method was one hundred percent fail-safe.

Not this time, I vowed. Not if she takes me around the world a dozen different ways. Not if she swears to become my sex slave, to commit acts of perversion beyond my wildest fantasy. Not if she . . . whoa, I thought, slow down before you wind up throwing yourself at her feet.

CHAPTER 16

The Briny Breezes Motel is crescent shaped, three stories, and sits just off the service road at the Sheepshead Bay exit of the Belt Parkway. An "adult motel," the dive is a mecca for every persuasion and combination. Whether you're straight, gay, or into cocker spaniels makes no difference to management, provided, of course, that you have the cash for the room (no charge cards, please) and that you're not squeamish about the screaming going on next door.

Running the length of the building was a parking area containing a dozen cars, including Jackie's white Ford. I pulled into a slot and got out of the car. Grimm took up a post nearby but he didn't get out. Instead, I saw him writing feverishly in his daybook, probably recording my time of arrival: TOA—3:33 P.M. Anyway, he stayed put and that was okay because by now I couldn't wait to see Jackie.

I hurried inside to the front desk. Behind the counter sat a burly character dressed in overalls and a plaid flannel shirt. He looked more like a lumberjack than a concierge but I figured he hadn't been hired for his suavity. His face was partially hidden behind the early edition of the New York *Post,* I wondered if it carried the story of Carol Antonucci's murder. Possibly a cut on page twenty, but no more. The Giants had made the playoffs and nothing short of nuclear attack could have dislodged them from the front page.

"You want a room?" said the lumberjack, lowering his paper. He reached for a registration card. "Thirty-seven bucks, good to midnight."

"Midnight?"

"This ain't the Plaza, pal. You want the room or don'tcha?"

"I already have a room."

"Then whataya want from me? You lose your key?"

"Nothing," I said. "Just wanted to see the headline."

He lifted the paper. "Now you seen it."

I thanked him and walked away thinking that a man could come in here with a whip over one arm and a battered broad over the other and still get a room, no questions asked. After all, this *was* an adult motel.

Room 133 was down the end of a long corridor with a low ceiling. The corridor smelled as though someone had just run through it with a can of Lysol. It was done in red: carpets, flock walls, and red bulbs. It made me feel like I was inside a submarine deep under enemy waters. Eerie. Especially in contrast with the natural light in the lobby. Still, I couldn't deny the effect of all that red. I felt it instantly. Red was the color of heat, symbol of lust and other scarlet transgressions.

I walked swiftly, silently, checking door numbers, imagining all sorts of adult games taking place inside each room. Sodomy in 127. S&M in 129. 131, water sports. Room 133.

I put my ear to the door. Nothing. I didn't know what I expected to hear but I wanted to be ready for anything. With Jackie, anything was likely. She might even have a man inside, in which case the friendly lumberjack would find himself refereeing a battle royal.

I knocked a few times, heard some movement behind the door, then Jackie. "Who is it?"

"Your husband," I said loudly, which no doubt caused a chuckle or two in the adjoining rooms.

She undid the lock and opened the door a crack. There wasn't an inch of light before I bulled my way inside like a cop busting a bordello. Startled, Jackie jumped to one side as I slammed the door behind me.

There was no sign of anyone except my lovely wife. But her presence filled the room with what it was meant for. She was wearing one of my silk shirts, protectively holding the collar around her neck as if the rest of her body was vulnerable. Which was a joke. Because the shirt was unbuttoned all the way down to the briefest pair of panties she owned—a purple string with a heart-shaped patch that barely covered her pubic hair.

She could see my eyes and she smiled with the smugness that comes from gaining a quick upper hand. Round one to Jackie. Unanimous!

"My, but we're feeling frisky this afternoon," she said, scoring the first blow of round two.

"Is that costume meant for me?"

"Who else?" she said.

By now I could feel my insides turning to silly putty. I knew the feeling too well, knew there was no way to control it; that mixture of panic and desperation that comes from loving a woman who doesn't give two shits and a holler about you.

Jackie saw it. She could always see right through this macho image I'd try to portray whenever she had me on the ropes. And at that moment she had me reeling.

"What's the matter?" she said. "Don't you like my outfit?" She held the shirttails apart and performed a delicate pirouette. When her back was to me she gave the shirt a cancan swish showing me her ass split by the purple string into a pair of flushed melons. Her upper thighs were as firm as a kid's, not one fucking flaw.

"Very cute," I said.

She steepled her fingers under her chin. "I thank you."

"Save it." I turned away. I had to take my eyes off her before she annihilated me completely.

Check out the room, I told myself. Stick to business, remember your vow. Sure, my vow.

I scanned the room. Kingsize waterbed, mirrored ceiling, an overhead strobe light for headtrippers, twenty-one-inch TV with cassettes of *Deep Throat, Porn Scandal,* and other Oscar winners. In the bathroom: a commode, a bidet, and a shower equipped with steambath converter and a stool attached to the wall.

"What are you looking for?" Jackie said. "You've seen all this before." She'd been standing by the door watching me look for something I didn't want to find—a trace of another man.

I pointed to her open suitcase on the floor beside the bed. "That!" I tore into it, throwing the contents over my shoulder. "What did you do with it?"

"Do with what?"

"Gideon's Bible," I snapped. "What do you think?"

"You don't think I'd be silly enough to have the ledger with me, do you?" She went to the bed and sat down. I turned around in time to catch the bed undulating like marshweed in a summer breeze.

"Where is it? No more games, Jackie. You're going to give me that book or . . ."

"Or what?"

I wanted to say I'll wring your neck, but what came out was, "I'll go to the cops and tell them you've got it."

"I'll deny it. Then what? It's too late to go to the police, Frankie. So why don't you come over here next to me?" She patted the bed and everything rolled, including my stomach.

"You're going to fuck me into submission, is that it? What do you take me for, an imbecile? I already know what you've done and it damn near got me creamed. I'm still not out of the woods, not by a longshot."

"What do you mean?"

"That telegram you sent to Gizzo: 'See F. F. for details.' You fixed me good with that one."

I wasn't used to seeing Jackie nonplussed, but she was now. "How . . . how did you find out about that?"

"Because Gizzo ran me in, that's how. Two of his pets picked me up this morning right outside our apartment. I'm surprised you didn't run into them on your way out. But I guess you were in too much of a hurry to notice. You're going to get me killed, you crazy bitch. Now stop fucking around and give me the book."

"Let me think," she said.

"Christ, don't think."

"Shhh." She waved her hand as if what I'd just told her was more a petty nuisance than a major setback to her plan. Then she began nodding her head. Trouble.

"So all right," she said. "That's what I wanted to tell you anyway. I just didn't expect Gizzo to react that fast. Besides, it doesn't matter. Not at all."

"Doesn't matter? I'll tell you what doesn't matter. Your whole cockeyed scheme doesn't matter because it's not coming off."

"Oh? Why not?"

"Because I'm not throwing in with you and I don't think you can pull it off by yourself."

"Maybe, maybe not."

"Let me tell you what I think," I said.

"Okay, but sit down here first." She patted the bed again and again everything rolled.

"No way. I think you're responsible for what happened to Carol Antonucci. Indirectly, maybe, but so what. I think you tipped off the cops about Dusty's book which caused them to ask a lot of questions. I think they let on to the wrong person that Carol knew about the book. And that got her killed."

"Don't be an asshole," she said. "I'm sorry about Carol but anyone could have tipped off the police."

"It was you. Tommy wouldn't do it. And it wasn't Carol."

"That's what you say."

"Can't you see what you're doing? Gizzo won't pay anything for that book. Whatever Dusty wrote has to be proved in court. Besides, we still don't know if it means anything."

"Maybe," she said. "Maybe there's no one alive that knows what it means. But who cares? Except for Gizzo."

"Yeah? Well suppose Dusty had another partner beside Gizzo? A silent partner that even Gizzo doesn't know about?"

"All the more reason why Gizzo would want to pay for the book."

"Or kill for it," I said. "You're sick."

"I'm hot, if that's what you mean."

"How do I get through to you?" I said. Then I made the fatal mistake of sitting next to her and her narcotic perfume, Essence of Woe. "Jackie . . . you . . . you have to give me the book. There's a good chance that it's not too late to straighten it out with Gizzo. I'll explain it to him."

She was rubbing my thigh, every stroke getting closer and closer to pay dirt. "Explain what?" she whispered. "That your wife is a lunatic? Take off your coat." I took it off. "Don't ruin this for me, Frankie. We can make it work, believe me. He'll pay us off. It's business. He's used to this sort of thing."

"But I'm not."

"You'll learn."

"You're dreaming."

"So what if I am? What else have I got? Life's a bore. I don't want to be like every other woman. The only people who get anywhere are the ones who take risks. The bigger the risk, the bigger the reward."

"And the bigger the consequences," I said. "But you're serious, aren't you?"

She had her hand in my fly, probing. "You better believe it."

"With you I never know what to believe. And cut that out!"

She was stroking me now, and I could feel my resolve slipping away. "Don't be scared, babe," she said. "It'll be all right."

"If only you'd lie *all* the time," I said. "Then I could figure you out."

"Then I'd be predictable," she whispered in my ear. "And that's no fun . . . is it?"

Fun! We were both one step away from a shallow grave and she was having fun.

"I brought some toys," she said. I groaned. "Oh stop," she said. "You know you love it."

Jackie's idea of toys was enough to send the guys from Hasbro scurrying back to their drawing boards. Toys? More like an arsenal for the sexually depraved: rubber and plastic vibrators of every dimension; lubricants, lotions that smelled like fruit and tasted like motor oil; leather ensembles replete with crotchless panties and cupless bras, elegantly matched with spike-heeled boots. And her special favorite—handcuffs. God, don't let there be handcuffs. Not today.

"Be right back," she said.

She went into the bathroom and came back with her tote bag, the one stenciled *Le Bag*.

With minimum effort she pressed me down on the bed. She fished in the bag and came out with a sixteen-inch rubber dildo, a four-battery job with two working ends for double pleasure. Or pain.

"Remember this?" she said.

How could I forget? Willie the Wonder Worm, she called it. A python was more like it.

"This won't change anything," I said though.

"Uh-huh."

She was busy planting kisses all over my face, neck, ears. Her tongue swished around inside one of my ears sending goose bumps right down to my heels. Almost inaudibly, I said, "Come on, don't do this," knowing that if she really stopped I'd have raped her anyway.

I stared straight into her pale green eyes which was

difficult at such close range without going cross-eyed. She lifted herself, shook free of her shirt, and began undoing the buttons on mine. Then I heard Willie. His buzz was louder than a 707.

"Let me get over you," she said wistfully.

I moaned. It was a half-hearted protest for I knew what "getting over me" meant.

With acrobatic ease she spun around on top of me. I knew I'd regret what I was doing, but for the time being all I felt was pleasure, as if I was being hit with morphine before suffering the wound.

She reached back. Willie was humming madly. I took the damn thing and did what she wanted. She bucked and squirmed but held on, gripping my legs, bending over till I felt her lips, her mouth. I laid there, shot full of pain-killer, eyes glazed, apprehension melting away. Her teeth caught me for a moment. I yelped.

We kept at it. I could have stayed like that until they condemned the place. But there were more toys in *Le Bag*.

Without missing a stroke, she reached one arm over the side of the bed and began fishing. "Shit," she said, "I forgot the cuffs."

I would have told her that Detective Grimm had a pair outside. Except Willie was winding down, his engines depleting. Like mine.

"Your belt," she said. "Quick, tie me up!"

She rolled over, throwing her arms over her head. I found the belt and bound her wrists. "Oh God," she said. "Do it now! Hurt me, you sonofabitch!"

I pulled tightly on the belt. She bit me several times on each shoulder and for a while I didn't know which of us was hurting more. Finally, Jackie stiffened. She shook for a few seconds then breathed that long heavy sigh. I sighed right along with her.

"What's wrong?" Jackie asked. She was lying beside me, arms and legs splayed.

"I was just thinking. You haven't told me anything about your plan. If you're so hell-bent on making a score at Gizzo's expense, you're going to need a tight plan."

She got up on one elbow. "Then you'll help me?"

"I didn't say that. All I said was you haven't told me how you expect to pull it off."

"I'll need you, Frank."

"I figured you didn't get me here for love."

"It could be that way . . . after."

"Tell me."

Her plan wasn't much different than any blackmail scam. She had the book which she'd threatened to hand over to the police if Gizzo didn't fork over $500,000.

Then she got to the scary part. "As for the actual exchange," she said—and I leaned closer because I knew this was where I came in—"you'll go to his house."

"Oh, peachy."

"Hear me out, will you?"

"So far it sucks."

"You go to his house. We'll have a rented car parked out front. You make sure he puts the money inside the car on the floor under the driver's seat. Then you go back inside. I'll be outside watching. If I see it's clear, I just get in the car and drive away."

"Into the Sunset? Jesus Christ, you don't think he's going to pay once I give him the book, do you?"

She grinned and her eyes lit up like she'd just been voted into the Liars' Hall of Fame. "Are you ready for this?"

"You want a drum roll, or what?"

"He'll pay because he won't have the book yet. As soon as I'm sure I haven't been followed, I'll call and tell you where the book is hidden."

I twisted around and struggled off the wavering bed. "See ya, Jacqueline."

"What's the matter?"

"Everything. I'm not going back to that house. Not without the book, I'm not. You don't even know Gizzo's phone number. That's not a major problem but it's a practical one."

"That's easy," she said. "He'll include the number with the money."

I aped her: "That's easy. He'll include the number with the money."

"Right."

"Wrong. Because once you're home free how do I get away?"

"Come on, babe, you're not thinking."

"I get that way when I'm being fucked."

"He won't try anything until after he gets the book. By that time we'll both be long gone."

I bent down like I was looking for something under the bed.

"What are you looking for?" she asked.

"Horse shit. Because if I'm the horse's ass you think I am, then there should be plenty of it lying around."

She didn't see the humor. "It'll work."

"You'll never get away clean," I said. "Gizzo will be watching that money like it's his life's savings. He'll find a way to follow you without you knowing."

"That's a risk, I'll admit it. But before he gets the book there isn't much he can do."

"Are you kidding? All the while you're flitting around in your rent-a-car he'll have his fucking hands around my throat. He won't have any trouble making me cough up the book, Jackie. I've got this thing about pain, you know?"

"You won't tell him anything."

"Don't be so sure."

"Oh, I'm sure. You see you won't know where the book is either until I tell you on the phone. That's why it's foolproof."

"Yeah? You haven't proved it with this fool. You're asking me to go into Gizzo's candy store without knowing where the book is or where you're going with the money. That's not a plan; that's insanity."

She said nothing.

"All right," I said. "Suppose I do go through with this and you decide to cut out with the cash?"

Her eyes flashed angrily. "We're in this together. I trust you, why shouldn't you trust me? You can always tell Gizzo that I'm in this with you . . . if that will make you feel better."

"That won't help much when Nunze starts crushing my larynx." I shook my head. "Gizzo's not going to pay a dime for Dusty's book. I'm not convinced it means anything at all to him."

"Then how come he killed Carol?"

"I don't think he did."

"But he is interested in what the book says," she said. "He wants to know that much, doesn't he?"

"Maybe. But not for half a million bucks."

"Hey, I'm not going to argue about it."

"Good. Give me the book and we'll forget the whole thing."

She bristled. "If you don't help me, you'll never see that book. I'll do it all without you. And Gizzo will still think you're behind it. He already thinks so . . . but I'll make sure in case he's forgotten."

I knew she would do it, which didn't surprise me as much as the hurt I felt when I heard her say it.

Sullenly, I said, "How do you do it?"

"Do what?" she snapped.

"Turn it on and off. A minute ago we were making love. I don't know how that made you feel but it made me feel like we meant something more to each other than partners in crime."

"I wasn't making love."

"Then what the hell were you doing? What kind of woman are you?"

"Don't be naive. People fuck every day. Does that mean they're all in love? To me being in love is a state of mind I can reach only after I've gotten the things in life I really want."

"Like $500,000?"

"An acceptable down payment."

"Suppose you tell me where I stand on your list of priorities. After the money, of course. Am I number two behind a Mercedes? Or three after a villa in Jamaica? And what about people? Where do they stand on your list?"

"Is all this necessary? Why do you always have to hear that you're the most important thing in my life?"

"I'm not 'a thing.' "

"Man, then. Man, all right? Why do you keep pressuring me? I told you that you're the one man I *could* love. But God, you're like a vise squeezing me in. I can't take you when you're like that."

"Don't worry about it, Jackie. I won't pressure you anymore."

"Oh, honey."

She'd been glaring at me but that dagger-look quickly changed to a soft smile. It reminded me of a game Brother James and I used to play when we were kids. "Crazy Faces." We'd move our hands up and down in front of our faces, changing expression each time. A grin, a pout; eyes crossed, tongues out. In moods and expressions, Jackie would have topped the two of us. It drove me nuts.

So she came into my arms looking bright and cheery.

"Do you mean it?" she said. "Really?"

"Sure."

She kissed me, a lingering open-mouthed kiss—her way of sealing the vow. Except she didn't know the way I felt about vows.

Finally she broke off. "You'll help me?"

"Yeah, I'll help you." I started putting on my clothes. "I'm going home to pack a few things," I said. "We'll set it up for tomorrow night. Don't call the apartment. If I have to reach you I'll call here and leave a number at the desk. Check it every hour. It's best if we don't see each other until after this is over. I'm being followed."

She raised her eyebrows. "Here too?"

"Yes, but don't worry. It's one of the cops that came up to see me yesterday. The black guy. I'm going to tell him

171

we're splitting up. This meeting was our last shot at reconciliation." I wondered how much truth there was to what I'd just said.

"All right," Jackie said. "But you'll have to shake him off so you can move around. You wouldn't want him tailing you to Gizzo's place. Meanwhile I'll send the last telegram. You'll see Gizzo tomorrow night?"

I nodded.

"What time?"

"How about midnight? That sinister enough for you?"

"Should I go ahead and rent the car?"

"Maybe I oughta steal one," I said.

"No, no." She honestly thought I would do it. "I'll get the car," she said. "Don't worry, nobody will trace the car to me."

"Uh-huh," I said, tying my shoes. "Well, I'd better get going before Grimm gets antsy." I went into the bathroom to wash up. I knew what I had to do. What I didn't know was how to accomplish it.

I rejoined her, slipped into my coat, and gave her a kiss. "Just one more thing," I said. "How did you know where to send the telegram? I never told you where Gizzo lived. I didn't know myself until today."

"Phone book," she said. No hesitation. Sign of a skilled liar.

"I wouldn't expect a guy like Gizzo to have a listed number," I said. "You wouldn't leave me holding the bag, would you, babe?"

"Stop it, will you? I told you, we're in this together."

"And we'll go down together, right?"

She beamed. "Yeah, Fontana." Hugs and wet kisses.

I said, "You'll love me twice as much after you've got Gizzo's money in your pocket."

"We'll make it," she said. "You'll see."

I was at the door where I turned to face her. "One thing for sure . . . we'll never know unless we try."

CHAPTER 17

Out in the submarine-lit hallway I fell back against the wall, my head spinning the way it sometimes does when I'm given a fast shuffle. Talk about con jobs. I felt as though I'd just driven off a used-car lot with a '58 Edsel. Was I that dumb or was Jackie that cunning?

Right now there were a few items I had to sort, analyze, and record. Like Jackie's cute phrase: "We're in this together." I knew I was being used but that didn't bother me as much as a certain question that kept buzzing around my weary brain: what would Jackie do if I walked out on her? Would she hole up somewhere like Tommy Milano?

Tommy, for all his maniacal faults, had shown a great deal of restraint by cutting out. I might have called it common sense if I didn't know him better. In a way I wished he was around. He knew exactly what his uncle was capable of doing and might have scared Jackie enough to change her mind. Even *he* would have had to admit that her scam was more than crazy: it was a one-way trip to oblivion.

That question came around again. This time it brought an answer. I didn't like it but I knew it was true. Jackie wouldn't bat an eye if I deserted her. She had her own black book with more names than Dusty's. One phone call, I thought, and I'm history. Christ!

I started down the hall. Someone called. A hushed voice from behind me. "Hey, numbnuts. Where you goin'?"

It was Tommy. He was at the end of the hall, one hand on the stairwell door, grinning at me like a Cheshire cat. "C'mere, you dumb fuck. There's an ape outside with a badge."

I walked toward him. "I know that. Jesus, Tommy, where the hell have you been? How'd you get here? How'd you find me?"

He opened the door. "In here."

We mustered on the landing. A meeting of the minds. I suppose it's true that misery loves company because I was happy to see him. I should have been angry, of course. But Tommy was in high gear, the way he always acted when closing in on a score. I didn't want to hear about it. Though I knew I would.

"I been tailing you," he said. "Not you directly. The apeman."

"You followed him here?" I couldn't believe it. Grimm seemed pretty sharp. "He didn't see you?"

"That jig couldn't spot his dick with radar." He leaned back against the wall and stuck a Kool in his mouth. Casual Tommy Milano, killing time with his good buddy.

"I heard about Carol on the radio," he said. "Dumb bitch."

"You didn't have anything to do with that, did you, Tom?"

"Fuck no. Think I'm nuts?" I nodded. "My man," he said.

"Since when? Last time we talked you were throwing me to the wolves."

He lit the cigarette and exhaled a blue cloud. "Hey,

look, I'm sorry, all right? I wasn't thinkin' straight. That book an' all. Woulda been great though, huh? Rippin' off Uncle Charlie?"

"A million laughs. We're not out of the woods, you know. Your uncle knows we have the book."

"We?"

"It's a long story."

"I got time."

I stalled for a moment, not sure if I wanted to tell him about Jackie's telegram. Part of the reason was lack of trust. Tommy's sudden appearance had me rattled. Mostly though, I was embarrassed over having the book lifted right out from under me.

I decided to chance it. Tommy listened intently, laughing about the laundry bag, scowling over my encounter with Gizzo. It went like that, up and down, till the story ended with Jackie in room 133.

"Figured that's why you were here," he said. "This was one your haunts when you first married the bitch." He ground the butt under his heel. "She planned this, eh?" He grinned. "The book for half a mil. I love it."

"I thought you would. Listen, Tommy, don't get any ideas."

"Rest your mind," he said. "Think I'm nuts? Why do you think I tracked you down?"

"I've been wondering about that. Friendship?"

He laughed for a long time. Too long, I thought.

When he calmed down, he said, "My life ain't the greatest. But I ain't gonna toss it away for no quarter of a million bucks."

"What do you mean?"

"Quarter mil. Half of a half. My share of the split." He grinned broadly. "And you a college man."

"I don't like what I'm hearing, Tommy."

"Relax, for Chrissake. I came here to tell you to turn the book over to Charlie. Mail it to him, anything. Give it to me if you're afraid. I'll get it to him. I think he'll let us ride if he gets it."

"You *think*."

"Get real, Frankie. The only guarantee I ever got from my uncle was that he hates my fuckin' guts. I'm playing the odds, that's all. He gets his shit, and there's no reason to put us away."

"I'll think about it."

"You do that. But not too long, pal-a-mine. You know me, I go with the wind."

"I know," I said. "Only watch you don't blow away permanently."

"No sweat. Okay, listen to me."

Grasping my shoulders, he pulled me closer. The rest of what he said came out of one side of his face, through a twisted mouth that dropped his lower lip like he had a toothache. "I'll get word to my uncle that we're coming in. Meanwhile, you get the book from Jackie. Kick her ass if you have to, but get it." He paused. "Otherwise I will."

I swiped his hand from my shoulder. "Stay away from her!"

He started toward me, then checked himself. For a moment he just stared at me like he was sizing me up. What he saw must have convinced him.

He smiled, and just like that Mr. Charm appeared. "You're really hooked on her," he said warmly. "Ain't you, Frankie."

"Try me," I said.

"Not me, pal. She's all yours and you're welcome to her."

"So long as you don't forget it, pal-a-mine."

He smirked. "I got enough headaches."

"How do I reach you when the time comes?"

"You don't. And don't give me that fisheye. I'm campin' out these days. Don't worry, I'll track you down."

I was plenty worried. Tommy had me going down a one-way street and I hated one-way streets. Particularly dead ends.

"I'll catch up with you," Tommy said.

He descended the stairs three at a time, opened the back door, peeked out, and took off.

I watched until the door shut.

I didn't care for Tommy's plan any more than I did Jackie's. Even without the shakedown, confronting Gizzo fell under the heading of hazardous duty. Having Tommy with me might have helped if his uncle had any regard for genealogy. Perhaps he did. Though in Tommy's case I feared it was unlikely.

I was mulling a course of action when something started up in the lobby, a ruckus between the lumberjack/desk clerk and my old friend Grimm. I slipped into the hallway. Grimm was shouting. "I *told* you, I'm a cop. Here's my ID"

"I don't give a fuck if you're Wyatt Earp," yelled the lumberjack. "You ain't goin' back there."

They sounded like a pair of bulldogs with distemper, and their growls went rumbling down the corridor with enough thunder to open a few doors. Room 133 wasn't one of them. Farther down several male heads did pop out and one guy charged out of his room naked as a jay sporting a huge hard-on. He was pissed and I understood why.

"Hey!" he hollered. "What the hell's going on out there? I'm losing the mood with all that noise."

The lumberjack hustled toward him. "S'all right, sport, everything's under control. You can just pole-vault right back into your room."

The guy mumbled something but when he turned around I could see that he wasn't going to vault anywhere.

I caught Grimm moving in alongside the lumberjack. "There he is," he said. "That's the guy."

The lumberjack waved in disgust. "Yeah? Well, just get him the hell outta here." He headed back to the desk shaking his head. "Fuckin' joint's a nut house."

I walked up to meet Grimm who'd already started toward me with a menacing look on his face. "What are you trying to pull now?" he said. He checked his watch. "You're supposed to be working. What the hell are you doing hanging around this place?"

Let him think what he wants, I told myself. I'm not in the mood for explanations. Not any more.

"Get lost, Grimm." I started to go around him. He yanked me back. We were eyeball to eyeball. "I quit my job," I said. "Is there a law against that?"

"Ryan wants you where he can keep an eye on you. In case you forgot about it, buddy, you're still our bait. Me, I don't care if you quit your job or not. Tonight you're working. I'm not going to let you fuck up this investigation just because you caught your wife screwing around."

That did it. I didn't wait to ask how he knew Jackie was inside, I hit him with everything I had. A right hook to the mouth which should have laid him out. It didn't. It split his lip open, which evened the score from last night. But it didn't knock him flat. Instead, he just rocked back a little and then he was on me.

When you've just smacked a guy the way I'd smacked Grimm, and that guy doesn't budge, there are only two things you can do: run like hell or just keep throwing punches until one of them connects. I couldn't run so I started swinging, wild looping shots that caught nothing but air. Meanwhile, Grimm was doing a Marvin Hagler, bobbing and weaving like he'd spent his whole fucking life in the gym. Finally, when he'd had enough dancing, he locked onto my arm and twisted it into a hammer-lock. He forced me forward and held me so the side of my face was jammed against the wall. It was goddamn degrading.

I kept struggling, against Grimm and against the needles that were jabbing up my arm into my shoulder.

"Hey!" The lumberjack again. I could see him out of the one eye that wasn't stuck to the wall. He was coming at us on the run. "You crazy bastards wanna fight, take it outside or I'll call the cops."

"I am a cop, you ignoramus," Grimm said.

"Well you ain't on our payroll," said the lumberjack. "Now break it up or you'll be out in Staten Island doin' twelve-to-eights at the fuckin' dump."

"Yeah," I piped. "The fuckin' dump."

With the hammerlock still intact, Grimm shoved me down the hall, through the lobby, and out the front door. As we passed the lumberjack, Grimm said, "I'm gonna check this place out."

"You do that. But you guys are doing better on this joint than we are."

"Shit!" Grimm replied.

It was dark. Snow flurries were whipping around the lot. Grimm escorted me to my car, pulling up my arm every now and then just to remind me that he was the boss. I wasn't disputing the point.

"I'd love to work you over, Fontana," he said. We reached my car. "But that'll wait. Right now I want you to get in your car. You're going to work and I hope to Christ they come for you tonight." He opened the door and pushed me in none too gently. "So let's go!"

Using the one arm that still had life, I cranked down the window. "Hey, Grimm." He stopped a few feet away and came back.

"Yeah."

"I want you to know that if I have to kill someone to protect myself, I will."

"What does that mean?"

"It means that I'm not counting on you to save my ass."

He shrugged. "That's up to you. But if you're in my way when the shooting starts . . . well, that's not my fault, is it?"

"Funny," I said. "I was about to tell you the same thing."

He looked at me quizzically and I couldn't help wondering what he'd say if he knew I'd let Tina Webb clip my gun.

Seconds later he pulled out and motioned me to follow,

which I did, trailing along like live bait off the stern of a troller.

I resented the indignity of being pushed around by Grimm, by Gizzo, and by Jackie. Yet what really grabbed me was that I seemed to have no control at all over my own fate. They were each pulling a different string that had me twitching and jumping around like Popo the fucking puppet. I was so disgusted that I was wishing something *would* happen tonight. Of course, I didn't wish too hard. I mean I was disgusted, I wasn't suicidal.

Grimm drove quickly. I kept pace, maintaining a safe distance between us, close enough to let him know I was there, yet far enough to tell him I wasn't too thrilled with the situation. Something about that man just didn't sit right. It seemed his reasons for hating me went beyond his mere contempt for fingermen. It could have been the color thing, though I didn't think so. Somehow I couldn't picture Grimm and Dusty sharing high-fives and calling each other bro. Still, he'd been assigned to protect me. Why had he cut me loose so quickly last night? It was that move that had opened the door to Gizzo's men. But maybe that's what Grimm wanted.

The more I thought about it, the more certain I was that Grimm was ad-libbing, stretching Ryan's orders for reasons known only to Grimm. Perhaps Ryan didn't care any more about what happened to me than Grimm did. In which case no one would give a damn if the bait was swallowed whole as long as they hooked the big one.

Fuck, if it was bait they wanted, I'd give it to them.

We were on the Van Wyck Expressway, about twenty minutes from the Skyview. Twenty minutes from . . . what? Gizzo would have the place staked out, so would Ryan: a reception committee I had no intention of meeting. "Sorry, Grimm, this is where I get off." He'd just passed an exit. I knew he couldn't double back till he reached the next one so I swung onto the service road letting Grimm go on his merry way. I pulled into a Texaco station, left the motor running, and raced to a phone booth.

A moment later my brother was saying, "What's the matter? Don't you earn enough in that bar to pay for your own calls?"

"I'm in a booth."

"So get change."

"Cut the lecture, James, I'm in trouble."

"I might have known. Mom wants to know why she hasn't heard from you. You know, Fran, it wouldn't hurt you to pick up a phone once in awhile."

Fran. My brother was named after my father. Not to be outdone, my mother decided unilaterally to name her next child after herself. Back home everyone called me Fran. The second reason why I'd left Akron.

"James," I said, "will you shut up and listen to me."

"You're a waste, do you know that?" My brother had this thing about college grads who blew their degrees on unrelated careers. Particularly bartending.

"I want you to do me a favor."

"For how much?"

"No," I said. "No money."

"I told you to lay off those silly cigarettes."

"James, will you stop being a wise-ass and just listen? I sent you a package. Send it back to me right away."

"Indian giver."

"James!"

"What's in it?"

"Bait."

"What?"

"They're important papers. Do me a favor and send them back to me Federal Express. Do it right away, will you, James?"

"What's going on, Fran? You sound . . . panicky." If he only knew.

"I've got to have that package by Tuesday."

"Life or death, eh?"

"Something like that."

"Hey, you're not kidding, are you? Is there anything I can do? Legal advice?"

"Yeah, you can check my last will and testament."

"Come on, Fran, no jokes. What's wrong?"

"Just do as I ask and don't get involved."

"I don't like the way you sound. I think I'd better . . ."

But that was all I waited to hear. Grimm's Plymouth went barreling by, the red light flashing on the dashboard. He must have spotted my car because he hit his brakes and spun into a one-hundred-and-eighty-degree turn.

He was still about a half block away when I dropped the receiver. There wasn't much chance of shaking him off. Not by car anyway—he was too close and too good with the wheel—so I snatched the keys from the ignition, left the old bucket where it sat and took off on foot.

I saw a one-way street and headed for it. It was a dark street with old houses and driveways built for prewar automobiles. I ran until I felt a kink in my side, then ducked into one of the narrow driveways where I hid between a sloping garage and a cyclone fence.

It was pitch black, cold as Eskimo pie, and the wind kept blowing shards of ice off an old snow pile and into my face. I pressed myself against the garage and peered out at the street. A car whizzed by. I didn't know if it was Grimm. Not that it mattered. I wasn't going anywhere until I was sure it was safe or until frostbite forced me out.

I played the name game for about thirty minutes and was up to forty-two names of old flames when I began to wonder if I'd ever reach forty-three, I was so cold.

I crept out of hiding and down the driveway. The street was quiet, no cars, no flashing lights. Stamping circulation into my near-frozen feet, I started back to the Texaco station. My car was where I'd left it. Only now there was another car parked next to it: a blue and white cruiser with two cops, snug and warm inside.

I crossed the street to an underpass walking as casually as my numbed legs would allow. I sensed their eyes on me as I teetered self-consciously toward the service road, ready to run if they pulled out. They didn't.

When I was safely out of their line of vision I began

jogging with the traffic, holding out my thumb, glancing over my left shoulder just in case the cops had caught on.

By now the snow was coming down in wet flakes the size of frozen pizzas. It was what we used to call "packing snow." Good for snowballs and snowmen, lousy for sleds. It was the kind of snow that sticks fast and accumulates faster. And it was already higher than my shoetops. Not what you'd call ideal weather for jogging.

Several cars sloshed by without slowing down. No surprise. The way things were going the only ride I'd likely get would be in the back of an ambulance, a victim of hit and run.

I was on the verge of convincing myself that a stay in the hospital might not be such a bad idea when a car eased up beside me. The driver, whose face I couldn't see, called through an open window. "Wanna cab?" I kept trotting. He kept pace. On the door I read: J. James—Deluxe Taxi Service.

"So what is it?" said the hack. "You wanna ride or you trainin' for the winter Olympics?"

"Okay," I said. He stopped and I jumped in. It was one of those private cabs, no meter.

"I ain't suppose to do this," the driver said. "But I'm on my way home so it's okay." Which meant this fare would wind up in his pocket. "Whatsa matter, your car break down?"

"Yeah."

I thought about my Camaro sitting out there under an inch of snow. I hated to leave it, but what bothered me more was not having any wheels. There wasn't much I could do without them.

"Weatherman says we got a good one coming," the driver said. "Like he knows, right? Yesterday he said today would be sunny and mild. Asshole!"

The cab was thick with cigarette smoke. I tried rolling down the windows but they had those safety gadgets on them. I never understood why cab companies installed the damn things. I mean who'd be crazy enough to bail out the window of a moving cab just to beat the fare?

"Where can I take you?" he said, lighting up another smoke.

"I don't know the address. It's in Astoria."

"Righto."

I was almost thawed out by the time we got to Tina's apartment house. It was close to nine o'clock and enough snow had already fallen to make the weatherman look like a champ. Why are they always right when you don't want them to be?

"That'll be twenty bucks," the driver said.

"Twenty dollars? It only took five minutes to get here."

"That's about two hours less than it woulda taken you to jog it, mister."

I looked at the name stenciled across the dash. "J. James," I said. "Sure that doesn't stand for Jesse?"

"Hey, that's good. But it's still twenty bucks."

I gave him twenty and got out of there before he had a chance to curse me for not tipping.

"Good evening, sir." The doorman, the one from last night.

"Looks like we're in for quite a . . . oh, it's you." He turned around and went back behind the plate glass. He'd shoveled a path to the door. I went up to it and tried to pull it open. The sonofabitch was holding it closed from the other side.

"C'mon, man, it's snowing out."

He was eyeing me like I was the regional salesman for Soviet War bonds. Reluctantly, he poked his head out from behind the glass.

"I don't know if Miss Webb is in."

"Well why don't you try her, then we'll both know."

He grumbled, walked slowly to the intercom, and pressed a button. I stepped uninvited into the lobby.

"Yes?" Tina's voice hummed through the speaker like a one-word lullaby.

"That character is here to see you, Miss Webb. The

one from last night. Should I send him away?"

Hesitation. A few seconds too long perhaps. I inched closer to the doorman. "I have to talk to you, Tina," I shouted over his head.

He gave me a quick, dirty look before turning back to the intercom. "Sorry, Miss Webb. He's very persistent."

"I'm coming down," Tina said.

"Are you certain?"

"Frederick, will you just tell him to wait, please?"

We heard a click. Frederick shook his head. He had the look of a man whose instincts had failed him completely.

"Sorry, Frederick," I said. "Some days you just can't catch a break. Believe me, I know how it feels."

Tina emerged from the elevator dressed for a two-day trek across a frozen tundra. Woolen hat, scarf, boots, gloves, and a down ski coat. I was wearing a thin leather jacket over a V-neck cashmere sweater, and Regals that felt more like sponges than shoes.

Striding briskly toward me, she had the implacable look of a schoolmarm closing ground on a troublemaker. She scooped up my arm and hustled me outside.

"What gives?" I said.

"I'll ask the questions. Where's your car?"

"Getting a tune-up."

Her lips formed a straight line. She nodded a few times, looked up at the sky, and said, "We'll walk."

"Where we going?"

"My studio."

"What studio?"

She took my hand and we headed west, toward the river. She walked quickly, her head down against the wind. It was too cold to talk so I pulled up my collar and tried to keep pace.

"One more block," she said to her boots.

"Thank God."

It was a long windy block that got worse as we approached the river. Manhattan Island was out there some- where though I couldn't see through the flakes.

In the "personals" there are women who appeal to men who enjoy quiet walks in the snow. I used to wonder about those women. Until tonight. They're nuts and that's all there is to it.

Tina's studio was on one of the upper floors of a converted loft. I had heard that aspiring artists were migrating to this area from Soho, where a single month's rent was more than most painters would earn in a year, a lifetime in many cases.

She unlocked the outside door and showed me in. The building had an ancient elevator. One of those metal cages that rattle and creak and never quite meet the floor evenly. You have to step up or step down and either way it's a frigging hazard. Tonight it was out of order. Thank the Lord for small favors.

We climbed the five flights of stairs without talking. Tina was clearly annoyed and I wasn't sure why. I knew she'd tell me in her own time so I went with it. If nothing else, I'd be out of the cold for a while.

"Very nice," I said, meaning the studio which appeared in flickering segments as the hanging fluorescents sprang to life.

She locked the door behind us. "I share it with two other girls," she said. "I live closest, which makes me the custodian." She removed her gloves and waved them at me. "Give me your coat and take a seat."

I looked around. What I saw was something that was once part of a warehouse. An entire floor used for storage, probably. The brick walls had been painted recently, and I imagined four other floors like this one, spruced up and leased by a sagacious landlord anxious to accommodate the refugees from Soho and Tribeca. The ceiling, about sixteen feet high, was bordered with pipes for heat and water. Except for the floor, which was lacquered to a sheen, the only significant change was the windows, where the ancient steel-framed, corrugated glass had been replaced by huge, clear panes.

Sidestepping the easels and frames cluttering the floor, I drifted toward an old love seat that faced the windows. Paintings of every size were stacked vertically against the walls. They seemed to be grouped into three sections.

"Which are yours?" I asked.

Tina pointed to one of the stacks. "Those. But we didn't come here to look at paintings."

She was hanging our coats in a portable closet. "I suppose you want a drink."

"If you have one."

She crossed the room to some makeshift cabinets over a badly stained sink. I looked out the window while she clinked and fussed. "I guess you're into skylines," I said. "Must be a nice view from here. We're facing Manhattan, right?"

"Here." She handed me a small snifter. "Benedictine," she said. "It's all we have."

I swirled the drink around in the tiny bell-glass and then gulped it like a shot of fifty-cent rye. It burned all the way down but it felt good, stimulating yet relaxing at the same time. "Thanks."

I sat in the love seat and gently punched the cushion beside me. A playful invitation to Tina who was having none of it. "All right," I said. "What is it? You've had a bug up your ass since you walked off the elevator."

"You mind explaining that phone call?"

"Oh that."

"Yes, that. I've been a lunatic all day. You were in trouble and there wasn't anything I could do about it."

I took her hand and pulled her down alongside me. "I'm sorry," I said. "I didn't mean to shake you up but there was a detective standing right next to me and—"

"I knew someone was there. I thought it was Gizzo. What happened? They're still after the notebook, aren't they?"

"That's all they've got."

"Except for you. That's why I brought you here. They

know you spent the night with me. I can't have cops running in and out of my apartment. It's hard enough to find a place."

"What if they track me here?"

"They won't. Besides, what can happen?"

"The cop from last night," I said. "He's been dogging me. I shook him off on the way to the Skyview. I'm not a lawyer but I think that makes me a fugitive."

"And I'm aiding and abetting, eh?"

"If I let you. Which I'm not."

"Then why did you come to me?"

She had me there. "I'm not sure. No place else to go . . . I guess. I don't know, I'm confused."

"There's nothing confusing about it," she said. "You need help and I'm . . . available."

"There's more to it than that."

"I'm flattered."

Her golden hair dipped low on her forehead. I leaned forward and kissed her. We were nose to nose and I could see her blue eyes misting over. "Tell me what happened today," she said softly.

Tina seemed quite concerned as I related my day. She didn't utter a word during my narration; instead she let her facial expressions speak for her. Anger, sympathy, indignation, her pretty face contorted like she had a flea inside her ear. Until finally she found an expression to lock onto. Incredulity. Total disbelief over what I was now telling her—my plan of action.

"So tonight," I went on, "tonight I'm going to see Gizzo. I won't let myself become part of Jackie's scheme. I've got to get to him before she sends another one of those wacky telegrams."

Tina looked wide-eyed. "You're out of your mind. You can't go back there after what happened this morning. The next time this Gizzo gets his hands on you . . ." She shook her head and let the thought hang in midair.

"I know," I said. "Listen, this isn't something I want to

do. But I don't want to spend the rest of my life running from the man."

She went silent, pensive. I could hear the starter buzzing in one of the lights like a dying cicada. Finally she said, "Let's get one thing straight, Frank. Do you want help or don't you?"

I shrugged.

"Then will you at least admit that you *need* help?"

"Yeah, yeah. What do you think?"

"Then from now on we're in this together, the two of us."

There it was again: "we're in this together." With two beautiful women willing to share my trouble, how come I felt so alone?

"Wrong," I said. "Where's my gun?"

"Frank! No guns."

"Why not? The bad guys have guns."

"They know how to use them."

"That's what I'm afraid of," I said.

"What would you do with a gun? They'd only take it away and use it on you."

"I'll risk it. What did you do with it?"

She lowered her face. "I couldn't keep it in my apartment so I brought it . . ." She let the words fall away.

"Here? It's here now?"

"In the closet."

"Get it," I said.

It took a few moments to extract the weapon from the junk she kept inside the closet. "At least take the bullets out before you shoot yourself," Tina said, handing me the revolver. I would have expected her to treat it like a dead rat, but instead she gripped it firmly by the barrel and slapped it into my palm as if she was a nurse and I'd just asked for a scalpel.

"You handle that gun like you know what you're doing," I said.

"I've been around them a long time," she said. "My father was a cop for twenty-five years."

"Oh that's great."

"He thought so." She rubbed her eyes. "Not in the City. Upstate. He was the sheriff in a burg called Haynesville. I got out when I was eighteen. My husband was a weekend hunter. Came up from Yonkers looking for deer and found me instead. But you've heard that before."

She sat. "Now, tell me exactly what you expect to do with that. By the way, it's a thirty-eight caliber."

"Thanks. I'm going to convince Gizzo that I've got nothing to do with blackmailing him. That if he wants Dusty's book so bad, I'll give it to him."

"You have it?" She seemed excited.

"A copy," I said. "I told you Jackie's got the original. That's why I've got to see Gizzo tonight before she does anything. Otherwise he'll think I'm in on it."

"What about Ryan?"

"Screw Ryan. He's using me. He knows I'm not involved in any murder. It doesn't matter to him what happens to me as long as he gets his man. The same goes for Lawson. And Grimm, that bastard, he'd love to see me get my ass blown off."

"And with that thing," Tina said, pointing at the revolver, "he's likely to see it happen."

I stared vacantly out the window of Tina's studio. All dressed up and nowhere to go. Tina stood beside me, her thumb hooked inside my back pocket. She had the radio on and the DJ was advising motorists to stay put. I hoped Grimm was listening. And Jackie. And Gizzo.

"What we've got here is the storm before the storm," Tina said.

I grunted.

I was right about the view. Even with the snow I could see cars crawling along the FDR Drive. Tina pointed across the East River. "We're opposite Gracie Square. If you look south, you can see the Citicorp Center."

I squinted.

"Four to six inches of snow," the DJ was saying. "Turning to freezing rain by morning. A great night to stay home and cuddle with your honey."

"So why don't we?" Tina said.

"I'd love to but I can't just sit around here all night."

"You won't be sitting."

"Yeah," I said balefully.

"Look, if *you're* snowed in, what makes you think your wife will have an easier time getting around. She's not supposed to send the telegram until tomorrow night anyway. Right?"

"Yeah, but—"

"No buts. If it bothers you that much, why don't you call her up, see what she's up to."

"We agreed on telephone silence."

"I don't believe it."

"I know. I just don't want to hear any more lies. I know what I have to do and there's nothing to gain by talking to her."

"So?"

"It's the storm," I said. "I was ready to go tonight, had myself psyched."

She kissed me. "Then let's not waste it."

She walked back toward the studio door. Against the wall was a large rectangular shaped object covered by a bedsheet. She removed the sheet to reveal a kingsize mattress. One of those blow-up jobs.

"We've got blankets and pillows," she said. "Come here and give me a hand with this."

I took one more look out the window, flakes whirling around like so many moths, a tugboat braving the icy currents.

"Ah, what the hell," I said. "It's no night for a gunfight anyway. You could catch cold out there."

CHAPTER 18

Dawn arrived with a rhythmic tapping on the windows. The snow had changed to freezing rain.

I had dreamed I was back in the sub-red corridor of the Briny Breezes Motel, standing in a long line of men that began at the lobby and wound its way along the arching hallway right to a revolving door. Over the door a neon sign was flashing—133—133—133. We each had our hands on the shoulders of the man ahead of us as we shuffled toward the door. In front of the door stood Tommy Milano dressed like a Good Humor man. A change-maker hung from his belt and he was clicking coins into his hand. "Step right up, gents, don't be shy. Only thirty-five cents for missionary. Blowjobs half a million bucks." Then I heard Gizzo's mechanical voice. "You think I'm responsible for this? I came here because she sent me a telegram. Show him, Nunze."

Tina had taken me into her arms. It was just before dawn. "I'm here, Frank. It's all right. Sleep," she'd whispered. But I didn't. I couldn't take the chance on going back to that nightmare. So I let Tina comfort me while I fought off the fear that had me shivering uncontrollably.

Despair. I hadn't really felt it until that moment. It seemed that while I was awake I'd been too preoccupied with survival to realistically weigh my chances of getting out of this alive. Sure I'd thought about it, but the considerations had fallen far short of an unbiased appraisal. Waiting for the first morning light, running the events through my mind, it all seemed quite hopeless.

I nudged Tina.

"Huh? What is it? What's wrong?"

"Where do you think I'll be this time tomorrow?"

"Shhh. Go back to sleep."

"There's not much moving out there," Tina said. She was standing by the window wearing a gray sweatshirt that said "I Love NY"—a red heart took the place of the word "love." Until Thursday night I'd felt the same about New York. Now I found myself wishing I'd never left Akron.

The pre-dawn despair had begun to wear off, replaced by other feelings, jumping beans in the pit of my stomach, a rumbling somewhere in my lower bowel. Fear.

I went to the window and looked out. Manhattan glistened under a layer of ice, light traffic moving up and down the FDR slowly—but moving. "If they can make it, so can I."

"You're going through with it?" Tina said. "You won't change your mind?"

"There's no other way. I've got to get out to Long Beach before Jackie contacts Gizzo. It's Sunday," I said. "Do you think you'll have trouble renting a car?"

"They're open," Tina said. "There's a Hertz office a few blocks from here. I'll get us something to eat and get the car on the way. When do you want to leave?"

I looked out again at the sleet now falling in diagonal

lines like thousands of tiny glass missiles. "Never," I said. "But we'll go as soon as you get back."

She started to say something, changed her mind, then went for her coat. "If the phone rings, don't answer it," she said. "Keep the door locked. I'll be back soon." She gave me a little hug and then left, locking the door from the outside like she was securing the family jewel. Some jewel. Wanted by the police, sought by gangsters, and going off on a suicidal errand prompted by a wife who couldn't care less how I got myself killed as long as I netted her enough cash to retire in the Caribbean.

I stood there for a while at the closed door. Nothing to do now but wait and worry. The worrying I was used to, the waiting drove me nuts. I kept wondering what Jackie was doing and the more I thought about it the nuttier I became. I glanced at the phone. "Fuck it!"

I dialed information. "Briny Breezes Motel, in Brooklyn," I said. A recording gave me the number.

I wasn't too surprised to get an answer after the first ring. Not because my luck was changing; I just didn't expect their switchboard to be buzzing with action on Sunday morning.

"Yeah," said the male voice, harsh, intimidating.

I never answered the phone with anything other than a "hello." In business you hear "Mr. So-and-So's line," and in the movies you get "Yes?" "Hello," just seemed more civilized.

"Is this the Briny Breezes?" I asked.

"That's what you dialed, ain't it?"

It could only be the lumberjack. Not even a class place like the Briny could afford two men with such savoir faire.

"Room 133," I said.

"Hold on." A few seconds went by and he was back. "No answer."

"Can you tell me if the room is still occupied?"

"Far as I know."

"I'd like to leave a message," I said, sensing impatience at the other end.

"Hey listen, slick, this is the Briny Breezes, ya know? Our guests don't check the desk for messages."

"She's expecting this one."

"What was that room again?"

I told him, then gave Tina's studio number. "Just give that to the party in room 133 and tell her to call Frank right away."

"Frank," he said. "Okay. Only I'm tellin' ya, our guests don't check for messages."

"This one will," I said. He clicked off. "I hope."

For the next hour I paced the floor while WLTW oozed Billy Joel, Ronstadt, Genesis.

The phone rang at eleven-thirty, a shrill timbre that made my heart speed. I was sure it was Jackie calling, could see her with the receiver cradled between her neck and shoulder.

"Hello," I said.

No answer.

"Hello," I repeated. "Answer goddamnit!" The phone went dead in my hand. I shouted, "Hello, hello, you sonofabitch."

I was still grumbling when Tina came in, cheeks flushed, nose like a ripe chili pepper, upsweep falling in wet stringy wisps. She had several small bags inside a large one which she dropped with a thud on the counter by the sink. She studied me. "What happened? Did the phone ring? You didn't answer it, did you?"

"Something, yes, and yes," I said.

She grimaced. "What?"

"Three questions, three answers. I got bored watching the weather so I called Jackie."

"And?"

"She wasn't home. I left your number. That's why I answered the phone, thought it was her."

"What did she say?"

"Nothing. She hung up."

"Could have been a wrong number," Tina said. "Or one of the girls. We don't make a habit of bringing men up here." She was unpacking the bags, laying stuff out on the counter. "If it rings again, let me answer it. Now, how about something to eat? Roastbeef on rye. Potato salad. Coke."

"Coke?"

"Soda," Tina said.

"Did you get the car?"

She removed a set of keys from her purse, tossed them at me. "It's a gray Cutlass. We can take it right off the lot when we're ready."

"I'm ready."

She was shaking her coat out. "After we eat. Besides, it's still pretty icy. Let's sit tight for a while, it might clear up."

Sitting tight for a while turned out to be lunch, followed by a marathon of lovemaking that continued right up until nightfall. At first I protested, told her I could never get it on, that my head was fraught with the perils of murder and blackmail, money and guns—my appointment with fate, doing what I had to do. Right.

"You always do what you have to do?" she asked. Which was all the convincing it took.

Ply him with potato salad, weaken his resolve, and screw the dummy senseless until he agrees to what you want. I knew what Tina was about, having only a short time ago gone through the same routine with Jackie. The difference was that Tina was trying to keep me alive.

"Just stay there, let me do the work." And then she was bouncing up and down as hard as she could. "Tell me you won't go." More. "Say it!" Then more, harder, and faster.

It was a noble but futile effort that ended not in climax but with Tina simply toppling over as though her bones had given out. "Well," she gasped, "I tried. At least I tried."

"So did I." I started to get up but she pulled me back. "No more," I said. "You're wearing me out."

"Apparently not enough." She rolled over on her side,

draped an arm around my waist. "God, I wish there was another way."

"You don't think there's a chance for me to pull it off, do you?"

"Not much," she said.

For a brief moment I thought I detected mist in Tina's eyes. But she turned away quickly and placed her head on my chest. She stayed that way and after a while she said, "There's something I have to tell you, Frankie."

"You're crazy about me."

She pinched me. "Stop it! You can't joke your way out of this. You're scared shitless and you know it."

"Of course I am. But I'm mad, too. I'm tired of getting dumped on. Ever since this thing started I've done nothing but counterpunch. Mostly at shadows. I've got to do something back."

"You're not kidding me," she said. "You're not showing initiative by going to Gizzo's. That's what your wife wants you to do."

"Think whatever you like."

"My God, Frankie, can't you see what she's gotten you into?"

"I'm not doing this for her. She's in the clear. I'm the one that's out on a limb."

"You love her, don't you? You still love her."

"C'mon, for Chrissake. What do you want me to say?"

"Admit it."

"I don't love her, I'm infected by her. A shot of penicillin, two weeks in the sun, and I'd have her out of my system."

"And then what? What happens when this is over?"

"According to you I won't make it anyway, so what difference does it make?"

"I want to know. If suddenly you were free of it, this thing with Gizzo and Ryan, would you leave Jackie?"

"What is it?" I said. "Are you trying to rationalize what you're doing with me? Listen, I appreciate everything you've done, everything you're doing, but I still think you're crazy to get involved. The timing's all wrong and you know it."

"No one twisted my arm," she said. "And you've got it all wrong if you think I'm looking for assurance about what we've got here. I don't expect you to walk out on your wife for my sake. I just want to know how badly you're hooked. Tell me honestly, could you leave her?"

Could I leave Jackie? I remember asking myself that precise question back in the days when I was cocky enough to think I had the upper hand. At that time I had answered with speed and certainty, yes. I would take Jackie to the Briny Breezes and tell myself it didn't mean a damn thing. She was a whore, like Tommy said. A few weeks, a month, and both of us would move on. It wasn't until after our marriage that the question of leaving Jackie became something more than hypothetical. Which was why I was having trouble giving Tina a straight answer.

"Well?" Tina asked. "Would you leave her or not?"

"I think so."

Tina looked skeptical.

"It's the only way," I said. "I've let it go too far, I think. There's no balance anymore. Maybe there never was."

"What do you mean?"

"The hokey qualities you need to keep it going—love, I mean. Ideally, the scales balance, or close to it. But each time you give a part of yourself without getting anything in return, the scale tips a little. Each put-down, each humiliation takes some from your side and puts it on hers. Finally you've got nothing left to give, your ego's whittled away and the damn scale is so fucking lopsided that it takes whatever energy you've got left just to hold on. When that happens, it's time to leave. Yeah," I said. "I'd leave Jackie."

Tina was gazing at me like I'd just come down off Mount Sinai holding the Sacred Tablets. "Most of us don't wait that long," she said.

"Depends on your capacity for abuse."

She smiled a thin smile. "She doesn't deserve someone like you."

"No," I said. "It's the other way around."

"It's time," I said, checking my weapon, spinning the chamber and snapping it shut with a flick of the wrist. I felt like Clint Eastwood doing Dirty Harry.

I put the gun in my pocket. "All set?"

Tina had already put on her coat and was pulling her boots over heavy woolen socks. Between grunts she said, "I wish . . . you would . . . leave that . . . here!"

"You know," I said, "I can understand how people get gun fever. You feel sort of immortal when you've got one in your hand. That's dumb, isn't it?"

"Retarded is more the word. The cemeteries are filled with immortals and none of them ever died from a fever."

"Let's go," I said.

The phone rang as she was locking up. Instinctively I reached for the gun. I had the fever all right. Me, jumpy?

"You go on," Tina said. "I'll catch up."

I stepped back inside and shut the door. "I'll wait."

She picked up the receiver. "Hello . . . yes, I know . . . no, I don't think so . . . A date, if it's any of your business . . . Good-bye."

"Who was that?" I asked.

"No one important."

"A man?"

"Yes. Now let's go if we're going."

I took Tina's hand and we left. She seemed angry. I didn't know if it was because of me or the last-minute phone call. I didn't press it. My mind was running an hour ahead—down to Gizzo's playroom.

Rain. A light mist that you couldn't get away from no matter which way you cocked your head. Tina kept hers down, stepping nimbly through the slush while I watched the street. I was looking for hostile vehicles, like Grimm's for instance.

"I'll bet Grimm got his ass reamed by Ryan," I said. "I wonder if he went to your place looking for me."

Tina grumbled. "I wish he was here now. There's our car." She pointed to a gray Cutlass parked alongside the Hertz office on the front side of a chain that cordoned off the lot. I opened the door for her and went around the other side.

I got in and glanced over at Tina. "Here we go."

I took the expressway to Woodhaven Boulevard, made a right, and headed for Long Beach. All the while Tina sat brooding.

"Why don't you let me take you back?" I said.

"Forget it! I'm giving you fifteen minutes with Gizzo. If you're not out by then, I'm calling the police. You're not getting killed while *I'm* around. So just keep quiet and drive."

I did, for about a half hour. Then, as though thinking aloud, Tina said, "I wonder if they tried the Briny Breezes. If Detective Grimm knew your wife was there he'd likely go back. Maybe they took her in for questioning. Maybe they're holding her until they find you. What do you think?"

I hadn't thought about it and I told her so. But I liked it. "At least she'd be out of circulation for a while."

Tina scowled. "I'd like to put her out of circulation for good."

It might be an outstanding match, I thought. A five-star attraction for Sunday's Wide World of Sports. Jackie Fontana and Tina Webb squaring off for fifteen, the loser getting me for life.

"Maybe that's why she never called back," I said. "I can just see Grimm dragging Jackie's ass out of that motel. You know if she hasn't reached Gizzo yet there's a good chance he'll believe me."

"You're dreaming," Tina said. "You had your chance yesterday when he sent you home for the book. But you ran away. He won't believe anything you tell him. Not now."

"Why? Why can't I make him believe that I'm not a threat to him? I'll appeal to reason."

"God. It doesn't matter anymore, can't you see that? Men like Gizzo kill people to get what they want. And what Gizzo wants is that book . . . and *you* out of his hair."

"That's exactly what I want."

She shook her head. "You're ridiculous. Just drive, all right? Concentrate on the road. Can you see all right?"

I know zilch about jet streams and low-pressure troughs but something weird was happening with the weather. The temperature had shot up so quickly that the roads had suddenly become awash with melting snow. Adding to our misery was a soupy mist now blowing in off the Atlantic, ghostly puffs of vapor like cosmic snowballs that obscured all but a few yards of river flowing beneath our headlamps. We'd break through one cloud only to get swallowed up by the next. "Christ," I said. "What else?"

"He's trying to tell you something, Frank. Like maybe you oughta turn back."

I was thinking the same thing though I didn't say that to Tina. I knew it was impossible. I couldn't have turned back any more than I could have stopped a dive in midair. I'd already bounded off the highboard, I was out in space with nowhere to go but straight down. The problem was some wise-ass had emptied the pool.

Ahead of us I could just about see the Cross Bay Bridge, its tollbooth engulfed in a pale yellow nimbus. Easing slowly into the one open gate, I checked the rearview mirror. Nothing. Only the fog. Murky, unreal.

"It's tough going over," said the man in the booth. "Be careful."

I gave him a buck. "I'm more concerned about what's on the other side," I told him, envying his antisocial profession, a job where you don't come in contact with people for more than several seconds at a clip. It gave me an idea for a new career . . . if and when.

Up and over the bridge, closer to God, and the heavy jet screeching angrily somewhere above us. It sounded enraged by the lack of visibility, flying blind the way Tina and I were at that very moment.

"Wherever that plane is going," I told Tina, "I wish we were on it. How does Tokyo sound?"

"Not far enough," she said. She looked at me. "Not if Gizzo wants you."

"Is this Rockaway or London?" I said. We were on the downside of the bridge approaching the exit to Far Rockaway. Tina was up on the edge of her seat squinting out to her right, into the fog where Riis Park should have been. All I could see were the skeletal limbs of the roller coaster snaking through the clouds. "We just crossed the River Styx," I said.

Tina was silent for a moment, then she said, "You know there's irony in this. Crossing the Styx into Hades—the underworld—where Gizzo lives."

"Knock it off, will you please."

"Just a thought," she said. "Hey, be careful!"

I'd almost missed the exit to Beach Channel Drive, swerving suddenly, knocking Tina back in her seat. "Keep your morbid thoughts to yourself," I told her. "Hades!"

We moved east through the subterranean soup at a snappy twenty miles an hour, wipers thrumming ineptly against the inexorable mist. It was close to nine P.M. and I figured at the rate we were traveling I just might reach Gizzo in time for brunch.

There was plenty of time for Jackie though—provided she wasn't cooling her heels in police headquarters. I could see Gizzo fuming over the telegram, croaking orders to Nunze and No-Neck: *Gulp—brrrr*. "Bring me that bartender! Dead or half-dead, it don't matter." Wouldn't he be surprised to see me walk in under my own power? So surprised that he might have me crippled just to conform reality to what he'd envisioned.

I clung to a ridiculous faith in persuasion, anyway. By speaking the plain truth I would beat the odds, overcome misfortune, and walk away a winner. In short, I was prepared to spill my guts. I would give him his lousy book, I'd give him Barney, and his low-life nephew if that's what he wanted. About the only thing I wouldn't give him was my wife.

Forty minutes later we were driving down Park Street. The way the fog was dropping and with steam rising from the wet street it looked more like Transylvania than Long Beach.

"We're almost there," I told Tina. "It's just before Lido. Keep your eye out for an ugly pink house with a wall around it."

She pointed. "Like that one over there?"

"Where? It's like looking through gauze."

"Over there, turn right."

I made a very slow turn, no longer in any rush to see Gizzo. I strained my eyes and what I saw made my mouth go dry. I said, "That's it."

"He's got company."

There were two cars parked in Gizzo's driveway. Two shimmery lumps of metal and chrome that couldn't have looked more foreboding had they been a pair of tanks with thirty-millimeters zeroed in on us. It was the second car that caught me off guard, a blue job that looked very much like a car I'd sat in a few days ago. A Toyota to be exact, the one with a concise pattern of bullet holes in its rear seat.

"That's Barney's car," I said. "They've got Barney Rubbles. Gizzo told me he'd be talking to him. I wonder if they brought him or if he came on his own."

"Who knows?" Tina said. She sighed. "Listen, we can't just sit out here like this. They might see us from the house. Pull back a little."

I backed up and parked between street lamps about fifty yards from Gizzo's driveway. From here we couldn't see much of the house. But we still had a good view of the two cars which seemed less menacing now that we were out of cannon range.

"Can you see anything?" Tina asked. "This damn fog!" She didn't appear to be frightened but I could tell by her tone she wasn't taking this lightly. "The other car," she said. "Is that Gizzo's?"

"It belongs to the two apes that picked me up the other day. Some guy named Nunze and another palooka named Al who doesn't have a neck. They're the ones that roughed me up."

"That settles it. You can't go up against all of them. This whole idea is insane anyway. Now let's just get out of—"

"Here they come," I said. "Get down!"

I slid low in my seat much the way I had scrambled for cover the night Dusty was killed. Tina sat firm.

"You can't see anything from down there," she said. "It looks like three of them but it's hard to see." She looked down at me cowering in my seat. "For Godsake, will you get up and look!"

I pulled myself up and peered stealthily out at the gloom. There were three of them, all right, and I knew them all. "The fat one's Barney," I said.

He looked a little wobbly but at least he was walking on his own—though closely followed by Nunze and Al. One of them must have shoved him because he lurched forward, stumbling comically toward his car. But this wasn't meant to be funny. There was no humor in what was happening to Barney.

He opened the car door and got in. No-Neck, after a brief rap with Nunze, went around the other side. Nunze waited momentarily and then ambled to the Caddy, got in, and started it.

Tina was up on her seat, face close to the windshield, straining her pretty blue eyes. "Where do you think they're taking him?"

"Swimming lessons."

"Don't be glib. We can't let them do that." She was serious.

"I'm too scared to be glib," I said. "Besides, I've got my own problems. I don't know how to swim either."

She looked stunned. "Do you realize they might kill that poor man because of you?"

"I do. But there's also a chance *I* might get killed because of *him*. That kind of evens it out. I don't know what Barney said in there, but whatever it was, you can bet your easels he didn't raise my stock any. That poor man, as you call him, is one of the oiliest s.o.b.'s you'd ever want to meet."

They were pulling out of the driveway. I wanted to shrink into nothing but Tina wasn't about to duck. So I grabbed her, pulled her to me, and kissed her. This way at least they couldn't see our faces.

With my lips against Tina's, I muttered, "Are they coming this way?"

She muttered back, "How can I see with your face in mine?"

I turned to look just as they'd cleared the driveway. "They're going the other way."

"That was close. If they'd have seen us . . ."

"They didn't. Now's my chance. Gizzo's alone. If I can get in and out of there before they get back . . ." I let the thought hang for a moment, riding the high so to speak. It didn't take long for Tina to shoot me down. "And if you can't get out, what happens then?"

"You can make a contribution to the Home for Wayward Barmen," I said.

"That's not funny."

She was telling *me?*

"It's the only way," I said. "You think I want to do this? Just stay here and keep an eye open. If I'm not back in a half hour, you can call Ryan."

"Fifteen minutes," she said. "That's all you've got. And what happens if while I'm calling, they take you for swimming lessons?"

"Will you stop being so damn morbid? I'll work it out. I'll tell Gizzo that someone knows I'm here. I'll stall for time, give you a chance to get help."

"We'd better synchronize our watches," Tina said. "I've got ten after ten." I grinned. "What's so funny?"

"I've got five to ten. You know, my brother and I used to do this when we were kids. We'd play war games. Never could get our damn watches straight."

"Well this is for real, Frankie. Remember, fifteen minutes. Fifteen. Then I'm calling Ryan, Grimm, and the goddamn National Guard."

"Don't worry, I'll be out before then." But she was worried. So was I.

She said, "And be careful with that thing," meaning the gun I had just taken out of my pocket. It didn't feel anything like the warm plastic pistols James and I used to play with. This one felt more like a chunk of ice, like I was holding hands with Death. "Put it away," Tina said. "And promise you'll only take it out if you have to." I reached for the door handle. "And Frank . . . Frank, I . . . I . . ."

"What, for Chrissake?"

"I think I love you," she blurted.

I got out, but before closing the door I leaned back in. "Do me a favor, will you?"

She nodded.

"Try to make up your mind by the time I get back."

She smiled and started to reach for my hand. Then she changed her mind and blew me a kiss. I closed the door gently, waved good-bye.

And made a mad dash for Gizzo's house.

CHAPTER 19

I suppose it would have been easier just to walk up to Gizzo's front door, ring the bell, and announce myself. It certainly would have made more sense than racing across a soggy lawn with a gun in my hand like I was attacking some gook stronghold. But at that moment nothing made sense, least of all my being there.

I reached the wall, opened the gate, and sprinted, dodging pretend bullets and cannon shells, stepping gingerly through the mine field. I kept running, finally reaching the side entrance where I stood breathless and weak in the knees. I was on the patio under the arches, it was dark, and I couldn't actually see the door, just a black hole like the mouth of a cave that led to a bottomless pit. Walk in, take the big fall, and wave good-bye to Frank Fontana.

There should have been a nightlight, a sign over the door, perhaps: "Through these portals pass the lowest and meanest in New York." Of course there were no signs, no warnings. Not even "Enter at your own risk."

Funny how small things can upset a plan. Like a

doorbell for instance. There wasn't any, or if one existed I couldn't find it in the dark. All this and I couldn't even get past the door. I could see myself walking slowly back to the car, dejected, game called on account of no bell.

I ran my hands over the door frame, then the door itself. There had to be a way—a brass knocker, a nickel clapper, a gold triangle, anything to let Gizzo know I was out there. I came up empty. "What the hell," I said to no one and started pounding the door with my fist. What came back was a sound that told me it would have been easier to punch my way into Fort Knox. What I needed was something hard, something metallic. Like my gun.

Clonk! Clonk! The butt end of the revolver made a nice loud thump as I tapped gently at first, then bolder. Fearing a hair-trigger, I held the barrel to one side and kept hammering until I heard someone fussing with the inside lock. I stepped back and pointed the thirty-eight at the door. My hand was shaking and the gun felt like a ten-pound sack of potatoes. I wondered if I could hit anything even from this range, or if Gizzo would answer the door with a gun of his own. More importantly, I wondered if I'd have the nerve to pull the trigger.

The door opened.

I could barely see the shape not more than a foot away. For a moment I wasn't sure if the man was Gizzo. Then I heard that Cuisinart voice box of his go *gulp—brrr* and some mumbling I couldn't make out.

"Mr. Gizzo?" I said tentatively, which was kind of crazy considering I had the gun leveled at him. "I'd like to talk to you."

Either he was accustomed to having guns pointed at him or he didn't see it, because he came toward me without the slightest hesitation. I backed up until my buns were pressed against the stucco wall. I could see him now, dressed in a white shirt and tie, no jacket. He looked around as if to satisfy himself I was alone, then said, "You're late."

"Late?"

"Yeah. I've been waiting. For you. Come inside . . . before I get a chill."

I figured he still hadn't seen the gun and I felt stupid holding it out like that so I put it back in my pocket and held onto it while I followed him down the narrow staircase. At the foot of the stairs, he said, "Take your coat off. Sit down."

Big shots like Gizzo never ask anyone to do anything. They speak in edicts and the peasants obey. I took a chair from one of the card tables, removed my coat, folded it over my arms, and sat down. My right hand stayed under the coat near the gun.

There was a pause while Gizzo monkeyed with a thermostat on the far wall. He had to stand on his toes to read it. Even with the specs he'd slipped on, he was still having trouble seeing the temperature.

The room seemed smaller, the pool table dominating most of the floor space. Over it hung an expensive Tiffany light suspended on a brass chain. There were no windows or clocks; you couldn't tell whether it was day or night, if the weather was fair or foul.

Satisfied with the temperature, Gizzo placed his glasses on a table and came toward me. He teetered a little as if looking up had made him dizzy.

Gulp—brrr. "I just had a talk with your friend Barney Rubbles. Very interesting. And lucky for you."

"I . . . don't understand."

"It's simple," Gizzo said. "Before I talked to Barney I wasn't sure if the book really existed. Now I'm sure. Even better, I know what it says." He chuckled to himself, gulped, and said, "Old Barney was real cooperative. You shoulda heard him."

Gizzo studied my expression, which was running somewhere between pain and confusion. "Whatsa matter?" he went on. "You're getting the five hundred grand. That's what you want, ain't it?"

"Mr. Gizzo," I said, shaking my head like I was

coming out of ether, "I don't think you understand why I'm here. I came to explain that I—"

"No need. Your partner's already explained it. What I can't figure is what makes a guy like you fall in with a creep like that."

"Barney?"

"Come on, kid, it's over. You think I wouldn't know my nephew's voice? That call this afternoon. Strictly third rate. He put a hanky or something over the phone, but I could tell that little shit's whine through a bale of cotton." *Brrr.* "Five hundred grand in the back seat of a fuckin' car. That's a joke in itself. The best though is when he tells me to hold onto *you* until he gets the cash."

He chuckled again. I would have laughed, too, if my throat didn't feel like I'd just gargled with alum.

Gizzo took a moment or two to stare me down. I needed only half that time to realize what had happened. The lure had been too much for Tommy. I pictured him doubling back to the Briny, watching while Grimm and I tussled our way out the door. He had heard Jackie's plan, thanks to me. Jackie's greed was matched only by his own. After that it was easy. I would be coming to see Gizzo. The only question was how soon. Gizzo would get his book, they would get their money, and I would get a free ride to Lumpsville.

One thing for sure, Jackie wasn't being detained at police headquarters. Doubtless she was cooping in room 133 at the Briny Breezes where, comfortably at rest on the huge waterbed, she awaited a package containing $500,000 in blood money: Gizzo's money, my blood.

Gulp—brrr. "You look kinda green, Frankie. The money don't look so good anymore, does it?" He grinned broadly. "Cheer up. I'm a nice guy. You asked for five hundred and that's what you'll get. Of course there ain't nothing says I can't take it back later. Eh? Fuckin' kids." He tapped a finger against his temple. "You're all *botz.*"

Was there no getting through to this man? "Mr. Gizzo," I said, "please, you have to listen to me. I don't have anything to do with this. I came here for one reason and that's to tell you not to pay a dime for Dusty's book. I'll give it to you for nothing."

"For nothing?" He paused. "Now I'm confused. You had your chance . . . yesterday. And why the call? Eh? If you don't want money . . . what do you want?" *Brrr.*

"All I want is your guarantee that you'll leave me alone once I give you the book. I still don't know what it says. I'll forget I ever saw it. I can't hurt you. Shit, I'm no threat to you at all."

"Ahhh," Gizzo said, "now I'm getting the picture. My beloved nephew sold you out. Maybe you don't know about the call. Eh?"

"That's right," I said, nodding in rapid succession.

"Looks like we both have a score to settle, Frankie. Of course you're in no position to do anything . . . But don't worry. I'll do it for you."

I was starting to think that Gizzo's brain was completely warped. A lifetime of double-dealing could do that to any man. Still, I had to push. "Tommy doesn't even have the book," I said. "All he knew was that I was going to give it to you. He must have figured I would go along with his . . ."

Gulp. "Blackmail."

"Yeah. Once I got here, I'd have no choice."

"Sure," Gizzo said. "You're just a babe in the wood. You don't know nothing. Hey, schmuck, whataya think, I was hatched out of a fucking easter egg? I don't have to see the bull to know bullshit when I smell it. You've been had, Frankie boy. And you'll pay for it . . . believe me."

"You won't do anything to me," I said.

"Yeah, says who?"

"Someone else knows I'm here. The cops will know, too, if I don't leave soon."

Gizzo started to laugh. No mere whirring chuckle but muted guffaws that came from the deepest part of his belly. "You poor simpleton," he said. "The whole fucking city knows you're here."

My temperature took a sudden dive. I kept staring numbly at Gizzo whose toothy grin had summoned up the face of that same damn crocodile I'd seen here yesterday. And closing my eyes did nothing to clear the image. It only made me aware that there were just two areas of my anatomy that were still functioning: my feet—because that's where all my blood had settled—and my brain. Though I wouldn't have taken book on the latter.

Gulp—brrr. "You gonna stick to your story?"

"Huh?"

"I thought you might try another one. Like your old lady's the one behind this."

For an instant I was bolstered by the thought that it wasn't me Gizzo wanted, but Jackie. How had Gizzo managed to tie her into this?

"My wife's got nothing to do with it," I blurted, not wanting to believe I'd let myself die for the bitch.

"Oh, I know that," Gizzo said, his crocodile grin getting wider. "No man would let a broad call the shots on something like this." He walked over to a candy machine, dropped a coin in the slot. A Hershey fell out. "No," he said, "it was that little bastard nephew of mine."

Gizzo had it figured even before the phone call. He'd guessed right when he said Tommy and I had seen something the night Dusty was killed. He wasn't sure then what we'd seen but it didn't take much to dope it out. And since Tommy and I had been together in this at the start, wasn't it logical to think we were still working as a team?

But there was one thing I knew about Tommy that even Gizzo didn't know. I knew where he was hiding.

I was coming around now, fitting the pieces into a picture that had all the earmarks of a triple-cross. How could Gizzo know about Jackie's involvement without someone telling him? Only two people knew about Jackie's scheme—Tommy . . . and Tina.

Jesus H. Christ. Was it possible? Was Tina working for Gizzo? It explained her life-style, the clothes, apartment, the studio. How was she paying for all that?

212

Defying gravity, my blood slowly began to work its way upward, flooding my veins with the vital fluid I would need for my next move. Escape. Run. Haul ass! Beat a path up the stairs, out the door, across the street, and right out into the cold Atlantic.

Why not? There wasn't anyone there beside Gizzo. And unless he pulled a piece on me, I knew I could outmuscle the runt. One thing for sure, he wasn't about to yell for help. By the time he finished *brrring* I'd be long gone.

Door chimes pealed. A mellow resonance, it sounded more like high mass at St. Pat's than a doorbell. Doorbell! How the hell had I missed it?

Gulp—brrr. "Sit tight for a minute while I get that."

Sit tight. Was he kidding? If I sat any tighter I'd need exploratory surgery to locate my rectum.

Gizzo started up the stairs and I began looking for another way out. I ran to the back of the room. No door. No windows.

My brother James once told me that nothing ever seemed to happen to me in moderation. He used to say I was the inherent subject of extremes. And so it was now as my luck went from bad to horrendous. I'd prayed for a cop, and a cop I got. Ryan!

I knew it was old moonface when I heard him sneeze coming down the stairs. At first I thought I'd been saved. But that fleeting notion died as soon as I saw him walk into the room. He didn't even bother to look at me, he just went on talking to Gizzo as though I wasn't there. It made me wonder if I was.

"We've got to be neat about this, Charlie," Ryan was saying. "No loose ends. If he gets a chance to talk to the wrong people it's all over."

First Tina, now Ryan. Gizzo wasn't a mobster, he was a frigging conglomerate.

My eyes were fixed on the kind lieutenant from homicide. What I saw was a metamorphosis that rivaled the caterpillar's. Unlike the butterfly, however, there was nothing pretty about the new Ryan. Sure, I'll get you the book, pal . . . so you can hand it over to your boss for a pat on the back and an envelope stuffed with bonus money. Too bad Tommy wasn't here to see this.

"Don't worry," Gizzo said. "He's not going anywhere. I'm bringing Peppy in and as soon as he gets here we'll wrap this up. How about a drink?"

Ryan shook his head and sneezed.

"Take brandy," Gizzo said. *Brrr*. "Helps with the cold."

"No thanks. What did Reuben have to say about the book?"

"Plenty. But you'll find out when Nunze gets here."

"No, no. I'm taking a chance as it is. Grimm's been asking questions. He's not as dumb as you think. You know he's got a hard-on about getting bumped off Organized Crime. And if he gets Lawson's ear, I'll have plenty to answer for."

"Yeah. Too bad we couldn't buy Lawson. I'd feel a lot better with a narc on our side. That fucking Sands was ripping me off pretty good. According to Barney Rubbles, he had a sweet setup with Peppy. A special arrangement."

"Skimming."

"Yeah, right off the top. A shrewd article, that Sands. Figured he'd have something if he put it all down in writing. Too bad he didn't have a chance to use it. I don't know how much they got, but I'm gonna find out in a few minutes. I'll make a soprano out of that fucking DeSimone."

"So he wasted Sands."

"Looks that way. I guess he didn't appreciate how Dusty was separating the cream he was skimming. The pricks deserved each other."

I couldn't believe they were talking that way in front of me. I didn't want to believe it. Because it meant that, as far as they were concerned, I was already dead.

I couldn't accept that. No one was going to kill *me*. People like me don't end up on a missing-persons list. They raise families in split-level homes on Long Island, they read about this kind of stuff. Entertainment for the law-abiding masses. I waited for my miracle.

"Well, that's your business," Ryan was saying. "I have to leave. You handle DeSimone any way you want. As for this guy," he said, flicking a thumb at me, "the heat was too much. Must have gone with the wind. Tomorrow we'll put out an all-points on him."

Gulp—brrr. "I don't think you're gonna find him."

They laughed and shook hands. From over Gizzo's shoulder I could see Ryan looking at me now for the first time since he'd arrived. I searched his eyes for remorse and found nothing. It was as if he were viewing a corpse on a slab in the city morgue—a nameless stiff with a tag tied to his toe.

Together they walked to the staircase. "Check in with Nunze tomorrow," Gizzo said. "I might have something for you."

"Right." Ryan sneezed loudly.

"God bless you," I piped. He shot me an empty look, placed his fedora on his head, and clomped up the stairs. A moment later I heard the door close.

I was alone with Gizzo again, only this time I wasn't about to mince words. I had given up trying to convince this grinning crocodile that my intentions were honorable. He was going to eat me up regardless of what I told him. I had to start believing it, fast.

I shut him out and tried to concentrate on what was going to happen to me. Me on my knees, hands bound behind my back, mouth gagged, eyes bulging in terror. Nunze and No-Neck smiling, standing over me with their guns pressed against my temple. Guns, streams of blue-white smoke curling from each barrel. Me, lying face down in the mud, the back of my head like a squashed jelly apple.

I opened my eyes. I'd seen enough. My shirt was drenched, my hands cold and wet. I was melting. Like the Wicked Witch of the West in Oz I was disintegrating. In another few minutes there'd be nothing left of me but a soggy pile of clothes.

Gulp—brrr. "Whatsa-matter, kid, feeling woozy?" Gizzo was over by one of the machines feeding his sweet tooth. "Can I get you something? Drink? Candy bar? Gives you energy, candy does."

He looked so goddamn smug, stuffing his gaunt face like he didn't have a care or worry in the world. Me, I'd had it. I couldn't take him for one more second, his exhaust fan voice and his goddamn candy. I jumped up, wrestled the gun from my pocket, and aimed it as his chest like before. Only now I was sure he could see it. I had him this time. Or did I?

He seemed startled but I could tell he wasn't scared. His mouth slacked open and I got a close look at the brown goo he'd been chewing. Then he sported that irritating grin of his and I knew, gun or not, that Gizzo still held the upper hand. His *gulps* and *brrrs* were a bit irregular but he kept his cool.

"What . . . are you going to . . . do with that?" *Brrr.*

"I don't know. I know what I'd like to do with it."

He shook his head slowly, the incessant grin jabbing me in the eyes. "But you can't, right?"

"What makes you so sure?"

"Look at yourself. Shaking like you got Saint Vitus dance." My arm was weaving all over the place and my wrist looked like it was connected by thread to a handful of Mexican jumping beans. "Besides," he said, "I know guys like you. How do you think I got where I am? By knowing the kind of people I'm up against. Why do you think I didn't ask the dick to shake you down? Because it doesn't matter that you're packing heat. You couldn't pull that trigger any more than you could chop the head off a chicken."

He was right about the chicken. I fought off the shudders and threw out my chest. I'd show him. "Oh yeah? Listen, you cocky bastard, I'm getting out of here and you can't do shit about it."

"Who's stopping you? Go on, see how far you get.

You and my nephew. Ryan might be worried about you, but I'm not. Go on, run. I'll have the two of you by tomorrow."

I could feel my finger tightening on the trigger. Christ knows, I wanted to pull it, shoot the son of a bitch right where he stood. But Gizzo was right about me. I'd never do it. "You gotta find me first," I said instead, and turned and dashed up the stairs, taking the steps three at a time. If the door was locked I'd blow it open, that much I *could* do. It was a bolt lock. I slid it aside, threw open the door and flew out of there like one of those headless chickens Gizzo had conjured.

I ran, slipping and sliding on the wet grass. I put the gun back in my pocket so I could pump my arms for speed. My eyes still hadn't adjusted to the dark and I was running blind. That's why I never saw them.

Wham!

I slammed into Peppy. Both of us went down. I'd hit him so hard that I felt his breath wheeze against my face, heard him grunt. We sprawled across the lawn and I kept rolling until my head crashed against the iron gate.

"What the fuck?" someone said.

It was Nunze. I caught a glimpse of him just before I blacked out.

CHAPTER 20

The only time I had ever been hospitalized was when I was nineteen. Nothing serious, just a simple slice of a surgeon's scalpel. "Cosmetic surgery," was the way James had put it. Though at the time I'd failed to see any aesthetic value in having my foreskin snipped.

I refer to my circumcision not out of some latent penis fixation but because of the light over Gizzo's pool table. The way it was hitting me as I lay supinely on the felt surface reminded me now of the light over the operating table, the way I'd squinted up at it through eyes glazed by Demerol.

I squinted, partly from the light, mostly from the pounding in the back of my head. I could almost feel the egg mushrooming under my hairline. I let out a long, silent sigh and tried to get my mind back in working order.

I'd been running, I remembered that much. Yes. It was all coming back. I had made it to the front lawn and then I'd plowed into a stone wall. Except the wall had had bad breath. I remember catching a whiff of garlic just before I started rolling across the grass. I'd caught Nunze and Peppy as they were coming in. Perfect timing. Either Gizzo was blessed or I'd been living under a storm cloud.

". . . when he wakes up." I had missed the start of Gizzo's utterance but I knew he was referring to me. They were somewhere behind me, Gizzo, Nunze, and Peppy.

"I still don't see why you wanna take a chance with all that dough," Nunze said. "We got him and we'll get Tommy. You'll get your book and you won't have to risk a fucking dime."

"I got my reasons," Gizzo replied. "Just do as you're told. We pick up Tommy as soon as Al gets back."

"What about him?"

"Peppy? We ain't gonna worry about him. Are we, Pep?"

"I swear to God I didn't—"

"Stuff it!" Nunze snapped.

Gulp—brrr. "No more bullshit, Peppy, I got you cold."

"Come on, Boss, you know me better than that." His voice carried a whine I'd never heard from Peppy. I could understand it though. He was pleading for his life and a man naturally whines in that position. I knew from experience.

"Jeez," Peppy said, "I been witcha too long to pull somethin' that dumb."

"Sure, and the longer you work for somebody the more ambitious you get. You see the boss getting rich and you get to wanting some of the wealth for yourself. We got no pensions in this organization, you know what I mean? How much of my dough you got stashed away for your retirement, Pep?"

"Nothin'. I got nothin'."

"You mean you got nothing left. You popped Dusty, didn't you?" No answer. "Not too bright getting him on his own porch. Our boy over there saw you do it."

"Did he say that? Get him up. Let him tell me to my face."

I shut my eyes. I wasn't ready to face Peppy. I wasn't ready to face anything, except sleep.

I heard footsteps coming toward me. "Leave him be, Nunze," said Gizzo. "I don't need him to tell me what I already know."

"Yeah, but—"

"Nunze, for Chrissakes!"

"Okay, okay."

"Just keep your gun on this bastard. You still gonna deny it?" No answer. "Tell me how you worked it with Dusty. I think I know but I want you to tell me. And don't look so scared. I'll give you a break if you say the right things."

"I . . . I don't know." Peppy said, slowly. Then in a gush: "It was him, that fuckin' Sands. It was all his idea. He had his own pushers, some niggers from the Bronx and a couple of greasers from Jackson Heights. He was over-chargin' them. Built up a reserve and then took it off the top. Then he started buying his own shit."

"And you found out about it."

"Yeah." Peppy sounded disconsolate, a kid telling his father he'd been caught cheating on his math test.

"You were working for me," Gizzo said, raising what little voice he had to its fullest capacity. "You shoulda come to me about it. He bought you off, is that it?"

"Yeah."

Suddenly there was a sickening thud, like a fist or something harder smashing into bone and flesh. Peppy groaned. A chair fell over and I heard him hit the floor. "Later, Nunze. We'll finish him later."

I could only imagine what was left of Peppy's face. The hook nose that had haunted me the last three days was probably smeared all over his face. I shivered, wrinkled my nose and tried to slip back into unconsciousness. It didn't work.

"Hey," Nunze said, "I think the roadrunner's wakin' up."

"All right, bring him over here."

I opened one eye just enough to see Nunze standing over me, smirking. He had dimples, deep crescents on both sides of his mouth, half-moons that were probably cut out with a switchblade. His nostrils flared and I could see black hairs growing out of his nose. He also had a long-barrel revolver in his hand, a Magnum, maybe. I wasn't sure. From my angle it looked more like a howitzer.

"Have a nice nap?"

I smiled, sporting dimples of my own. I started to get up and my head felt like I'd spent the night on the Bowery guzzling muscatel. "Ooooh." I brought my hand to the back of my head. It felt wet and sticky.

Nunze turned to Gizzo. "He got blood on your table." He took my arm and pulled me onto my feet. "Come on. Come on, move it."

"Easy," I said. "Take it easy."

He gave me an impolite shove and I staggered toward Gizzo who was still munching chocolate. The guy was a dentist's delight. Peppy was slumped in a chair covering his face with a handkerchief. I couldn't see his nose, just the hanky stained with blood.

Gulp—brrr. "Feel up to taking a drive?"

I looked quizzically at him. "Is there a hospital around here?"

"Don't worry, you ain't gonna die from a bump on the head. I thought we'd pay a visit to my nephew. I think we both got some business with him, don't you?"

I nodded slowly. I hurt too much to do anything fast.

"You know where he is, right?"

Another nod, this one slower than the first.

"And you'll take us there, right?"

"Yes," I said, unable to manage one more nod.

"Who's picking up the money?"

"Tommy, I guess. I don't know, you talked to him."

Gizzo turned to Nunze. "Man, do you believe this kid? Anybody who'd fall in with my nephew has to be a few cards short. Is that what they teach you in college, how to be a schmuck?"

"Guess so." I was too spaced to argue. Besides, he wasn't too far off the mark. I hadn't been playing with a full deck. If I had, I wouldn't be here.

Chimes again. "That's Al," Gizzo said to Nunze. "Watch them while I let him in."

I sat down next to Peppy. He still held the hanky to his face so all I could see were his eyes. They looked vacant, distant, like he'd been sniffing coke all night. He glanced over at me and I could see he didn't have the slightest idea who or what he was looking at. Peppy and I were two guys from different sides of the world with nothing in common except a gravesite. I wondered if being killed with someone meant your spirits would be linked forever. I shuddered at the thought. Peppy DeSimone wasn't the sort you'd want to spend five minutes with, much less eternity.

Gizzo was back. "Al says there's a car outside. What's Tommy using for the pickup?"

I shrugged. "Must be a rental."

He walked over to the stairs and called up to Al. "He don't know the car. Get the plate number." He went upstairs and a few moments later I heard them talking it over. They were on the landing and their conversation drifted down.

Through his police contacts, Gizzo would trace the registration. He made the call from upstairs somewhere. It took about two minutes to learn that the car outside belonged to Hertz. It was pretty damn scary, the pull this man had.

He came back down with a pragmatic look like there wasn't an obstacle in the world he couldn't overcome. Perhaps there wasn't. He strutted to the table next to ours and sat down. To Nunze, he said, "I told Al to put the money on the front seat and lay low until the wheelman shows up. I hope it's my nephew. It'll save us a trip. But it won't matter who it is. We got 'em, don't worry."

Nunze looked perturbed. "Why shouldn't I worry? That's half a million bucks you're fooling with. You mind telling me what you're doing?"

"The money's gonna find its way to my nephew. And when it does, I won't have to wait anymore."

Nunze nodded. He looked enlightened, almost pleased. A smile touched his lips. "Yeah. Yeah, I get it."

Which was more than I did. I didn't get anything. I had no idea why Gizzo was taking a chance with all that cash. It made no sense at all. Like Nunze said, he had me and he would get Tommy, and there was no doubt that he would soon get the book. So why this? I kept my mouth shut. I'd find out soon enough.

Gizzo produced a deck of cards and began playing solitaire. Silently I watched him, occasionally glancing over at Nunze, who was leaning against the near wall eyeballing me. He'd holstered his magnum and for the first time I began wondering what had happened to my doorknocker. Then I saw the thirty-eight tucked inside Nunze's belt and the wondering stopped.

Meanwhile, there was nothing to do but watch Gizzo cheat at solitaire. He did it so matter-of-factly, pulling whatever card he needed from the unturned piles, reshuffling the dead ones. He played the game the way he lived, by breaking the rules to win. And from where I was sitting, he was pretty damn good at it.

For almost a half hour I watched Gizzo's bony fingers fly over the cards, mesmerized by a pair of dazzling pinky rings that stuck out like two diamond knuckles. Peppy must have had a concussion because he remained in a trance, his face so swollen even his mother wouldn't have known him.

Nunze was the only one fidgeting. Finally he said, "I don't like it. Al should have been back by now."

Gizzo looked up, then checked his gold Omega. "Yeah. He should have made contact. Leave me your gun and go check."

Nunze pulled my gun from his belt, placed it on the table in front of Gizzo, then hurried up the stairs and out the door.

"I hope Tommy didn't chicken out," Gizzo said to me.

"I'm looking forward to seeing his face when I catch him with my money."

"I don't understand," I said.

He didn't answer.

"Why are you going through all this?" I asked.

Gizzo thought it over for a moment. He knew the reason so it was just a question of his wanting to tell me. He did.

"He's my sister-in-law's son. Been causing me grief for a long time now. But I had to look the other way 'cause he's got my wife's blood in him. She's a pain in the ass, my wife, but she's no jerk. If Tommy ever got hit she'd know where it came from."

"So what does that mean? He gets a slap on the wrist while I get a bullet in the head?"

He laughed. "No. You're both getting bullets. Like I said, my wife's no jerk. She finds out her nephew pulled a half-million-dollar ripoff on me and she'd go after the little prick herself. Money talks, my friend. Especially with females."

I knew exactly what he meant, though I didn't waste time thinking about it. A light had gone on in my head. Gizzo was playing this out just to frame Tommy. Get the money to him and then kill him for having it. Weird. But to me, everything about Gizzo's world could not have been weirder.

"Hey!" Nunze shouted. "They decked Al!" He came thundering down the stairs. Worry lines were etched on his forehead and he was breathing hard.

Gizzo tossed the cards across the table, snatched the gun, and went quickly to join him. "He's okay," Nunze said. "He's upstairs shakin' it off."

Gizzo was pissed. "I don't give a shit about Al's marbles. Did he get a look at the driver?"

Nunze shook his head. "He got nailed from behind, right after he put the dough in the car."

Gulp, gulp—brrr. "Sonofabitch! Bastard! Here. Take this." He gave my gun to Nunze. "Okay. We go. You," he said to me, "off your ass! You're taking us . . . to Tommy. Right now."

Nunze pointed over at Peppy who was still having trouble focusing. "What about him?"

"That's all set. Jake'll meet us on the way. Let's go."

"The Briny Breezes," Nunze said. "Yeah, I know the joint."

He was behind the wheel of the Caddy. Al, rubbing his head and cursing under his breath, rode shotgun. Peppy sat squashed between them, his head lolling around as if his neck were made of rubber. I was in the back seat alone with Gizzo. Apparently, a semiconscious Peppy posed more of a threat to them than I did wide awake. It was an insult, sure, but the kind I could live with.

By now Gizzo had regained most of his composure. He'd managed it once he saw how cooperative I was being, taking them right to the Briny where Tommy Milano would be counting out his uncle's money.

But Gizzo was still plenty sore. Not because Al had gotten himself cold-cocked before glimpsing the wheelman, and not because he'd temporarily lost sight of all that cash. Gizzo was sore because something had happened that was not part of his game plan.

"Make tracks," he told Nunze. "And watch out for the law. We don't want to get stopped for running a light."

The only thing consistent was the inconsistency of the weather, for the night had turned clear and crisp. The streets were dry and only a trace of snow remained along the curbs.

Gizzo was staring pensively out the window. No one said a word. The tires hummed along the roadbed.

I had made numerous mistakes in my life and the worst, it seemed, was believing that decency could ever overcome greed. In Jackie's case, I had believed that love and marriage would suffice. With Tommy, it was basic loyalty. In a way, I guess, I couldn't blame them for the fix I was in now. Being deceitful was inherent in them and I was a fool to think they might change because of me.

The one person I couldn't figure was Tina Webb. Could I have been that wrong about her? That blind? The way she made love to me, selfless, uncomplicated. I had looked into her eyes and what I'd seen was integrity. I may have been swinging at shadows lately, but there was nothing unreal in what I perceived in Tina's eyes. Where was she now? I wondered.

Meanwhile, I could feel myself getting drowsy. It was like waiting my turn in the dentist's chair. I knew pain would soon be inflicted on me and so I tried to escape it by falling asleep.

It must have worked because I don't remember crossing the bridges or any other part of the drive that got us to the Belt Parkway. It was Gizzo who brought me around. He spoke: "Get off at Pennsylvania Avenue." And I jumped.

Nunze pulled off and we eased to a stop behind a parked car. He left the motor running. It was dark and deserted.

Two men got out of the car and walked over to us. My throat felt like I'd just run the Boston Marathon. Al got out, pulling Peppy with him. Nunze slid over. Gizzo pressed a button and the rear window slid down silently. "He won't give you no trouble," he said.

One of the men leaned in, looked at Gizzo, then at me. He had a square jaw and a mouthful of pure white enamel. "Him too?"

Gizzo shook his head. I sighed and fell back in my seat. Later, I thought. I'll face it later.

"Okay," Gizzo said, "let's move."

Nunze got back behind the wheel while Al jumped in. I watched as square-jaw and his companion escorted Peppy to their car. His head was bent forward, his feet dragging.

Now I was alert, brought to a state of acute awareness by the ease with which Peppy was being dispatched. He'd gone off meekly. Of course they'd softened him up considerably, but still, Peppy was a fighter, a mug. What happened to his instinct for self-preservation? One last gasp at defending himself. If he couldn't muster it when it counted, how would I?

I felt Gizzo's eyes on me and turned to meet them. "Just like that," I said, snapping my fingers.

He snapped back. "Just like that." He saw the look on my face. "Whatsa-matter? You don't think he deserved it?"

"That's your business."

"Right. Then you'll understand why I've gotta do the same to you."

"That's different."

He smiled. "It always is."

"He's one of your own kind," I said. "He knew the score. But I'm not part of this. I didn't do anything to get killed for."

"You hold me up and you say that to me? What was your share going to be?"

"You have a one-track mind. I told you a dozen times: I'm not in on it. I'm being set up."

"Then you're a menace to yourself. I should kill you just for being so fucking stupid."

"A kick in the ass would do just as well," I said.

Gizzo laughed. "I don't know," he said, a little dreamy. "An educated kid like you. Why'd you get hooked up with a shit like my nephew?"

"I've been asking myself that same question."

"We have a few minutes."

I shrugged. "You familiar with Akron, Ohio?" He shook no. "Canton?"

"Football, right?"

"Yeah, Hall of Fame. Every August they put on the Hall of Fame Game. Parades, celebrities, it's a big deal all week. A midwestern Mardi Gras. And that's it for the action. I used to read the New York papers, see the advertisements for the Eastside clubs, Broadway shows, the whole scene. I wanted to be part of it. When I started bouncing with Tommy, I couldn't believe the people he knew. They all seemed big time to me. Especially guys like . . ."

"Like me."

"Yes. You people all have an air about you. You fuck over the system and get away with it. Even come out better for it. Guys like me step out of line once and the roof falls in. Why is that?"

Gizzo looked at me in a peculiar way, almost fatherly. "You do much gambling?"

"Some. Small stuff."

"Ever hear the expression 'never gamble with scared money'?" I nodded. "They say that because every time you do, you lose. It's that way with us. We win because we're not afraid of the stakes or the consequences. What can they do, put us away for awhile? You know the right people and doing time is like a paid vacation."

"Can I ask a question?"

"You want to know why I got into this."

"Yes."

He motioned toward Nunze and No-Neck. "You should ask them. They had a choice. When I came to this country I was so dumb I used to shit in the street. No kidding, right out on Mulberry Street I used to do it. One day I'm over by the curb, pants down over my shoes, shittin' and strainin'. A couple mustachios caught me and rubbed my face in it. 'This is America,' they say. 'Over here you don't shit anywhere unless we tell you.' You get what I'm saying?"

"I think so."

"Well that's the way it was. We came from Palermo to get away from the pricks and we wound up living right next door to them. I did what I had to do. For thirty years I did whatever the mustachios wanted. I didn't make my bones until I was almost forty. Today it's different. A kid gets kicked out of school for smoking and he comes to us looking to be made. Thinks he's tough. We even got these new guys, guys with business savvy. Commercial buttons. Ever hear of them?"

"Tommy told me about them but I didn't think it was true."

"Well it is. Bankers, builders, Wall Streeters, guys who know how to launder money. We make them. But they don't have to do it. They've got good jobs and plenty opportunities. I never had either one. But I'll say this, I hope I'm around to see these sharpies pay their dues. Shit, they think the only way they can die is from eating too much cholesterol. Just squeeze them a little and they'll juice up like an Orange Crush. They're not ready to die for us. And that's the difference."

"Were you ready to die at my age?"

"Hey," Gizzo said, "I wasn't born with this box in my throat. I don't have much time, but I'm not afraid. Never was. I'd go today without a gripe, and that's the way I was when I was a kid. I never gambled with scared money . . . and I never will."

He turned away and went back to looking out the window. "Now that's enough . . . talk, we're almost there."

CHAPTER 21

There wasn't a soul around when we pulled into the parking field at the Briny Breezes Motel.

I scanned the lot for Jackie's car. It wasn't there, and I wasn't surprised. She was probably on a plane for the Ivory Coast, getting as far from this mess as possible. A good general in retreat.

Gizzo doped out his plan. It offered the least amount of risk to him. Naturally. He'd stay in the car, keeping a gun on me while Nunze and No-Neck made mince pie out of Tommy. Then Nunze would return for the two of us and they'd mince *me*.

If I was going to make a move, it would have to happen while I was alone with Gizzo. After all, he only weighed a hundred-twenty pounds, was old and sickly. I'd destroy him. Hope soared, and, for the first time since arriving at Gizzo's, I began thinking about tomorrow.

I should have known better. In the up-again-down-again world of Frankie Fontana, hope loomed anything but eternal. Gizzo didn't stay in the back seat with me. He made me get in the front and lie face down on the floor with my head under the steering wheel. So I lay there kissing the gas pedal, wondering which gun Gizzo was holding on me. Including mine, there had to be at least three in the car. I tried to sneak a peek and every time I did Gizzo *brrrrd* me back the way I was. I decided it wasn't worth the gamble. Not when I was gambling with "scared money."

"He'd better be in there," Gizzo said. "It'll go bad for you if he's not."

"How much worse can it get?"

"You'd be surprised. Lots of ways to waste a man. Think how it feels having a car roll over your belly. Or having a garden hose crammed down your throat."

I keep telling myself I was a damn fool for lying there. Jump the s.o.b., take a bullet. With luck he'd get me right in the heart. Instant death. But my body would not comply. I lay frozen, nailed to the goddamn floor, envisioning the horror he'd just described. Then I threw up.

"Christ!" Gizzo said. "Jesus Christ. Well, now you'll just have to lay in it, that's all."

My throat was on fire. Half my stomach lay in a liquid mess right under my nose. I dry-heaved a few times until finally Gizzo backed off. "All right, get up out of there before you drown in your own puke. I'm not ready for you to die yet."

Slowly I got to my knees. I was on the floor on the passenger side and I rested my head against the glove compartment. "Air," I groaned. "I need air."

"You'll get air in about a minute. Here comes Nunze."

Nunze opened the door and looked down at the floor. "Oh shit."

"Never mind that," Gizzo said. "Did you find Tommy?"

"We got him. His ass is already starting to twitch. Better get in there quick or we'll have another spill on our hands. Jesus."

They made me clean myself up. I did the best I could with only a handkerchief. My coatsleeves were stained but that was all the damage. Except I felt that I'd spent the night in the blood bank replenishing stock.

"Here," Gizzo said, handing me a spearmint Life Saver. "Suck on this. It'll straighten you out."

I popped it in my mouth. It did little to straighten me out but at least it took away some of the acid taste.

Nunze clutched one of my arms and we started across the parking field. Gizzo kept a few paces back. "You clear the front desk?" he asked.

"All set."

There was no one around when we went in. A small transistor sat near the switchboard, playing rock. A newspaper was spread out on the counter. No doubt the lumberjack would be sleeping off the rest of his shift.

Down the hall we went, footfalls muffled in the carpet. I didn't have to be told where to stop.

"133," Nunze said. He tapped a code on the door and it opened by itself. Nunze shoved me inside. Gizzo followed us in.

"You ain't gonna like this, Candy," No-Neck said.

Gizzo looked at Tommy, who was doubled over in a chair holding his groin. I could see the pain on his face. In an abject way it kind of gave me a lift. Not only had I wanted to kick Tommy in the chops myself, but with him here it meant they'd have another toy to play with. It might split their attention long enough for me to do something beside throw up.

Gulp—brrr. "Where's my money, you little whoremonger?"

Tommy didn't answer. The best he could do was shake his head.

"He doesn't have it," No-Neck said.

"You sure? You checked?"

"Don't have to. If he had it, he'd give it over."

"Bring him over to me." Gizzo turned to me. "You get your ass on that bed. Move one finger, we'll bust you apart." I got on the water bed, waited for it to stop rocking, then settled back to watch the show. On violence alone, I would have rated it triple-X.

They stuffed a washrag into Tommy's mouth. Then they held him against the wall, took down his pants and shorts. Tommy's eyes were darting around in their sockets, looking for a place to hide. But that was all the fight he had in him. After getting kicked in the balls there wasn't much else he could do.

"Razor," Gizzo said. He sounded like Dr. Gillespie.

Tommy went banjo-eyed when he saw Nunze pull a long-handle razor from his breast pocket. It was one of those Oriental jobs you see in the martial arts stores on Forty-second Street. The blade was about a foot long.

"I'm going to do something your mother should've had done when you were born," Gizzo said. Tommy shook his head furiously. "Whatsa-matter?" Gizzo went on. "I'm doing you a favor. This'll do wonders for your sex life. Make a new man out of you." He looked at Nunze. "Ever do a circumcision with that thing?"

Nunze grinned broadly and his jowls seemed to puff out like a frog in heat. "Nope, but I'd like to try." He brought the razor toward Tommy's limp pecker and as he did I could feel my stomach doing a Mount Saint Helens'.

Gizzo reached up for a handful of Tommy's hair, jerked his head back. "Nod if you know where the money is." Tommy nodded so hard that Gizzo lost his grip. "Take the gag out."

Nunze yanked the rag. Tommy coughed. "His old lady's got it."

"*What?*" Gizzo spun around and glared at me. "What the fuck's he talking about?"

"That bitch wife of his," Tommy piped in soprano. "It was her idea. I didn't want any part of it."

"But she twisted your arm, right?" Gizzo said. He was still looking at me, watching me turn green on the sea bed.

"You gotta know this broad, Uncle Charlie. She's got ways that fuck up a guy's head."

"You were born that way," said Gizzo. "All right, now suppose you two gabrones cut the shit and start telling me what I want to hear."

"That's the truth," Tommy sing-songed.

"He's a liar," I said.

"You scumbag! Listen to me, Uncle Charlie. His old lady comes to me with a story about this book. She tells me it belonged to Dusty and it's got enough shit in it to put you away forever. Then she lays it on me! 'Got it all figured,' she says. Her and numbnuts are going to shake you down. Well, shit, I'm family, I ain't about to let them pull that on you. But the heat was all over me so I figured I'd coop here until they ease up. Then I'd come to you and lay it all out. Honest to Christ, that's the truth."

"He's lying through his teeth," I said. "I'll tell you what really happened."

"Don't listen to him, Uncle Charlie. He's weaseling out."

Gizzo's head was snapping back and forth like he was working a kink out of his neck. "Hold it!" he said, angrily. To Tommy, "Button it up for a minute. I want to hear his side. Your side sucks anyway."

"Can I get up?" I said. He nodded and I struggled off the bed. "Barney told you that he gave me the book Friday afternoon. Right?"

"Go on."

"Well that night I phoned Tommy, told him about it. We set up a meet at the diner before work. I told him then that I wanted to bring the book to you. I never said a word about a shakedown."

"Why didn't you take it to the cops?"

"I didn't think you'd appreciate it. I don't want to spend the rest of my life ducking shadows. Besides, I had another reason for helping you out. I wanted your help. You were right about us, what we saw that night. We were so close we heard Dusty hit the ground. I figured if Ryan found out, he'd try to frame me into an accessory rap. In fact, his partner came right out with it. You have clout, so—"

234

"So maybe I'd pull some strings, take the heat off."

"That's right."

"So far I like it. Keep going."

"Hey, *wait* a minute!" Tommy shouted. "You ain't gonna swallow that shit."

Gizzo eyed Nunze and the rag went back in Tommy's mouth. Nunze was a handy guy to have around.

"So tell me," Gizzo said, "who tipped the cops about the book? And why?"

"Carol Antonucci," I said quickly. "She knew about the book because she was the one put me onto Barney. I think after Dusty got clocked she just panicked. I don't know."

"Peppy didn't get her. Who do you think did?"

I looked hard at Tommy who was squirming vigorously in Nunze's grasp. "Yeah," Gizzo said, "that's what I think, too. Tell me more."

I had the audience in the palm of my hand. I kept rolling. "Before the phone call," I said, "you got the telegram. Who knew your address? Are you in the phone book?"

"What are you, crazy?"

I let out a heavy sigh. I didn't know if it would help me, but for sure it sealed Tommy's fate.

Gizzo took a step toward his nephew. "Douche bag!" He slapped him good. Forehand, backhand, again and again until Tommy's nose and mouth were pouring out blood.

No-Neck, who was taking it all in, finally said, "We can do this all night except we still don't know who's got the bread."

"Don't worry," Gizzo said, adjusting his rings and checking his hands for damage. "Nobody can spend big bucks around here without us finding out. Besides," he winked at No-Neck, "they're going to be disappointed when they open that envelope. Half a million, shit, I wouldn't pay that much to get my wife out of a Mexican jail."

"How much?" Nunze said.

"Not enough to get crippled, but enough I don't want

to give it away." To me, he said, "You got any ideas?"

"I've been with you all night. Far as I knew this was a one-man show." I head-moved toward Tommy. "His." One more nail in the bastard's coffin.

Another eye command and the gag came out. Tommy couldn't get the words out fast enough: "That's all a pile of shit. It's him and his wife, they brained it. I was coming to you. Just didn't get the chance, that's all."

"The money," Gizzo said. "Who picked it up? Who's your wheelman?"

"I swear to God I don't know." I'd seen Tommy lie often enough and there was something in his eyes now that told me he wasn't lying this time. He honestly didn't know who had made the pickup. He could only assume, as had I, that it was Jackie . . . or yet one more sap of her choice. "It must have been his old lady," Tommy said. "Who else?"

"She strong enough to take Al out with one shot?" Gizzo said. "Who you shitting?"

Now there was a point I hadn't considered. Whoever zonked No-Neck had to know what he was doing. In the movies, a guy gets rapped and he's out cold. In real life, you smash a guy, he shakes his head and smashes you back. Harder.

"All right," Gizzo said. "Here's what we're going to do. We'll take a drive, see. You guys can have the whole back of the car to yourselves. Talk it over. By the time we get where we're going, you'll tell Nunze who's got my money. Capeesh?"

I capeeshed, all right. This was the end of the line. Worse than Peppy, I'd be spending eternity with Tommy Milano.

CHAPTER 22

Gizzo wasn't kidding when he said we'd have the whole back of the car to ourselves. You can't get any farther back than the trunk. That's where they put us, packed away like a couple of spare tires.

We were in Tommy's Buick, Nunze and No-Neck riding up front in first class. They'd brought us around the back of the motel where Tommy had hidden his car. Gizzo, in no mood for slipups, would follow in the Caddie. "I wanna see your faces when you get it," he'd said just before Al slammed the lid on us.

They were taking us to the Family's secret burial grounds, an unconsecrated piece of real estate somewhere in New Jersey. We were barely five minutes out when Tommy started in with me. "Satisfied now, you hard-on?"

I couldn't see him. I didn't have to, he was so close I could have reached him with my tongue. His head was somewhere around my knees and my face was buried between his thighs. Our arms were wrapped around each other's legs. I had the jackhandle in my back while he was sandwiched against the doorlock.

"They're going to kill us," Tommy said. "I only wish I had enough time to do a number on you first, you squealing little prick."

I didn't reply. Being in the trunk had reminded me of *White Heat* and Jimmy Cagney playing psycho Cody Jarrett. There's a prison break and Jarrett takes a hostage, some guy named Parker (a squealing little prick), and puts him inside the trunk of a big roadster. Later, on a country road, Jarrett gets out, goes over to the trunk, and says: "How you doin', Parker?"

"Air," comes Parker's muffled voice. "Gimme air, Cody."

"Sure, Parker, I'll give you air." And Cody Jarrett pumps six shots into the trunk in that inimitable Cagney style.

I always wondered if Parker was killed by the first shot or the sixth. Maybe he hadn't been hit at all. Maybe he'd curled himself into a ball in the corner. There would have been plenty of room inside the trunk of a '41 Lincoln.

"What's the matter?" Tommy was saying. "Too scared to talk? You never did have any balls. That was Jackie's complaint. She had to have balls for the two of you. That was a great idea she had. Too bad I didn't know about it before I talked to Carol. Crazy cunt wouldn't tell me anything. That goddamn book. If you had given it to me in the first place I never would have roughed her up. She had a soft head. I didn't think she was dead. But fuck it, she got what she deserved.

"Now that wife of yours, man there's a chick. Shame it didn't work out. 'I'll get the money,' she said. 'You wait here for me.' That's how come we fucked it up. Neither of us trusted each other enough to do anything alone. I wouldn't let her go without me and she wouldn't let me go without her. So nobody did nothing. That's a joke, eh? After all the bullshit . . . Listen, my uncle didn't leave any money 'cause we never got the car there. He wants my nuts on a platter, that's all. And if it wasn't for you, he wouldn't have found me."

I lay there quietly seething.

"Still not talking? Try this. Your wife and me had ourselves a ball on that big-ass bed yesterday. That was just before you got there. You got sloppy seconds, man. You know she gives the greatest head I ever had. Those lips of hers, man they—"

He never finished. I'd moved my head up, biting as hard as I could on the first thing I felt. I wouldn't need a razor to circumcise this prick.

He screamed and started pounding his fist on my back. With no room to draw the blows, his hands kept hitting the top of the trunk. The thudding must have carried up front. The car suddenly lurched to a stop and I could feel and hear the front doors slamming. My teeth were still dug into Tommy's dick when they opened the trunk.

"Will you look at this," Al said. "Guy's trying to give him a blow job back there."

Now that the trunk lid was raised, Tommy had more room to swing his fists and they were raining down on the back of my sore head in rapid succession. It hurt but I wouldn't let go.

"All right, knock it off," Nunze said.

I bit down harder and Tommy started screaming again.

From the background I heard, *gulp—brrr*. "For Chrissake, what's going on? Shut 'em up, will ya?"

And Al did. He rapped me on the kneecap with the butt of his gun. It felt like I'd hit my funnybone except I tingled from my left foot to my left ear. My mouth snapped open while Tommy's clammed up.

"Why don't we do it right here?" Al said. "Nobody's around."

From my angle it was like looking out from inside a grave. All I could see were stars in a cloudless sky. I raised my head just enough to peer out, felt the cold air blowing across my face.

It might have been Canarsie, I wasn't sure. The Belt

was above us to our left and way out I could see the ribbon of lights on the Verrazano.

"Maybe he's right," Nunze said. "They act up at the toll, we might have some explaining to do." He glanced at Gizzo. "Okay?"

"Do it," Gizzo said.

This was it. Thirty-four years down the drain. A decade from now they might find some bones, but more than likely they'd never identify my remains. I'd end up as part of the foundation for a new shopping center. One helluva tombstone. Good-bye, Mom, so long, James.

"Hail Mary full of grace . . ."

Al leaned in and moved his gun toward Tommy's head.

I threw my arms over my eyes. "Blessed art thou amongst women . . ."

And then Tommy did something I'd been trying to do all night. I felt him lunge and I uncovered my eyes just in time to see him nail Al with an uppercut. Caught off guard, Al went sailing into Nunze. Gizzo reeled backward, more out of shock than contact. I heard a gun hit the ground. I couldn't get up because Tommy was using me for leverage, one hand on my face, pushing himself out of the trunk.

Gizzo *brrrd* like a defective blender. "Get him!" he finally managed.

"Fuck," Al muttered.

I popped my head up in time to see Tommy tear across the street toward the embankment that rose to the parkway. He didn't see the cyclone fence until he was right on top of it. He leaped and started to climb, scrambling swiftly to the top. He moved like Spiderman, even better.

By now, Al was halfway across the street. He yelled something to Tommy, then got down on one knee and took dead aim. Tommy had just reached the top, had one leg over the fence when the shot rang out. A sharp cracking noise that could have passed for thunder over Staten Island. Tommy hung there for a moment, then his voice came back to me. "Aaaahhh, Jeeesus." Then he slumped forward and lay there impaled on the pointy little X's on top of the fence.

Meanwhile, Nunze was down on his knees searching for the gun he'd dropped. He had the Magnum in his hand so I figured he was looking for my thirty-eight. I wasn't about to help him find it; I had only seconds.

I started to get up but fell back down. Al had done something weird to my knee. It squished when I leaned on it. I was going down for the third and final time when Al came hustling back. Gizzo poked his head inside the trunk. "C'mon," he snapped at Nunze. "What the fuck you doin? Whack him and let's get outta here."

"I dropped my fuckin' piece," Nunze said. "My prints."

"I'll do it," Al said. He looked at me cowering inside the trunk, then slowly, carefully, he aimed his gun at my face.

"Police! Hold it right there or you're dead!"

I got up on my haunches as quickly as I could and banged my head on the trunk lid. "Grimm," I shouted, "Grimm, over here . . . in the trunk!"

"Cops!" Gizzo said.

Al spun on his heels while Nunze got to his feet.

I don't know who fired the first shot, whether it was Nunze or Al. It didn't matter. As soon as it went off, I pulled the lid down over me like it was dawn and I was Bela Lugosi. I rolled myself into a fetal ball and braced myself.

There were four quick shots from close by. Then Grimm opened up. Maybe he had brought the SWAT boys with him; from where I was lying it sounded like qualification day on the pistol range. With so much lead flying I hardly had time to muse over what I was doing in the middle of it. It seemed redundant anyway.

"Over there," came Nunze's voice. "Two of them." He must have been down behind the rear fender, right beside my head . . . and the gas tank.

One of the bullets zipped through the trunk not more than an inch over my ear. Thhhpp, like a blowgun. Then another, and one more close to my feet. I kept thinking about Parker thrashing around in the trunk of that '41 Lincoln and suddenly I realized that he hadn't been killed by a bullet. It was heart failure that did him in.

I couldn't just hold my breath while they played shoot-out at the O.K. Corral; one of those shots was bound to find me. I had no idea who was winning, but I had to do something to help the good guys. After all, it was my ass they were trying to save.

Then someone yelled, "I'm hit. I'm bleeding. Hey, where you goin'? Come back, come back!"

If my ears were true, it meant that Nunze was down and No-Neck was beating a hasty retreat. Time to move.

I struggled free of the trunk and hunkered down as low as I could. A shot whizzed over my head. "Halt!" someone yelled. I looked behind me. No-Neck was heading for the fence where Tommy's body was folded over the top rung like forgotten laundry.

A door slammed.

"Halt!" Whoever it was didn't wait and no one else did either. A score of shots whistled in the night and kept on whistling until No-Neck screamed.

An engine sprang to life. The Caddie! Nunze was gone and so was Al. Which meant they had killed the body but not the head. That was my job.

The Caddie started to move. The cops were clustered around No-Neck. Forget about him, I wanted to shout. Gizzo's the one we want.

The Caddie's brights flooded over me like footlights. Something shimmered at my feet. The thirty-eight. I scooped it up. The engine roared. And headed right at me.

I leaped toward the curb. Gizzo swerved the other way, but he was too late. His fender caught Tommy's trunk and the Caddie stopped dead. I hobbled and hoped, reached the door, opened it, and hauled him out by his scrawny neck.

Footsteps. Voices shouting, getting closer. ". . . what we got here!"

"What is it?"

"Come see for yourself."

They had to pry me away from Gizzo. I was still babbling about how I was going to "kill the bastard" when Grimm appeared, puffing and grinning like he just finished the Marathon.

"Nice work, Fontana."

I blinked at him. Then swooned.

He caught me. "Easy now." He was holding me by the shoulders. "You okay?" I nodded. "How do you feel?" Grimm said.

My knee and head were throbbing in alternate beats. "Like I just got a reprieve from death row," I said.

Grimm laughed. It was the first time I'd seen him look any other way but sour. "You did. Another minute and you'd be out of it."

"How did you know they had me?"

"I'll give you the whole story in a minute." He gestured toward one of the squad cars. "Take a load off while I clean this up."

He started walking toward the group of cops that had pulled Tommy off the fence. He looked back ·over his shoulder. "You were lucky, my friend. Damn lucky."

"Yeah," I said wearily. "I'm just a lucky guy."

He waved and I couldn't help thinking that Grimm was all right, a stand-up guy. What else would you call a man who'd just saved your ass?

While they were throwing a jacket over Tommy's face, I took the time to check things out. Both ends of the street were blocked by blue-and-white cruisers, lights spinning, doors open. Uniform police were scurrying in all directions, shouting at each other, holding back the rubber-neckers who'd abandoned "Sunday Night at the Movies" to watch the better show out here.

Their attention was focused on one of the cruisers. The police had it surrounded, half of them facing the car, the other half looking out. The interior light was on and through the protective screen between the front and rear seat, I could see a drawn, bewildered old man. He was shaking his head as though he still hadn't figured out how he got there.

"How you doing?" Grimm said, splitting from the pack. He had returned to check on the hero.

"Okay."

He looked me over. "Don't worry, you'll live."

"It was touch and go for a while though."

He chuckled. All warmth, all heart. Where was this guy when his double was punching me in the mouth, twisting my arm, promising death if I got in his way?

"I'll have someone take you home," he said.

Home. Now there was an unpleasant thought. I was jobless and close to eviction. To say nothing of divorce. Which seemed like a certainty now that Jackie had blown the score of a lifetime.

Grimm circled the car, opened the door, and got in. "Smoke?" he said, holding out a pack of Winstons. I shook him off.

He lit up and I opened the window. "Questions?" he said.

I sighed. "Start with Ryan."

"Yeah," Grimm said, blowing smoke against the windshield. It snaked its way along the dash and out the window. "That's the one thing about this case that really hurts. We go back a long way, Ryan and me. He was my partner in Organized Crime. Then he got his gold bar and everything went to shit. It was Gizzo. I don't know if he pulled strings, or what. But Ryan made lieutenant and after that he buried his head in the sand whenever Gizzo's name came up in a shake. I pegged it right away. But what could I do? Turn him over to Internal Affairs? Shit. I had no proof. Even if I did . . . ah, what the hell. It's history. Anyway, something happened. We were assigned to protect a witness against Gizzo. It was Lawson's bust. You know Lawson."

"I know him."

"Yeah. Well . . . we blew it. The witness disappeared and me and Ryan wound up with transfers." He shook his head and smirked. "Some system. Six months later they got us teamed up in homicide." He looked at me. "You figure it out, I can't."

"So you were suspicious of Ryan all the while," I said.

"Bet your ass. He had to be on Gizzo's pad. Lawson never knew it but Ryan was the last person to see that witness before he vanished. You had to know Ryan to understand what that meant. I'll tell you, if it wasn't for Webb, Ryan and Gizzo would be playing footsies right now."

"Webb? Tina Webb? Are you talking about—"

"Yeah. The little honey that likes to fall out of car windows and play house with our marks. You're lucky. I know guys been trying to get into her pants for months. How is she?" He looked over. "Bet she's a handful, huh?"

"She's a fine artist," I said.

"Sure, and my name's Van Gogh." He put a hand over one ear and laughed. "That chick is a cop, first, last and always. You know, you can thank her for saving your life. If it weren't for her, I'd still be riding around Queens looking for you."

I must have looked astounded. I was.

"You had no idea she was a cop?" He reached over and flipped his cigarette past my nose. "Man, you're something else. Why do you think I wasn't casing her apartment house? She had us in touch with you all the time."

"I thought she was working for Gizzo."

He broke up. "Gizzo? Oh, that's funny."

It meant I was right about Tina all along. She had deceived me about being a cop but she had tried to protect me from myself.

I said, "Did you call Tina's studio tonight? About eight o'clock?"

"Yeah," Grimm said. "She called me when she went out for groceries. Told me you had ideas about going to Gizzo's, that she was going to talk you out of it. That pissed me off but there was nothing I could do. I called back later to see how she made out."

"But she wouldn't tell you."

"No. I went up to the studio but you had already gone. I couldn't believe she'd go to Long Beach with no support.

245

That's why I was late getting out there, it took time to work it out."

"Where was she when you got to Gizzo's?"

"On your tail. Right behind you, putting her ass on the line. I don't know what you got, friend, but you sure turned her head around."

"I never saw her. They never noticed."

"They weren't supposed to." He coughed.

"We got to Gizzo's and nobody was there. We couldn't have missed you by more than five, ten minutes. We didn't know where they took you but it boiled down to two possibilities: your place or the motel. We figured you were still okay, though. Gizzo wanted the book and he wouldn't waste you 'til he got it. By the way, where is the book?"

"Someone's holding it for me. Go on, finish."

"Okay, but Lawson gets the book. That's the deal. I get the collar for the Sands hit, Lawson gets Gizzo."

"I don't care about your merit badges, just tell me about Tina."

He smiled slyly. "She got to you, huh?"

"You could say that."

Grimm shrugged. "She's got lousy taste but that's her business. Anyway, we took a shot at the Briny Breezes. We get over there and who do you think is hawking the place?"

"Tina."

"Correct. That's when we spotted them taking you and your former friend out for a ride. We would have jumped in sooner but my gut told me something like this would happen."

"Your gut told you."

"Never wrong."

"Lucky you. Where's Tina now?" I said.

He shook his head. "Not sure. You know, she wanted to come along but I wouldn't let her. Webb might be great at surveillance but she's still a she. If you get my drift."

"Yeah, I get it. Look, if it's all right with you, I'd like to go." I was suddenly very anxious to get home. Like

246

Detective Grimm, my gut was sending me a message, telling me if I went home now, I would find two women there. Jackie, because she had nowhere else to go. And Tina, who had several places to go, but would never go to any of them until she settled up with Jackie. I could see the two of them tearing each other's hair out while poor Mrs. Schimmel listened downstairs, convincing herself to sell the house and take residence in the Sunnydale Home for the Aged. Not a bad idea, I thought, wondering if they accepted applications from thirty-four-year-old ex-bartenders with accounting credentials.

Grimm was talking out the window to a patrolman. "I want you to take Fontana home," he said. "Stay with him until you're relieved. We have to take better care of him. He's going to put Charlie Gizzo on ice for us."

"Wait a minute," I said. Grimm's head snapped toward me, his mouth turned down. This was the Grimm I knew. "What are you talking about?" I said.

"What do you think? You're going to testify once Lawson gets that little prick into court."

"Now wait—"

"No, you wait. If you don't testify I'll personally put you back in that trunk. Only this time you won't walk out. Did you think you were getting a free ride? Nothing for nothing, friend."

He sounded very much like a fellow I used to work with, a buddy who recently died climbing a fence. "I get it," I said sullenly.

"Hallelujah," Grimm said. "It's about fucking time."

I was back on the roller coaster, plunging abruptly from the height of good fortune to the depths of futility. I raised my eyes toward the sky. Why? Why allow me these meteoric flashes of hope?

Grimm was staring at me, waiting for me to say something.

"Tell me something, Grimm," I said. "Do you think it's possible that God could be a woman?"

CHAPTER 23

Patrolman Kevin Cullen was an affable young fellow with an obvious aversion to speed.

"Can't you go any faster?" I said to him.

"The man said to take good care of you," Cullen mumbled, his voice broken up by the police radio crackling under the dash. There was a 722 in progress at 227 Coney Island Avenue, or maybe the other way around. I wasn't interested.

I was already working on a short-term plan, one that promised to get me and my thirty-eight as far from the Big Apple as finances would allow. No way was I going to testify. Not now, not ever. An hour ago I could have killed Gizzo with my bare hands. But that was an hour ago. The rage was gone and Gizzo was alive and well enough to have me buried from inside the slam. I could testify. But where could I hide after the trial? And forget all that garbage about new identity for the State's witness. What I needed was a change of luck, not identity. I could never warm to the notion of becoming Homer Plotz, hardware clerk from

Timber, Oregon, forever vulnerable to an FBI clerk's selling me for a retirement nest egg. I closed my eyes and tried to dream about a life of flannel shirts and boarding houses.

We finally made it to Cross Bay Boulevard, where I directed Cullen the rest of the way. I was clinging to the slim chance that Tina wouldn't be there when I arrived. I had a parting gift for Jackie and I wanted to give it to her in private. Having failed in two attempts, I decided that this time my resolve was implacable.

"Pull in over there," I told Cullen, pointing to the fire plug. "Don't worry, I've already cornered the market on parking tickets."

While he pulled in I looked across the street. My heart began racing at the sight of Jackie's car parked in front of the apartment, boxed between a station wagon and a gray Cutlass. Lights were burning brightly from the upstairs window as were the lights from Mrs. Schimmel's rooms on the ground floor.

"Someone throwing a party?" Cullen said.

"No, my wife always keeps the home fire burning for me."

I got out of the car, flexed my sore leg. Cullen got out and I looked at him inquisitively. "I'll have to go in with you," he said. "Orders."

"There's a cop up there already," I said, pointing to the Cutlass.

"Sorry, but orders are—"

"Yeah, I know. I'm going to be alone with my wife, though. If I have to throw you out to do it."

He smiled. "Grimm said you might get a little feisty. Excuse me," he said, "but do you know that woman?" He indicated Mrs. Schimmel who was peeking through the venetian blinds. She'd done this a hundred times before but always surreptitiously enough to make me think I wasn't supposed to notice. This time it was different.

"That's my landlady."

"She looks upset."

More like devastated, I thought.

With Cullen at my side, I limped toward the house. We'd reached the sidewalk when Mrs. Schimmel yanked up the blinds and began making fierce gesticulations, hands to her throat and then a finger pointing upward. "Hurry," she was saying in pantomime.

I acknowledged her with a raised hand and with Cullen close on my heels struggled as quickly as I could up the front stairs, through the door and into the vestibule. The door to her apartment was wide open and she was standing well inside as though afraid to come out.

"Are you all right, Ma'am?" Cullen asked politely.

Mrs. Schimmel was many things at that moment but "all right" wasn't one of them.

Wearing a thick granny robe over a flannel nightdress, she had one hand on her heart and her eyes looked like white Frisbees. She blinked several times as if to satisfy herself that Cullen and I were really there. Her mouth was forming words but nothing was coming out.

Again Cullen said, "Are you all right, ma'am?"

He took a step forward and then the caterwaul came crashing down on us in a series of shrieks and screams and a litany of obscenities.

"Jesus," Cullen said. "What's going on up there?"

I glanced at Mrs. Schimmel whose mouth kept moving wordlessly. Her face was growing paler by the second. She took a deep breath, placed both hands to her throat, and said in a small, choking voice, "I can't . . . take this . . . anymore."

"That makes two of us. Come on," I said to Cullen.

Awkwardly I rushed toward the stairs, hopping and skipping as fast as I could. I could hear Jackie shouting: "Keep away, stay away from me or I'll let you have it." With what? I wondered.

In our haste, Cullen and I had gotten ourselves wedged against the side walls so neither of us could move. I could feel his holster pressing against the gun in my pocket. I shoved him back, grabbed the banister and pulled myself the rest of the way. Cullen clambered up behind me.

I threw open the door and froze.

"Holy shit," Cullen muttered.

"Yeah, holy shit."

From where I stood it looked like the earth had slipped its axis. The breakfast table was pushed awkwardly against the sink, chairs overturned, cabinets open to empty shelves. The entire floor was covered with shards of glass; pots, frying pans, service trays, and a variety of canned goods were strewn all over the kitchen.

Tina was nearest to me, coiled up in some impossible stance, shoulders hunched, knees bent, elbows tucked to her sides. Her forearms were straight up and her wrists were bent with fingers hideously wrenched to resemble the fore-limbs of a praying mantis. Except for the obvious differences—like her blond hair now in complete disarray and a bra strap peeking through the shoulder of her torn sweater—she was performing a flawless imitation of Bruce Lee in *Return of the Dragon*. Dragon Lady would have been more appropriate, except Tina didn't have the title role. That honor had to go to Jackie.

She was standing in the middle of all that rubble, holding her weapon—a carving knife, like in *Psycho*. It was one of the few items Jackie had brought with her when she moved in. She'd never touched it. Until tonight.

She was holding it close to her ear, her chest heaving, gulping air in convulsive spurts. Her head twitched each time she inhaled and a slight whimper escaped from deep inside her throat. One side of her face was scored with serpentine tracks, claw marks that trickled blood onto her blouse. Her eyes were squeezed into slits just wide enough to disclose a glint of venom.

She'd been on the short end of this battle, but the war was far from over.

I started toward her. "It's all right, Jackie."

"Frank," Tina said. "Thank God you're all right." I edged closer to Jackie. "Be careful with her," Tina panted. "She's crazy."

Jackie's eyes opened wide as I got closer to her. "They

want to arrest me, Frankie," she said in a whisper. "They can't do that." She tried a smile, it faltered, then dissipated into a capricious tic that tugged at both sides of her mouth.

"Easy," Cullen said. "She's flipped out."

She did appear deranged. Yet I couldn't help thinking that this was just one more performance for my benefit. Bring in the clowns for the grand finale.

Cautiously, I said, "Leave her alone, she's all right."

"Like hell she is," Tina said, moving in threateningly.

Jackie jumped back. "Frankie, Frankie, stop her. She's not in love with you. She told me so. She tricked you, Frankie, played you for a fool."

"*I* played him for a fool?" Tina said.

I looked at Tina and she must have seen the questions racing through my mind. She said, "You're a diehard, aren't you? How much are you going to take?"

"It's not that. It's just . . . look, I don't believe what she's saying."

"Then what the hell is it? If it were up to her, you'd be dead by now."

"I know, I know," I said, annoyed by being reminded.

"She's not even sorry for what she's done. Look at her, Frank. Take a good look. She's so sure of you that she still lies, knowing you'll buy it."

I gazed at Jackie, trying with all my power to see behind those green eyes, glistening now, imploring me to do . . . what? Understand? How could I understand? She must have known that because of her I had come within a whisker of being killed. Was I supposed to accept that as a consequence of loving her? My God, she hadn't even shown a glimmer of relief that I'd come out of it in one piece. It was Tina who'd seemed relieved.

Yet there she was, still trying to manipulate me.

"He's *my* husband," Jackie railed. "Tell her, Frankie. Tell her you'd never take her side against me. Tell her, Frankie." She screamed "*Tell herrrrrr.*"

Jackie stood there, shaking uncontrollably. If she wasn't totally deranged, she was damn close to it. I took a

252

step toward her. She waggled the knife at me. "Stay away. Don't touch me."

"Don't go near her," Cullen said.

I looked at Cullen. "She won't use it."

"Look out!" Tina yelled.

My arm went up. The knife descended. It missed by inches, but Jackie's wrist caught my forearm. She yelped, clutched her wrist, spun around, and ran for the bedroom.

"Get her!" Tina hollered.

Jackie had a step or two on me. I went after her but my knee buckled and I went down. The door slammed. Tina rushed to it. She tried the knob. "Shit!"

"Go away," Jackie said from inside. "Leave me alone."

"Now what?" Cullen said.

They helped me to my feet and drew me away from the door. We listened for a while, heard nothing. "I'm going in," I said.

"In a pig's eye," Tina said. "You'll wait like us. We'll get help. We've got people who do things like this."

"Emergency Services," Cullen piped.

"Get 'em," Tina said. Cullen rushed out.

"That's my wife, Tina."

"For better or worse, right, Frankie? What is it with you? Are you a masochist or what?"

"How about pride?" I said. "A little something for what's left of my ego. Ever since I met Jackie she's had me jumping through hoops. I need a reason to justify it. For Godsake, there's got to be something decent in the woman for me to have put up with her, to have married her in the first place. I'm looking to get out of this in one piece, in body and in mind. And in my heart.

"I told you I would leave her, and I will. That hasn't changed. But if she owns up to what she's done, if she shows just a modicum of regret, at least then . . ."

Tina was shaking her head. "I'm afraid you're in for a jolt, Frank. I'm not a psychologist but I've seen enough corrupt people to know that she's rotten to the core. So you can't see it, so what? Can you understand people like Gizzo? Or even Tommy Milano? Jesus, Frank, you're not expected to understand them."

"Jackie's not in Gizzo's league."

"She's a lot closer than you think. People don't mean anything to her unless she can use them."

"I know that," I snapped, "but I'm still her fucking husband."

I moved closer to Tina. She had to understand that I wasn't doing this because I was pussy-whipped. Those days were over. "Weren't you the one talking about commitments?" I said.

"Yes," Tina said. "Between rational people."

"I am rational. The fact that she isn't has nothing to do with it."

Tina started to say something. She stopped. The bedroom door had opened. Jackie was standing on the threshhold. "Send her away," she said softly. The knife was still in her hand.

Without a word I shoved Tina backward and dove at Jackie, catching her around the waist, the two of us tumbling into the bedroom. The knife fell to the floor. In one motion, I pushed myself up and kicked the door closed. Tina was a step away from reaching it when it slammed shut. I lunged for the door and pushed the button.

"Frankie!" Tina shouted. "What are you doing?"

"It's all right," I said. "I'm okay. Give me ten minutes."

"You're an idiot," Tina said. She paused. "All right. Watch yourself."

Jackie was still on the floor, dazed but unhurt. I helped her up and guided her onto the bed.

"I'm cold, Frankie."

I took off my coat and covered her with it. There was something I wanted to hear from her. I wanted her to tell me that she didn't love me, that she'd never cared about me except as someone she could use. I didn't need convincing, what I wanted from her was a single honest statement. Just one.

"Don't leave me, Frankie. Please." She held her arms out to me and I went to her. She hugged me tightly and began to sob. I didn't know whether I wanted to cry along with her, or slap her in the mouth.

With difficulty, I broke the hold she had on me. I looked around the room, trying hard to recall the good times we had had here. All I could see was the inside of Room 133 at the Briny Breezes Motel. Jackie and Tommy Milano rolling around that goddamn waterbed.

"Make them go away, Frankie," she said. "You can do it." Her eyes were fixed to a point on the ceiling, her pupils seemed to be dilating. If that's an act, I thought, it's brilliant.

She groaned and her eyes grew darker, misted over. No, this was real, this couldn't be an act. I didn't understand why but I was more frightened now than when Gizzo ordered me locked in the trunk of Tommy's Buick.

Impulsively, I bent forward, kissed her cheek and tasted the blood from the claw marks. "Don't worry, babe," I said. "I'll fix it somehow."

A rap on the door. "Frank? You all right?"

Jackie stiffened.

"It's okay," I said quietly. "I'm going out there, I'll talk to them."

She shook her head violently.

"Don't be afraid," I said.

Moving cautiously, I picked the knife off the floor, unlocked the bedroom door and walked out, closing the door behind me.

Tina was right there. I gave her the knife. "Thank God," she said. "They oughta be here any minute now. They'll take her to a hospital."

"What's going to happen to her? After, I mean." I must have had a hangdog look on my face because Tina took a quick glance and bristled.

"What kind of shit did she give you?"

"She's scared."

"A bit late for that, isn't it? God, Fontana, how gullible can you get? I don't know what she told you. But it's a lie, can't you see?"

"And what about you? A cop, for Chrissake. You could have leveled with me."

"What was I supposed to do? For all I knew, you could have been a murderer."

"And how long before you realized I was only a schmuck? You could have told me before I went to see Gizzo."

"Are you kidding? I did everything I could to stop you from going, practically tied you to the floor. I wanted to tell you. Believe me, I did."

"Why didn't you? One of the reasons I went was because Ryan was pressuring me. You and Grimm were together in this. You could have told me about Ryan, at least."

"I did what I had to do. Just like your walking right into Gizzo's hands. You didn't want to go in there, but you did."

"What are you saying? That you're a cop first and a woman second? Who did I make love to, the cop? You thought you loved me, you said. Was that the cop talking?"

"No," Tina said. "I meant it. I still do. Those nights together, well . . . oh, shit, Frank, I know the difference between lust and something decent—important. I thought you felt the same way."

"I did. Or I thought so. I'm all fucked up. Everybody has been lying to me since this thing started. I can't believe anyone anymore."

"Fine. Then you won't believe what *she* tells you."

"She's sick," I said. "I should have seen it all along. She's totally irrational."

"Irrational?" Tina said. "She's more rational than the two of us put together. She counted on your doing her dirty work, anticipated all your moves, manipulated you like a puppet. She'd be a widow right now if we hadn't spoiled her vacation plans.

"You should see the way she looks."

"I saw her, for Godsake. I saw her when she thought you might be dead. No remorse. Just disappointment that she didn't come away with Gizzo's money. She's in there scheming right this minute."

"She's afraid."

"Of what?"

"Going to jail."

"Don't be ridiculous. I just said that to rattle her. We've got nothing on her. I don't think Mr. Gizzo is going to accuse her of blackmailing him. Do you?"

"What about the book? She's got it somewhere. That's withholding evidence, isn't it?"

"You're the one that Reuben gave the book to. So far you're the one that's got to produce it and, if you can't, you're the one withholding evidence. No, she's clean. I'm sorry to say it, but that's the way it is.

"Go in there and tell her. See how quickly she recovers. Go on, try and get the book from her, see what she says. Go ahead. I'll wait right here."

CHAPTER 24

Jackie wasn't lying down when I went in. She was sitting on the chair next to the bed, my coat across her lap like a blanket. She looked like a patient convalescing in a hospital room. Her eyes were still glassy but I could see green in them again, the macabre gaze replaced by a penetrating stare.

She licked her lips. "Lock the door."

There was something in the tone of her voice that caused the hair on my arms to crackle and shoot straight up. Not even Gizzo's voice, weird as it was, had had such an effect on me. I did as she asked. I locked the door.

"Sit over here," she said, cocking her head toward the bed.

I reached out for her hands but they were under the coat and she kept them there. I sat down. "It's all fixed."

"Fixed?"

"Yeah. You'll have to answer some questions but nothing's going to happen to you."

"That's nice."

"Nice? What the hell's the matter with you? A minute ago you were hysterical because you thought you were going to jail. Well, you're not. It's all fixed."

"I don't believe you. You told them everything. They're blaming me, accusing me of conspiracy."

"No, no. All they want is the book." I glanced around the room.

"Sure, you'd like that wouldn't you? From the beginning you've been cozied up to the police. You and your girlfriend out there. I bet you both had a big laugh."

"You're crazy. I told you your scheme wouldn't work."

She lowered her eyelids. They fluttered. She clenched her teeth, took a deep, hissing breath. "My scheme?" Her eyes opened slowly like a doll whose eyes open when you stand her up. I didn't know what to make of this routine but I felt certain she wasn't going off the deep end, that she knew exactly what she was doing.

"It wasn't my scheme," she said. "You may have them fooled but I know better. You wanted the money as much as I did. More. That's why I hid the book, to stop you from—"

"Hold it! This is me you're talking to, remember? Don't hand me that bullshit. Don't make it any worse. It won't work. Besides, there's no reason for it. The cops have nothing on you, so let's drop the act."

"I know what you're doing."

"I wish I could say the same."

"You're putting it all on me to save yourself. Well, honey, it won't work."

"Jackie, what's wrong with you? I'm trying to protect you. Can't you see that?"

In the blink of an eye, the anger vanished, her expression softened by a thin, indecisive smile. "You know I love you," she said as though she couldn't make up her mind whether to laugh or flirt.

Listening to Jackie, watching her moods change, was like playing Russian roulette. Her mind kept spinning and each time it stopped you stood the risk of being struck by something lethal. I had the feeling now that I was staring directly into the loaded chamber.

"You can't say it, can you? Not even now."

She looked puzzled.

"You can't simply say 'I love you.'"

"I just said it."

"No. Putting the 'you know' in front of it is not the same as coming right out with it. Say 'I love you.' I want to hear it."

"You know I do."

"See what I mean?"

She didn't say anything.

"Then tell me you don't love me. Say that much."

More silence.

I said, "Why do you have to approach everything from an angle? It's so damn sneaky."

"It's not sneaky, it's safe. I don't want to get hurt."

I smirked. "You poor kid, the whole fucking world's looking to do you in. Well, you won't have to worry about getting hurt by me anymore."

"What does that mean?" '

"It means I've had enough. Tell me where you've put the book and let me go. I want out of your life for good."

"You can't leave me," she said without the slightest hint of desperation, as though she were stating a simple fact.

"Why not?" I countered.

"Because I know what your problem is."

I rose to my feet. "My problem? You're the one with the fucking problem. I don't have trouble accepting honest emotion."

"Oh no? Then why can't you accept me as I am? Why do you insist on poking around inside my head like some Park Avenue psychiatrist? The problem's not with me, Frankie, it's with you. I've never tried to change the way you are. Ever since you met me you've been on some kind of crusade, trying to convert me, to make a phony out of me. A phony like you. And don't look at me like I'm crazy."

"You are."

"Who do you think you are? Who gave you the white hat? If you were so pure of heart, why were you working for a man like Sands? There was enough shit going down at that bar. . . . I suppose you had no idea that Dusty was peddling dope? Or that Peppy DeSimone was an enforcer for Gizzo? And Tommy, that sick bastard . . . You were right in the middle of all of them . . . And then you marry me. You knew my track record. You knew all of that and yet you still pretend to be shocked. Like I said, Frankie, you're a phony."

She sat back like she expected applause.

"Maybe you're right," I said. "But that doesn't explain why you didn't just cut me loose. I know why I stuck it out, what were your reasons?"

She shrugged languidly.

I said, "For some reason you want to believe that you're one hundred percent rotten so you try to be as bitchy as you can. To you that's being honest. But you know what I think?"

"What's that?"

"I think sometimes you wish you could have a normal relationship with someone. I think that's why you've kept me dangling. You were afraid to let me go because I just might be the last chance you've got at living a decent life."

"You've got a high opinion of yourself, don't you?"

"If it was that high I wouldn't be here. The irony is that it's always the giver who winds up with the low opinion of himself. It should be the other way around."

"I should be ashamed of myself, is that it?"

"If you loved me, you wouldn't have to ask."

She sat there while I mustered the courage to walk out the door.

"Where do you think you're going?" Jackie said as I edged slowly to the bedroom door. "What about the book?"

"Keep the fucking book. I made a copy of it anyway."

Her face went scarlet and she began kicking her legs, thrashing wildly under the coat. It flew off her lap. "Just a minute, Saint Francis."

Another change in mood, one more spin of the chamber, only this time it was real. The trigger was actually cocked and I was staring down the barrel of a loaded gun. My gun.

"You," she said. She held the gun like it was a hairdryer. "You who comes home with a pistol in his pocket. Tell me about normal relationships. I want to hear again how you're my last chance at leading a decent life. Yellow bastard. Fucking hypocrite!" She flipped the gun from side to side. "You were going to force the book out of me with this, weren't you? You never made a copy of it or you would have told me. Honesty personified, that's you."

After what I'd been through with Gizzo's crew, having a gun aimed at me should have been old hat. It wasn't. Especially now, in our own bedroom, with Jackie looking to blow dry my brains.

"You know," she said, "I never felt guilty about anything I did until I met you."

I nodded toward the gun. "Do you hate me that much?"

"I hate that nice-guy routine designed to make me feel like shit. It won't work. I've fucked over better men than you, Frankie. I made them grovel."

"What's the matter, haven't I groveled enough for you?"

"It's what I get for being honest."

"Honest? You?"

"I told you about my mother and stepfather and you've been patronizing me ever since. I don't need it, especially from someone like you. Phony."

"I only wanted to understand. I loved you, for Chrissake."

"You wanted to change me."

"So what happens now?" I said. "You're going to shoot me because suddenly you can't accept the way you are? Because you haven't been bitchy enough? You're not making any sense. You need help, Jackie. Really."

"And you're going to help me?"

"No," I said. "I've given up."

"I said you couldn't leave me until I was finished with you."

"There's no way you can stop me."

"You don't think I can do it?"

"Shoot me. Spend the next fifteen years in prison."

"Shut up!" Her voice climbed an octave.

Tina, from behind the door. "Frankie. What's going on?" Tina was pounding on the door. "Let me in! Frank. Frank. Open the door!"

"You can't do it," I told Jackie.

I felt confident. I just didn't believe she would trade her looks for my life.

Meanwhile, outside the bedroom door, confusion, Tina shouting at someone: "Get up here! On the double!"

Jackie seemed perplexed, her head jerking several times from me to the door and back again. She got off the chair, gripped the gun in both hands and aimed it at me.

"Put down the gun, Jackie," I said. "Put it down before you get hurt."

"Before *I* get hurt? You've got it backwards, Saint Francis."

"Look at you," she said, shaking her head. "My salvation."

Cops were throwing their bodies against the door. "Open up!"

"Jackie," I said. "Give me the gun.

"I love you," she said.

The door crashed open. Jackie fired.

CHAPTER 25

I always wondered how it might feel to get shot. Surprisingly, it wasn't much worse than a sharp punch followed by a burning sensation that saps your strength. It's about the same as being kicked. Except this kick was slightly off target, high and to the left, striking my arm.

"I didn't mean it," Jackie wailed. "It was an accident."

Grimm and Lawson had arrived. They both came hurtling into the room right behind some other cops. For all they knew, I might have been bleeding to death. But what did they care? They were too busy whipping out their cuffs, and subduing the perpetrator before her next accident got one of them.

I felt someone tearing my shirtsleeve. Hands on my arm, cool, soothing. "All right?" Tina chided. "Had enough?" She pressed a wet rag against the wound. I winced. "I told you she was dangerous, didn't I?"

"No!" Jackie screamed. "It was an accident. The gun just went off." She was up on her toes trying to see over Grimm. "Tell them, Frankie. Tell them!"

Tina looked at me. "If you open your mouth I'll put my fist in it," she said. "Get her out of here, Grimm. Get her away from this idiot before he makes it seem like he shot her."

Grimm tugged Jackie's arm. "Come on, let's go."

"Frankie, Frankie tell them . . . it's your gun . . . not mine . . ."

Grimm and another cop had her on both sides, practically lifting her off her feet and out of the room. She looked back over her shoulder, her eyes wild with fear. "Frankie, please—please, Frankieeeeee—" She started to struggle but to no avail. From the kitchen I heard her shout. "Fontana, you miserable sonofabitch. I hate you! I hate you!"

She may have said much more but I didn't hear it. I couldn't hear anything over the siren wailing in my head. You know the sound, the one accompanied by vertigo and bright prisms of light that you see just before passing out.

For the second time that evening I felt myself falling helplessly into darkness. Only this time my head didn't strike anything hard. Instead, I fell face down into a black velvet glove the size of my bed. It caught me gently, enveloping my entire body with tenderness.

The bliss of insensibility. If only it could have endured.

". . . like he's coming around." That was Tina. She was bending over me, standing alongside a young man in a white jacket, stethoscope dangling from his neck like ice tongs.

"He's all right. Bullet went clean through his arm. No bone damage, nothing. He's lucky."

I groaned. "If I had any luck at all my car would still be in a garage."

"He's delirious," Lawson said from the foot of the bed.

"No," said young Kildare. "I gave him a shot, he'll be okay."

The room smelled of gunpowder and perspiration, of

madness and fear. "You from Bellevue?" I asked. "Tell me you're from Bellevue."

"Deepdale." He turned to Lawson. "He really should spend the night in the hospital."

"Just a few questions, then you can take him anywhere you want."

Kildare nodded, picked up his medical bag, and backed away.

"Fontana," Lawson said. "Where's the book?"

"Oh, fuck the book," I said.

"Just give it to him, Frank," Tina said. "Then I'll take you home with me. How does eggs for breakfast sound?"

"Now wait a minute, Webb," Grimm said. He'd slipped in beside Lawson. "We need his deposition."

"Send someone up to my place in the morning. We can do it there."

Grimm looked at Lawson and the two of them looked down at me with an expression somewhere between sympathy and disgust. "What do you think?"

"The book," Lawson said. The man had a one-track mind.

"All right," I said. "You'll get your book. My lawyer has it, don't worry."

"Who's your lawyer?"

"James Fontana, best lawyer in Akron."

"Your father?"

"Brother."

"I'll check it out."

"You do that, Lieutenant," Tina said. "In the meantime I'd like to take him home with me."

"Where's Jackie?"

"On her way to the precinct. She's got a few years facing her now. Attempted murder."

"Maybe . . . maybe I—"

Tina put her hand over my mouth. "Shut up. You're right, Lieutenant, he is delirious."